Heathen Girls

LUANNE JONES
Heathen Girls

MIRA®

MIRA®

ISBN 0-7783-2282-3

HEATHEN GIRLS

www.MIRABooks.com

Printed in U.S.A.

First Printing: January 2006
10 9 8 7 6 5 4 3 2

ACKNOWLEDGMENTS

First of all I have to thank my agent, Karen Solem, for believing not only that I could write but that I could tell and sell this particular story and for sticking with me until it happened.

I also want to thank all the editors along the journey who turned this book down with such thoughtful and encouraging words. They helped me work toward bringing out my best without crushing the joy of writing.

And my editor, Joan Marlow Golan—as always, her hard work made me look better, and I am grateful.

Thanks to my cousins, girl cousins and boys, but mostly girls (sorry, guys, you know how it is in this family) and my sister, Susan Shorter, and sister-in-law, Debbie Shorter, because they both do so much to keep our family a family. And most especially thanks to Patje Henneke Lentz for listening to me tell the good parts of this story and laughing at all the right stuff so I had the courage to press on with it.

Thank you, Mary Aiaka Lentz Coleman, for advice on hospices and dealing with a dying patient. Thanks to Lynn and Lynne, both good Lutheran girls who have not lost touch with their inner heathens, I think. Thanks to Stephanie Bond and Elizabeth Harbison for all the advice and support. And thank you to my uncle Dan Shorter, because something he said about the closeness of cousins started me thinking. Also for his famous reminder: Never let the truth get in the way of a good story.

And most of all to my own larger-than-life aunts by blood— Oleeva, Ruth, Ileene and Bette. And by marriage—Mae, Melba Deane, Suzie and Marge.

And thanks as always to my mother, Ida Maxine, for inspiration in every aspect of my life.

For all the women of my family, every generation.
For all the women who shaped my life.
The wise women, the wise asses and the
wistful—you are amazing.

1

"Jump, Charma! Jump into the water! Everybody here loves you. Not a one of us would ever let anything bad happen to you. You're safe. You're strong. You're free. Now jump!" The late afternoon sun glinted off Daddy's broad, tanned shoulders like he was made of pure gold.

And he was.

Golden.

And perfect. And wonderful. And, oh, how I wanted to live up to his expectations of me instead of just standing on the dock clenching my knees tight, trying not to pee in my brand-new hot-pink bikini bottoms.

"Jump wa-a-ay out, Charma Deane," he called. "Jump out past your fear."

I curled my toes against a warped plank.

In the distance Mama and my aunts draped themselves over lounge chairs like damp towels, soaking up the sun, drinking iced tea and listening to the Everly Brothers on the radio. Now and again one of them raised her head and peeked out from under her sun hat to make sure Nana Abbra, my daddy's mother, hadn't started out toward us, intent on spoiling everything.

It was Nana's house, after all. Nana's pond. Nana's queendom. And their husbands were Nana's boys, her princes.

"You can do it, brave girl." Ripples of green-brown water lapped at Daddy's chest. He stretched out his arms, his prized fishing hat in one hand and a beer can in the other. "Be bold. Be fierce. Show some faith, damn it, and live!"

I can still feel my cousin Minnie beside me at the edge of the water. Her dark almond-shaped eyes blinked. She slipped her tiny sun-browned hand into mine. "Let's go together, Charmika. You can do anything if you know you're not alone."

I wanted to believe her but...

Splash!

Scum-thick Arkansas pond water stung my soft, round belly.

Skanky water surged up my nose. It clouded my eyes and filled my mouth.

The awful taste.

The panic.

Then the all-consuming quiet.

And then my daddy's arms around me, pulling me close, holding me so tight that I thought he might squeeze the very life out of me.

Breaking the surface.

Daylight.

The rush of my mother and aunts onto the floating dock.

From somewhere, a trickle of warm blood down my arm, then I was whisked away.

Hours of not knowing. And then knowing the unthinkable.

Daddy was dead.

More than thirty-five years have passed. Some of the details may have blurred together in memory. But the one thing I have not forgotten—the thing I can never forget, though God knows I have spent enough years in churches and beds and bars and therapy trying—is the feeling of my older cousin, Bess, pressed close at my back that day.

"What are you waiting for, Charma Deane? God Almighty to kick you in the butt? Get out there."

Her cold hands on my sunburned back.

The push.

More of a shove, really—vicious and uncompromising in its determination. And afterward nothing in my world would ever be the same.

2

"I can't. I don't know what to do." My feet sank into the damp ground at the edge of the old pond. It was night, but not really night. Dark and forbidding. And yet familiar. Comforting, even, in its familiarity. "Please, just tell me what you want from me."

No answer came. Even the fat bullfrogs had stopped their resonant belching croaks and plopped into the inky-black water. Nothing. Just the whisper of leaves and the lap of the pond against the dock. Whoosh-whoosh. Whoosh-whoosh.

The same quiet, life-affirming rhythm of an unborn baby's heartbeat. Whoosh-whoosh. Whoosh-whoosh.

Someone was out there.

Someone who needed me.

Desperately.

"Mama? Mama, is that you?" Half a year after her death, had she had somehow breached the gap between heaven and earth and come to me? My heart ached with hope. "Mama?"

"Save me, Charma!" The cry ripped through my very being.

Not Mama but...

I strained to see into the night and mist. "Who's out there?"

Whoosh-whoosh. *The water rushed toward me on the shore, then ebbed away.*

"What do you want me to do?" I demanded.

"You know what you have to do." The answer came, soft and clear.

Whoosh-whoosh.

"Charma, it's time. Come on." The voice had changed, but the urgency had not.

"Come?" I stared down at the water. It had reached my feet and was rising fast. I clutched my throat. I could not breathe. I could not make a sound. I could only hear—

"Charma? Charma! I need you——now!"

I wanted to run. All my life, I never turned my back on anyone who needed me, but God in heaven I wanted to run away now. Run fast and hard and hide where no one, not even God, could find me. But I could not move.

And I knew that if I did not move—if I did not run or dive in and swim with all my strength—the water would consume me. Whoosh-whoosh. Whoosh—

"Charma Deane Parker, wake up, damn it!"

That quick, it was all gone.

The pond. The unknown voice. Gone.

My pulse thudded hard, high in my chest. I wiped a thin layer of sweat from my forehead and glanced around at the modest home.

Home. Home birth. That's what had brought me here.

"Wake up, girl."

"I'm awake." I fixed my gaze on my friend Inez Calaveras— or, more precisely, on the underside of her. "At least I hope I'm awake, because otherwise I am having that attack of over-flowing-D-cups-from-hell dream again."

"Overflowing D-cups?" She stood straight and gave her upper body a shake. "I'll have you know I am the same perky size C as when I got married twenty-eight years ago. D-cups my ass."

"No, darlin', if we're talking your ass, we are definitely talking a letter way beyond *D*."

"Charma!"

"What? I can't help it. I wake up endowed with the full force of my dazzling personality."

"And people wonder why you are divorced and pretty much always sleep alone."

I laughed. It shouldn't be funny, I know, but sometimes you have to laugh or stick your head in a blender, and my place is such a wreck I couldn't find my blender on a bet. So... "Nobody wonders about me, Inez. It's a small town. They all know my story."

Inez, a midwife in training, had gotten me out of bed in the middle of the night with a plaintive phone call. "Please, Charma, the girl trusts you. The midwife trusts you. And let's get real, any and all of the powers that be in this boys' club of a town trust you. If we should need to call on any of them for help, we'll need you to do it."

The woman did not tell a lie. People here knew me. They knew my family before me. Well, who the hell didn't know my family?

The Georges. Nowhere in the world could you have found a finer collection of droll, discerning, vain, vexing, cunning, coddled, coy and kick-ass women than in my family's gene pool. Queen bees every last one of them. Queen bees who understood that to survive you cannot just sting, you must also give honey.

My mother and aunts had given honey all over Orla, Arkansas, and parts beyond.

As the school nurse in a one-school-nurse town, I had, too, in a manner of speaking.

So my distress signal, whether to a doctor in the next town over or to the Orla police dispatch, would bring immediate and unquestioning results. It has always been that way—at least to hear the women of my family tell it.

Amend that. *Most* of the women of my family.

Bess did not grasp the legacy of strength through service and self-sacrifice.

Sometimes I envied her that even more than her looks, her fabulous lifestyle and her short but brilliant brush with fame. Right. Classic. I *envied* the person who had devoted herself to finding new and nasty ways to totally screw up my life.

I rolled my neck to one side, and the sleep-stiffened joints popped with all the subtlety of a sheet of bubble wrap being twisted. "Anyway, I am awake now. I must have just drifted off for a second."

"Some watchdog you make."

"Woof." I covered my eyes with my hand. "How's she doing?"

"It's hard for her. She'd do better if she could concentrate on the birth and not keep worrying that damn asshole will show up."

I nodded.

I'd known RoryAnne, the mother-to-be, since her first day of school, though I'd lost track of her after she dropped out at age fifteen. I'd never met the father of her child, but given the opportunity to introduce myself...

I am not by nature a violent person. But leave me alone

in a room with a redneck wife-beater, and I think I could go that way.

A low groan, deep and anguished, crept through the otherwise silent house.

I can't think of any sound save a bona fide ghost or a loved one calling out for help that could have chilled me more than that animal-like cry. I sat up and rubbed my hands over my face to hide any hint of my real inclination. To charge in there, grab that child and haul her out of here. "She really should have gone to a hospital to have this baby, Inez."

"She's a nineteen-year-old, convenience-store clerk with no insurance, in a town with no practicing obstetrician, married to an unemployed man with no mercy. What does the hospital offer her except a visit from the county social services, and a medical billing collection process sure to notify the maniac who has promised to kill her exactly where she can be found?"

"And you think she's safe here?"

"She has her mother, her midwife and us. We're all up for our part in it." Inez didn't meet my eyes. "Aren't we?"

"If you want me to make a phone call to bring help or to stand up to that piece-of-shit husband of hers, then yes, I'm up for my part."

"I was hoping you'd do more than that and you know it."

"Yeah, yeah." She wanted me to observe. Had the crazy idea I might make a fine midwife if I'd let myself try. Fat chance. "Probably not really room in there for all of us, anyway. And I should stay out here to keep watch."

"Used to be—I heard this from more than one person— used to be there was a place in this town where a girl like that could go and have plenty of room, help, dignity and feel safe, too."

I knew the place. I'd grown up in it. I held my hand up. "I don't have any sway over that household anymore. Not since Mama..." *Died.* Why couldn't I just say it? "Not since what happened out there at Christmas."

She muttered a phrase in her native tongue that I don't suppose you'd find in any polite English-to-Spanish dictionary.

"I have no idea what you just said, but I couldn't agree with you more," I told her.

Inez is Puerto Rican by way of New Jersey. She says that really throws your average Arkansas redneck for a loop, because they don't know *where* to sic their prejudices. Do they puff up, glower as she passes and mutter things about them dirty bean-eaters taking all our jobs? Or do they make with the silent treatment, showing their disdain with a subtle sucking on their teeth, a raised eyebrow and a pointed glance that everyone round here recognizes as code for "Damn Yankee"?

They'd never pull either around me, of course. They know I'd take up for the fiftysomething grandmother with the figure of a red-hot hoochie mama and wardrobe to match. Like fire I would, and take no prisoners. Nobody in Orla with any sense of history or self-preservation tangles with a member of the George family.

Nobody but Inez, that is.

"Come on, come and observe the birth. You're going to make one piss-poor midwife if you keep refusing to go into the birthing room." She thrust her arm out, pointing down a dimly lit narrow hallway.

"Midwife." I shook my head. "What the hell was I drinking when I agreed to consider *that* as a midlife career shift?"

"Bourbon."

I nodded.

"It was at your retirement party."

"*Voluntary* retirement." After twenty years of service and the realization that the school system could get a part-time nurse and a couple trained aides for what they paid me, it seemed the right thing to do. I didn't need the money and the others did. Besides, quitting work would give me time to pursue self-actualization. If you can get self-actualized by watching TV, shopping and e-mailing to your grown sons every lousy joke and doctored gag photo making the rounds.

"Okay, at your *voluntary* retirement party. You said you might just give midwifery a try because you were too flawed to preach the gospel and too fat to take up pole dancing."

I rubbed my temples. "God, don't I ever shut my mouth?"

"I've known you two years now, girl, and as far as I can tell, no, you don't." She laughed.

"Be honest with me, Inez."

"Always."

"You think my butt's too saggy for me to try that pole dancing gig?"

"I don't know. Stand up, and if it is, I'll give you a butt lift with my foot."

I believed she'd do it. So I stayed put.

"No more foolin' around." She tugged at my arm.

I took a deep breath.

"Aren't you excited to witness this miracle, Charma?"

"I'm a nurse, Inez. I've seen babies born before."

"In a hospital. It's not the same." She batted her hand in the air. "Home birthing is like... It's the way every baby should come into the world. Welcomed in an intimate setting, surrounded by love and comfort. What better beginning could a person have to prepare them for this life?"

"Prepared for this life?" I stood up and shimmied to smooth out my scrubs. I can't help it, after all those years of training I would have felt naked wearing anything but scrubs to attend a birth. Then I locked my eyes on Inez's blissed-out-on-babies expression and smiled. "You want to prepare a child for *this* life? Pry her from her comfort zone with salad tongs and throw her into the spotlight. A few coos, a few tears, a few tests for illicit drugs, then a slap on the ass, and before you know it she's carried away naked in the arms of a stranger. That, my friend, *that* is the way to prepare a person for life in *this* world."

Inez looped her arm around my shoulder. "Charma Deane, someday I am going to throw a salt lick into a kiddie pool filled with margaritas, and you are going to tell me the story of your life."

"Kiddie pool?" I barked out a laugh. "Honey, that'd barely take us through my formative years. You want to hear the story of my life, it's going to take—"

RoryAnne cussed a blue streak at the top of her lungs.

"I'm getting into the birthing pool with you, okay?" The attending midwife's words, intended to soothe her patient, rang hollow in my ears.

Water birth. That's what awaited me in the room at the end of this hall. A helpless child born not into light and air but into...

I tried to swallow, but my throat was dry.

No wonder I'd had that nightmare. No, more than a nightmare, it was so real. A portent, perhaps, if you believed in that kind of thing. I don't know if I do or not, only that if I closed my eyes, it all came flooding back to me.

Whoosh-whoosh. "*Save me, Charma!*"

The mother-to-be cried out again in pain.

"We'd better hurry." Inez rushed into the hallway.

"I can't," I whispered.

"Charma, you're going to miss it. What are you waiting for?" Inez called.

"For God Almighty to kick me in the butt," I murmured, my chest constricting and my knees weak. *Please, God, kick me. Get me moving one way or another before I stand here and turn into stone or find myself going under once and for all.*

Water splashed in the birthing pool.

Voices encouraged both mother and child.

I took one shaky step.

And the "Ride of the Valkyries" struck up in the background.

Thank you, Lord, for smart-ass sons who program ridiculous tunes into their mother's cell phones. I dashed back to my purse in the living room. "And while you're at it, God, bless whoever had the good grace and lousy manners to ignore my commandment not to call me today under any circumstances. I will be forever in his or her debt." I pressed the phone to my ear. "Hello?"

"Charma Deane! My lamb! My precious! Praise the Lord that you picked up. You are never going to believe what has happened now. It's nothing short of a travesty, I tell you. You know I'm not one to complain, but this...this goes too far. When you hear about *this,* Charma, lamb, you are just going to say—"

I put my aching head in my hand and muttered, "Oh, shit."

3

The Death Watch.

I heard it in her voice more than her actual words. But I had no doubt. My late uncle Kelvin's only legitimate widow, Fawnette Faubus George, wanted me to come out to the house where I was raised and tend to her while she spent the next week—or however long it took us all to realize she was perfectly fine—dying.

"What this family needs is an old-fashioned, big-assed bountiful funeral to return the George name to its proper place in Orla society," she would often say to anyone who would listen. "And God, in his infinite wisdom, has seen fit to choose me to provide it."

She got that notion a few years ago when a tumble down the stairs resulted in her life flashing before her eyes, the amputation of her left leg just below the knee and the revelation by nothing less than God Almighty of her role as George family martyr.

Now, steadfast as the semiannual going-out-of-business-blowout sales at Faymar's Boot-ique in downtown Orla, my aunt decrees that the family must gather for her last Christmas, Memorial Day or Arbor Day on earth. I've always found it a blessed mingling of wonder, absurdity, pathos and obligation. The Death Watch, that is, not the shoe sales.

Well, *usually* not the shoe sales.

See, I didn't just love the women who raised me. I was, in a sense, *in love* with them. Since my childhood they had been like great romantic figures in my eyes, leading by example, larger than life against a backdrop of small talk, small minds and small town society. I don't know how I could ever honestly deny them anything they truly, deeply needed.

"Aunt Fawnie, you know how I feel about you. You mean the very world to me."

"Oh, lamb, you don't have to say that."

"Well, it's true. You're like a...a..." I glanced down the hallway, praying no one was coming to drag me into the dreaded birthing room. "You're like a lifeline to me right now, Aunt Fawnie."

"You flatter me, precious, you do. I swanee, I don't deserve it. Not one bit. I'm good as worthless, you know, and for you to even hint otherwise..." She paused to take a deep draw on her cigarette. "But don't let me interrupt you."

"You are priceless, Aunt Fawnie." *Priceless like something you couldn't give away,* I could almost hear Mama muttering under her breath.

Mama.

Damn, there it was again. The awful reality of her passing pierced the delicate shell of my existence. Days went by, even weeks now, when I did not think of her, of all I lost, all I lacked and all I had been robbed of.

I clenched my jaw until my back teeth ached. *No.* I would

not give in to the pain. I would not let it—or Aunt Fawnie and her damn Death Watch—suck me under. "You know how much I love and admire you, Aunt Fawnie—and, of course, Aunt Shug."

"Oh." Another drag on the cigarette, a pause, then a long, hard exhaling breath. I could see the smoke curling through a tightly gritted smile at the mention of her husband's second wife. "Well, sure. *Everyone* loves Shug. Shug's a doll. Has been ever since the day your uncle Kel carried her back here from his tour of duty in Japan."

You'd think after more than forty years of playing the wronged woman, most of it sharing a home with Shug after Kel's death, she'd give that a rest. Of course, if Fawnie ever did straighten up and act right, I'd truly think she *was* preparing to meet her Maker. "I love you both and I'd do anything to—"

"I knew it. I said to myself, my Charma won't let anything bad befall me or my house. I told Shug if the earth opened up and the well went dry and hellfire started lapping at our feet, Charma Deane would spit on the flames to save us."

"But you also have to know—" I dived in before she could commit me to playing rock-paper-scissors with Satan for possession of the family souls "—I'd rather leap into the ocean buck naked with my true age tattooed on my ass—"

"Language, girl!"

"So that when they hauled my lifeless corpse up onto the shore," I continued, pressing on without a pause, "they'd post that damn age-ass photo all over the Internet for all the world to gawk at. I'd rather do *that* than come out to the farm right now."

"Charma Deane! I swan, I don't know what's got into you!

That kind of talk surely does not reflect your superior upbringing or honor your place as a member of the George family."

Screw the George family. That's what Bess would have told her. Bess never showed a lick of patience for the ever-ailing bottle blonde (yes, even in her seventies) with the perpetual smoker's rasp. It's sad, really, because though Fawnie dearly loves both her nephews and all three of her nieces, she damn near worships Bess.

Welcome to the club. Who doesn't adore Bess?

Besides me, of course.

Bess says whatever she wants. Bess lives however she pleases. And though she has no right even in the wildest stretch of imagination to it, when anyone calls her a Southern belle, she claims the title, always adding, "A belle with balls."

Most folks think she means it as a metaphor. Some part of me wonders, however, if she honestly does have a set—probably sitting in a jar on her vanity next to Nana Abbra's antique jewelry box.

Unlike some in our family, I never had the luxury of turning a blind eye to how selfish, hurtful and cold Bess can be when it suits her. I have forgiven her one too many times now and been repaid in heartbreak and treachery. If it were Bess alone in all that, well, I could deal with it. But after this last...event. After the way my aunts let my mother die, let Bess call the shots and never once picked up a phone, never explained, never came to me after to apologize...

"No. I can't come stay with y'all, Aunt Fawnie," I whispered.

"You can, you just *won't*." Her voice had turned hard.

"You could be right, but that doesn't change my answer." Nothing she could say could compel me to agree.

"Minnie is here, you know."

Except that.

Minami Annette George, now Raynes, the only child of Sugi Ichiuchi and Kelvin George, was named for a Japanese relative none of us ever met, and her daddy's favorite American beach-blanket bimbo. Our first grade teacher dubbed her "Minnie" to help the bashful, Asian girl "fit in better" among the slew of blond and buoyant Kathys, Debbies and Tammys swarming the school registers in late 1960s Arkansas.

I could justify to myself acting like a flaming donkey's patoot toward everyone else in my family, but not toward Minnie.

"Minnie? There? Since when?"

"She showed up this morning. Of course, her mama and I were glad to see her but..." Fawnie could convey true petulance over a phone line like nobody's business.

I exhaled slowly. "But there's only one of her and two of you. And you, old woman, can't stand the idea of Aunt Shug having someone home to fuss over her and you not having the same."

I heard the distinct rattle of ice in an upturned glass, then finally, "Shitfire, Charma Deane, how the hell did you get to be so damn ill-mannered?"

"Some flaw in my 'superior upbringing,' I suppose." I laughed. "So, can I speak to Minnie?"

"Minnie isn't taking phone calls." She said it in the same tone she might say, *Minnie thinks she's the danged-almighty queen of England,* then took a languid draw on her cigarette. "So there's no use you even asking to talk to her."

"No calls?" Minnie, the first of us girls to get her own private line and a pink princess phone to go with it? "Why not?"

"Maybe she's ashamed."

"What could Minnie possibly have to be ashamed of?"

"Her part in it."

Don't fall for this, my mind screamed, even as my lips formed the words, "In what?"

"That's what I called to tell you."

"Aunt Fawnie, you are not making any sense."

"Me? I'll tell you what doesn't make sense—throwing two helpless women out onto the streets. Now *that* don't make sense."

"I couldn't agree with you more." *There. All done.* She'd obviously called wanting someone to take her side in whatever imagined wrong had been dealt her. In one sentence I had given the old bat what she needed, and not had to pack clean underwear and leave my rented rat hole of an apartment to do it.

"It's not fair."

Feeling magnanimous, I threw in another nonspecific measure of support. "No, of course not."

"And with no warning. Leaves me without a leg to stand on, I tell you."

"Well, now that is bad, Aunt Fawnie, seeing as you only *have* the one leg."

Silence. One second. Two.

"Don't tell me you're picking now to start getting sensitive to my tacky remarks, Aunt Fawnie." I felt like such a jerk, and I didn't deserve that. Damn it, she'd called me when I'd specifically asked her not to. If anyone was the jerk here... "Aunt Fawnie? Honey? You okay?"

"I don't know what to do, lamb." A sudden quiet power seized the old woman's smoke-strained voice. "I never expected this, not from you girls, not from *her.*"

"Her?" The house had fallen silent as a tomb, but that did

not help me better discern the message buried in my aunt's hushed words. "Do you mean Minnie?"

"No."

I didn't want to ask. I didn't want to know. But as in so many things involving my family, something larger took hold, and I heard my own parched whisper. "Who?"

"Bess."

I knew it. I could have said it with her, and yet hearing it had all the impact of a blow to the gut. The wind was knocked clean out of me.

I could not feel a single breath enter or leave my body. I was still breathing, I knew. I'm an RN, after all—I know the consequences if you actually *stop* breathing, and much as I would have welcomed unconsciousness, a light at the end of the tunnel, the possibility of my mother greeting me, and finally getting some answers, it was just not happening. "What about Bess?"

"She holds the deed to the house, Charma."

"What?" My aunt might as well have been speaking ancient Aramaic for all the sense that made to me.

"Didn't you know that, either? *We* never knew. I swear, I always thought your mama had it. But after she went to be with Jesus..."

"Went to be with Jesus? Shitfire, Aunt Fawnie, you make it sound like she ran off to become a roadie for a concert tour of the Son of God," I lashed out in hurt and anger.

She said nothing in response and I got her message loud and clear.

"Aunt Fawnie, Mama just..."

"I have to push," the mommy-to-be in the other room wailed.

Water sloshed. Hushed tones followed.

I gripped the tiny phone as if it alone upheld me, and after all these months of denial, spat out the truth. "Mama just *died*. Okay? She...died."

"Well, she *died* without telling us that we didn't own this house. Your aunt Ruth owns it, or she did." This time the pause lasted longer and ended only after the flick of Fawnie's heavy silver lighter and the soft sucking breath of her starting a new smoke. When she spoke again her words came low and guttural, almost slurred. "That damn grandmother of yours. She hated all of us, you know."

For once Fawnie did not exaggerate. My grandmother had despised with every fiber in her being the women who had taken her precious sons from her.

"Okay, you can do this. Push." The midwife's reassuring tone carried down the hallway. "Push, but not too hard, now. Gentle…"

I massaged my temples. "Connect the dots for me, Aunt Fawnie. What do Minnie and Nana and the deed and...and Bess have to do with anything?"

"She's kicking us out, Charma Deane. Bess sent a letter. We have thirty days to vacate."

"That's not…" I wanted to say "not true," but after all the pain I'd suffered at the hands of my cousin I had no choice but to believe. "Why? Why would she do it? What does she want with the Aunt Farm?"

"I don't know, lamb. Tell me why our darling Bess does any-thing? Why did she write that damn book of lies about us? Why did she run off with your—"

"Stick to the house, Aunt Fawnie." The command rushed out in a controlled panic. Control, that was what was called for now, on both our parts. "Think. Did Bess give you any reason why she would do something like this? Why would she try to take the house?"

"She didn't say. Maybe she wants to turn it into some moneymaking venture. Set it up for some roadside attraction. You know, bring the whole family out for a day of fun at our newly renovated den of iniquity."

Home among the Heathens. Bess had taken the main part of the title of her one and only bestseller from Nana Abbra's penchant to tell us girls, whenever we got up to anything the least bit interesting or fun, that we acted no better than a pack of heathens. The subtitle, the stark white text under the bold red main title that still riled my aunts whenever they thought of it, she pulled wholly from her malicious imagination and twisted sense of humor. *My Childhood in an Arkansas Whorehouse.*

"Money from that vile book must have run out by now. Maybe she just wants to put the house on the market to raise some cash," Fawnie muttered.

"She can't sell it. It's our family home." Three generations of Georges had lived there in the house my grandparents built outside of Orla. When my uncle Kel died, Nana had insisted that Shug and Minnie move in with her. They say the best way to get along with anyone is to find a common adversary, so Fawnie came along, too, making it easier for everyone to choose up sides and not kill one another.

When Daddy died, Nana wanted me and Mama to join the brood. Mama agreed on one condition—that Nana get a house in town and leave us alone.

It seemed the ultimate generosity that Nana turned the eight-bedroom, double-balconied monstrosity over to her daughters-in-law, but everyone who knew the matriarch of the George family said she'd done it to farm the three aunts out and yet still be able to keep them under her thumb. From that day on, everybody in Orla called our house the Aunt Farm. "And as for taking it away to live in it herself...Bess has no right. Minnie and I grew up there, not her. She only came summers."

"I know, but seems your grandmother saw it different. She willed it to Ruth, and Ruth gave it to Bess a few years ago, to do with it what she would."

Ruth was Nana Abbra's only daughter. And Bess was Ruth's only daughter. Ruth resented the hell out of Nana for treating Daddy and Uncle Kel like a pair of precious petty princes. So she'd vowed to change that with her own children.

And she did. In a big way. By reversing the pattern of favoritism—full circle. So Bess grew up resenting Ruth for smothering her with affection, while her brothers starved for scraps of acknowledgment.

Seems when the women in my family love you, you can't win.

But Bess *had* won.

She made it a point to win, especially where I was concerned. From men to Mama's last moments, Bess had made it her life's work to steal them away from me.

Now she had gone after the Aunt Farm.

I couldn't make myself grasp it entirely.

"After more than forty years in this house, thirty days to vacate. It can't be done. It *shouldn't* be done. It's wrong, lamb, and I don't know who else to turn to but you. You have got to come. None of us can stand up to Bess—except you."

"No," I whispered, or I think I did. My mind said it over and over. *No. No.*

"Push."

Water sloshed.

RoryAnne moaned.

"There's the head," someone called out.

Inez appeared at the doorway. "Charma, it's now or never."

"This is killing me, lamb," Fawnie whispered. "It had ought to kill me, I tell you. What have I always said? They won't *put* me out of my house, they'll *carry* me out feet first."

Ah, back to the Death Watch. Somehow the damn thing had just lost all of its former luster.

"Charma?" Inez motioned frantically for me to come with her.

Water birth or Death Watch. Facing the future or confronting the past? Rock. Hard place. And me right in the middle— left to choose.

"Time's run out, Charma," Inez said, her hand held out to me.

"The baby is crowning, everyone," the midwife called above the quiet swishing in the birthing pool.

I turned my back and stuck my finger in my ear. "Is Bess in town, Aunt Fawnie?"

"We haven't seen her. She had a lawyer serve the papers on us."

"Do you have a lawyer?"

"I don't have anything—" her voice grew weak as a child's "—but you."

It would have been neater and so much more efficient if the old woman had just plunged a knife in my heart and got it over with. "I don't know what I could do to help."

"This is it," the midwife said.

"You could talk to Bess," Fawnie murmured. "She might listen to you."

"It's a girl!"

I shut my eyes. "Bess is dead to me."

"Don't say that, lamb! Don't ever say that. As long as there is life, there is hope. That's you, Charma Deane, you're our only hope."

"Welcome to the world!"

Whoosh.

Splash.

A baby's cry at last.

I dragged air into my lungs and held it for a moment before finally opening my eyes, exhaling and hanging my head. "Okay, Aunt Fawnie. Let me run by the apartment to get my things. I'll be there shortly."

"You won't regret this, precious."

I pressed the end call button and muttered, "I already do."

4

"Scoot over, sweetcheeks. I'm driving."

"Like hell you are." Sterling Mayhouse, a young—some people say too young—lawyer of my acquaintance, didn't budge an inch from behind the wheel of his sleek, ice-blue Jaguar convertible. He just leaned across the seat to pop open the passenger door. "You want my help? Get in. If not…"

"Extortionist." I plunked down into the leather bucket seat.

He laughed and gunned the motor.

I waved at Inez, leaving her standing on the porch with her hands on her hips and probably wishing she could have my head on a platter.

"Where to?"

"All I want is to get away from here." I slipped off my shoes and tried to guess how crazy it would make Sterling if I plopped my bare feet up on the dash. Yelling-about-my-white-trash-ways crazy or veering-off-the-road-in-a-fit-of-rage crazy. "Oh, uh, and to single-handedly rescue the Aunt Farm from the clutches of my cousin Bess, of course."

"How you plan to do that?"

White-trash-ways crazy, I decided, and kicked my heels up to rest on the charcoal-gray leather. "I don't have the slightest idea."

He glanced at my feet.

I wriggled my freshly painted toes.

He shook his head. "You are such a..."

"Low-down piece of common trash?"

"Liar," he finished.

I dropped both feet to the floorboard. Common trash I could have taken in stride, but for him to go flinging the truth in my face? What nerve.

"That you called me to come get you, the very fact you have us rushing off to the rescue, tells me you have a plan of some sort. Because no way would you go out to that house armed with nothing but your winning ways."

"Okay." Up went the feet again. "I do have a pretty good idea what to do, or at least where I can start to unravel Bess's plot. But since it involves doing something I find uniquely vile, singularly distasteful and—more to the point—personally humbling, I have no intention of doing it."

"None?"

"Never."

"Even if it meant those two old ladies got tossed out on their baggy behinds?"

I slid down in the seat and adjusted my shoulders. "Sure. Why not? I mean, what did Fawnie and Shug ever do for me?"

"Besides help raise you? And provide you with the foundation for everything you ever accomplished in life?"

"Hmm." I pretended a sudden fascination with the way the wind currents rushed over my outstretched hand.

Even so, my mind kept ticking off the list Sterling had started of all the ways my aunts had made my life richer. Like throwing me not one but two shamefully elaborate weddings—even though only one actually ended in vows being said. The wrong one. Which meant years later they got to throw me a wickedly wonderful divorce party.

And they were there when each of my sons was born, grew up and flew the nest.

And when my mother died.…

I sat up straight again and murmured, "It's been five months, you know. They still haven't said a word about Mama's death."

He didn't argue or take up their cause. He wouldn't dare.

Reaching a dead end, Sterling made a wide U-turn to get us headed toward Orla proper again, and changed the subject. "What were you doing out here, anyway?"

"I came to witness the miracle of life." I laid my hand over my eyes.

"*Miracle?* Out *here?* What? Did someone find an image of the Virgin Mary in a melted Tupperware lid?"

I laughed. Not because I found him especially clever, but because I had no intention of launching into a lengthy discussion of the long-submerged phobia that had sent me calling for him to come and get me. Instead, I focused on persuading the man to do battle with Bess on my aunts' behalf by veering to a topic I knew he'd find infinitely more interesting—himself.

"You sure are a cute thing, you know it?"

"I've heard talk." He chuckled. Not in arrogance, but smooth and warm and a little bit self-effacing.

Sterling is one of those rare breeds we grow in the South. He can walk the line between charming and charismatic and make you believe he is both when, down deep, you know he is neither. A potent mix of generations of ill-gotten gain and his own inexperience and good intentions, he calls himself an honorable attorney.

And that ain't the only thing he deludes himself about.

The darling, persistent fool has devoted far too much time and money to the impossible task of getting me to go to bed with him. So far all he's gotten for his trouble is my dazzling company, a couple home-cooked meals and now the unprecedented thrill of helping me untangle my aunts' legal woes pro bono. Lucky, lucky man.

It galls him no end that I have no desire to sleep with him.

Of course, I *do* desire him. I'm not dead. He's young and buff-ish, for an attorney, and menswear-model attractive— you know, casual and clean-cut, with his attention always fixed in the distance. I *want* to sleep with Sterling Mayhouse.

I just don't want him to sleep with me.

This was not a man who could deal with cellulite. Or two-decades' worth of post-baby belly. Or a stray gray hair in a place where angels and even Miss Clairol fear to tread.

That didn't keep me from playing the game, though. "I wonder why I don't latch on to you with both hands and never let go?"

"It's the age thing."

"*What* age thing?"

"Well, I'm thirty-four, and your two boys are twenty-one and twenty-three. So that means the age difference between us must be, what? A good ten years?" Sterling smiled, all rich and wry, like honey-butter and white lightning. He narrowed his eyes as if he had the power to see right through me. "Not that it matters to *me.*"

"Or me," I lied. "I'm not concerned about a few years here or there. Besides, have you forgotten about girl math?"

Some families have their own language. Mine has its own mathematical paradigm.

"It doesn't matter how many rules you and your cousins make up to shave years off your real age, the old clock still keeps ticking." Sterling flicked a helpless ladybug from the sleeve of his brilliant-white tennis shirt. "Tick-tock. Tick-tock."

"Don't talk. Don't talk." I echoed the rhythm of his mocking words. "In fact don't even bother to act like you understand the dynamics between me and my girl cousins."

He couldn't understand. Girl math was just one tiny part of the whole equation between Bess and Minnie and me.

We grew up together in a time and place that made us close in ways that blood sisters cannot afford to be. Close in ways that true friends seldom have the courage to be. Through our lifetimes we had forged a bond that only cousins could understand. Unbreakable as long as we each drew breath, even in the face of betrayal, even in the face of unrelenting anger, heartbreak and regret.

"You couldn't possibly get it, Sterling." I gritted my teeth. "To us, age is not about ticking clocks. It's about how we've lived our lives. How you live is far more important than how long you've been alive."

"Unless you've been alive ten years longer than the man who wants to date you."

All right. So I am a big fat hypocrite. If he really wanted to sleep with me, he shouldn't have pointed that out, though. "Oh, *dates* you can get from me, Mr. Learn-ed Counselor. Why don't you circle this one in red on your calendar as the day you blew any chance of getting in my drawers?"

"*Drawers,* Charma?" He laughed. "Damn, you *are* old."

"Shut up," I muttered. "And take the long way around, I need time to think."

"Think? It's too hot to think. Or to take the long way anywhere."

"It's just summer, you fool. It's supposed to be hot. I like it. Just drive."

I do like summer, especially in our little corner of Arkansas. It's special, you see, almost magical. I swear it is.

You don't know the South if you don't know its summers. Damp and slow, rich with the textures of life simmered down to its essence and haunted by the memories of every season past.

And hot? Hell, yes, it's hot, but that's not the whole of it. From May to September the South takes on both a veneer and a depth you don't find in any other season, any other region. It's hopscotching over a tar road to keep from burning bare feet and the slap of ice-box cold rushing out of a grocery store door on a sweltering afternoon.

To know the South is to know the smell of all things fertile and growing. Of earth and leaves. Of honeysuckle and lilac. And the sweet, sticky stench of rotting fruit. If you don't know that, then you don't know the South.

Even then it will fool you.

One merciless afternoon, just like this one was working itself up to be, the air will stir.

Followed by the swift rolling swell of clouds.

A sudden bolt of lightning.

A single earthshaking clap of thunder.

That's all the warning you get to scurry inside before all hell breaks lose.

Families are like that. They have their storms and their stinks. They have their sweet memories, their hot spells and the brief respite of rain. They have their growth and loss. And they have their roots. Unless you know these things about them, you don't know families at all.

And even then, they will fool you.

My family had sure fooled me.

I clenched my jaw. "Damn it, Dinah!"

"What, Charma?"

"Just thinking." I dredged up a feeble laugh and laid my head back. "My aunt Fawnie used to say "Damn it, Dinah" so often when talking to or about my mother that for a while when I was young, I thought that was her Christian name. Damn it, Dinah McCoy George."

"If your mama was anything like you, I'll bet she had a few choice names for your aunt, as well."

"Oh, yeah." I took in a good, long, deep breath and let it out real slow. "Even now that Mama isn't around to react, I'll bet that Aunt Fawnie still says it every time she thinks of my mama sitting down in that rocker on the back porch and just giving up like she did."

I blinked, and to my surprise tears stung the corners of my eyes. Tears? I hadn't cried over losing my mama in a couple months. Not like those first days when the smallest thing, like a song or catching a whiff of her old perfume, could reduce me to a sobbing six-year-old. It got so people were nervous just to see me walk into the market for fear I'd start shuffling through the aisles clutching Mama's favorite brand of toilet cleanser and bawling, "Damn it, Dinah, why the hell did you want to go and do that for?"

Sterling laid his hand on my shoulder, but instead of trying to ease my obvious pain, he said simply, "Fawnie and Shug must pine for your mother something dreadful."

"Fawnie and...*pine?*" His words saved me from sliding down that long, lonely, all-too-familiar slope that over this past year had frequently dead-ended with me on the business end of a spoon and fork poking down plates piled with comfort food. "I guess I hadn't considered that."

I felt ashamed to admit it. I had wrapped myself so tightly in my own grief and anger that I had shut out all thought of how the women who had lived with my mother most of my lifetime might suffer the loss. It must have been awful for them. And I hadn't done a damn thing to make it better.

And now came the trouble with the house and only me standing between them and...

I bit my lower lip. It felt like God himself had laced his hand around my chest and begun to squeeze.

Charma Deane, you're our only hope. Fawnie's plea gnawed at my very soul. *Only hope.*

Sterling pulled to a stop at the light, and I looked both ways.

In either direction Orla stretched out, ordinary and extraordinary all at once. I took a deep breath, as if I could breathe it all in but couldn't get my fill of it.

People often ask me why I stay here. And all I can say is, where else would I go? Even if I left Orla, Orla would always be in me. It's in the cadence of my speech and the coating on my pan-fried chicken. I couldn't exist without it, and in my arrogance I believe to the very core of my being that it could not exist without me—or my family.

I wasn't leaving.

And neither were my aunts. Not if I had anything to say about it.

And I did.

Even though that meant I now had to head for the one place in town I swore I'd never go.

"Where to?" Sterling rubbed his finely manicured hands together. "Shall I drive out to the funny farm?"

"Aunt Farm." Like he didn't know. I gave him an icy glare. "And no, I can't go out there yet. There's something important I have to do."

"What?"

"Get some ammunition."

"Ammu...what?"

"I'm going to need some pretty heavy artillery if I hope to blow Bess's butt out of the water. Luckily, I know just where to get it."

"You're not talking about real ammunition, are you? Because I can't be a party to actual gunplay."

I sighed. "Honestly now. Do I look like the kind of woman who would drag Bambi down to the Buckmasters' bonfire?"

"Honestly? Yes." He glanced around at Orla's quiet Main Street, possibly looking for an avenue of escape. When he turned to me again, he just shook his head and gave me that trademark sexy smirk of his. "If you thought it would serve a higher purpose—such as saving your family and besting your cousin once and for all—I think you'd do whatever you had to do to get the job done."

I smiled, gave him a wink and said, "I knew I did the right thing in bringing you. Now, make a hard right. We're about to do something dead wrong."

5

"A funeral home?"

"To hell with the hair salon. You get your best gossip in rooms with dingy green walls, the aroma of strong coffee cutting through dank air and a dearth of natural lighting." I held out three fingers and used them to tick off a list for his edification. "Church basements, bank offices and funeral parlors."

"Notwithstanding, a hair salon might not have been a bad choice." He grinned at me.

I glanced in the general direction of the side mirror and that was enough. Sinking my fingers into the caramel-colored mass, I muttered, "Damn humidity."

"Riding in the convertible doesn't help. I can put the top up from now on."

"Don't you dare. I love zipping around town topless."

"Now that conjures up a mental picture—"

"Well, commit it to memory, darling, because a mental picture is all you're getting."

"Tease."

"Horndog."

"Ah-ooooowww," he howled.

"Shh. Someone will hear you, you big idiot." I rifled through my oversize purse, grabbed my brush and began tugging it through the thick tangles. "Show a little respect. After all, we are at—" I gestured toward the black-and-gold sign in the plush green grass "—you know."

Chapman and Sons Funeral Home.

I stared at the words for a moment, unsure if I actually possessed the wherewithal to carry out my plan.

Chapman's sat two blocks off of Main Street, resting not quite square on a pie-shape lot down a narrow, angled street. On the brightest of days it looked cool and somber, its darkly tinted windows shrouded with heavy green awnings. I used to think they designed it that way to grant the grief-stricken some measure of privacy, but now I wonder. Who are they really protecting?

Most of us want nothing to do with the whole business of death. We don't want to know what goes on behind those smoky windows, under those covered walkways, deep inside those darkened rooms. We don't want to know.

Lord, at least I sure didn't.

We don't want to cross that threshold.

In fact, I had sworn a long time ago that I would never cross it. I would never walk through the door of Chapman's again.

"So, why are we here, Charma?"

"Because my family always does business with Chapman's," I murmured, gaze fixed on the place but seeing nothing in particular.

"Business?"

"That's what we always called it, doing 'business.' In fact, here in Orla it's a mark of prestige to say, 'We take all our business to Chapman's.'"

"You get prestige from your choice of undertaker?"

"Sure. On account of Chapman's has been in town the longest *and* they charge the most. Chapman's prices are more padded than their deluxe model satin-quilted coffins. So coming here is literally like throwing money into an open grave."

"That's just crazy, Charma."

"I *know.* My family even had our dogs cremated here."

"How is that going to help you gather ammunition to use against your cousin?"

"Let's just say I have a very long-standing—" *Difference of opinion? Unresolved issue? Complete and utter burn-in-hell-you-heartless-bastard contempt?* "—association with someone in this place."

"And that someone will talk to you?"

"Has to." I tossed my brush back in my bag, then squared my shoulders and stared at the old building, which looked deceptively like a place a freckle-faced boy with a lop-eared dog might live. I took a deep breath and said quietly, "He has my mother's ashes."

"Your...?" Sterling twisted in the seat. He grabbed my arm and gave it a shake as if that would bring me around and make me start talking sense. "Charma, honey, your mother has been gone since Christmas. Are you telling me no one ever came to claim her ashes?"

"It was in her will that they not be released to anyone but me. You haven't lived in Orla long enough to know this, but in my family we have a history of—" I cleared my throat "—not exactly treating the passing of family members with complete dignity."

I thought of Fawnie and Shug trying to outdo one another for the title of Most Wounded Widow over my uncle Kel's death. And how when they actually started to wrestle with each other over the open coffin, Mama shouted right there in the chapel for Daddy to go up and do something—preferably push them both in with the body and shut the lid!

Bess's mother, Aunt Ruth, had got all huffy over the incident, but upon viewing her baby brother laid out in his ripped-at-the-seams-to-fit army uniform, promptly fainted on the hand-tied Persian rug. She had to be carried out. Bess told Minnie and me that they'd stretched her out on the slab where they prepared the bodies, and the two of us, being all of five, pitched crying fits ourselves.

Two years later, when my daddy died, Mama let it be known there would be no such carrying on. Mama was the boss of everything in her world, and everybody did as she decreed—even my Nana, Abbra Esme Sullivan George. Except where her sons were concerned.

Nana Abbra made sure that the funeral of her most beloved boy would stand as a monument to excess, anguish and the eminence of the George family past, present and future.

A few years later Mama got back at Nana for that, but good. So designing, so disrespectful, so delightful was Mama and the aunts' revenge that Bess used the incident as the opening chapter in her book. It was one of the few things she wrote in that whole trashy tome that she did not embellish the hell out of or outright lie about.

Just thinking now of how they laid my Nana to rest still makes me shudder. It was so awful that Bess and I made a pact regarding our own demises right there on the spot.

That was back when I could still hope my cousin's word might mean something.

Heartache tinged with humor. If my family had one emotional tagline, that would be it. We always laughed and laughed hard, but it never quite made up for all the pain we inflicted on one another. Never.

I shut my eyes and raised my fingers to my forehead. My hand trembled, so I laced my arms tight over my chest and shook my freshly arranged hair back from my face. I didn't want to say anything more, but then again, I didn't want to get out of the car just yet. And there sat Sterling, waiting for me to do or say *something*.

So I forced myself to find my voice, soft at first, then stronger. "Nobody but me can collect my mother's ashes and, as you know, I was helping my youngest settle in his apartment in Tulsa when she lay dying, and nobody called me back to be with her or to oversee any...any *arrangements* for her remains."

"With no one claiming them, don't you think they'd have disposed of the ashes by now?"

"Guy Chapman would never do that to me." My hands fell to my lap. "Rest assured Mama's ashes are still right here."

"I hope you're right. Who's Guy Chapman?"

"He's..." The first boy I ever slept with. The man who left me at the altar. The mortician who last looked on my mama's lovely face, then burned her down to ash and bone without so much as a phone call to me until after the fact. "He's nobody."

The car idled quietly, ready for a quick getaway should my courage fail. My heart thumped hard in my chest and my thoughts became jumbled.

"What are you going to do? March up to the door? What if there's a body laid out in the front room?"

"What if there is?" What a stupid thought. It was a mortuary, after all. What did he think would be in there—a buffet? "I guess I'll just go in and see who it is. Maybe check out who signed the guest book."

"Okay, then." He popped open his door. "Let's do this."

"No. You stay here." It would be the first time I'd come face-to-face with Guy since... And to come dragging pretty young Sterling onto his doorstep like some prize-show pony? It reeked of a poorly plotted comedy where the desperate divorcée tries to impress her former lover. No, thank you. I'd like to think I had more dignity than that. "This is the kind of mission I have to go on 'unmanned,' as it were."

"What?"

"Let's just say I'll never get anything out of him with a stranger standing there." Code for *If I am going to make an ass of myself, I'd prefer as few witnesses as possible.*

"Okay. Fine. Then go."

"I am. I'm going. I can do this. I'll just pretend I'm paying a call on an old pal. An everyday, average friendly interaction with an ordinary neighbor."

"Yeah, an ordinary neighbor who has a corpse lying in the parlor and a crematorium in the basement." Sterling let his door fall shut with a thud. "Careful. You might find some ghosts in there, Charma."

I hopped out in a big hurry and headed up the walk, calling behind me as I went, "*Might* find some ghosts? Don't kid yourself—that's inescapable!"

The myth about small towns is that everybody knows everybody and they all cross paths day in and day out. The truth is, everybody knows *somebody* and they often expend a great deal of effort trying not to cross paths with *anybody.*

It seldom works.

Sooner or later you will see someone you wish you hadn't, and you'd better speak to them or there *will* be talk. That's the unwritten law. It's as unbendable as...as...as the rule about not buying anything from the hometown drug store that you don't want the folks at church or work to know you need. Hell, I don't know why they ever bother carrying men's hair dye or home pregnancy tests. A purchase like that half the town would know about before you had a chance to wash out the gray or pee on the stick.

So locals know to factor in an extra twenty minutes for the obligatory "God is good" and "Ain't that a shame" and "Bless his heart" exchanges on trips to the bank or post office, where you can't duck quickly out of sight. In Orla you don't have to *love* your neighbor, but at some point you'll have to look at him and be civil.

That's why I considered it a minor miracle that Guy Chapman had been back in Orla for over a year and I had managed to avoid running into him even once. A whole year. It had to be some kind of town record. And now here I was, marching up to the front door of his place of business for a no-holds-barred confrontation.

Damn that Bess.

I paused on the porch and glanced back at Sterling, who had his cell phone pressed to his ear.

What the hell is lacking in my personal makeup that I would waste so much time with a man like that? Was I that vain? That insecure? Yes on both counts, of course, but that wasn't the reason.

Strays, children and lost causes. My weaknesses. In Sterling I found something of all of those. Somehow I thought I could give the man, cut off from his family and floundering, a sense of direction. Yes, that I could rescue him.

He leaned away from his phone to check himself out in the rearview mirror, nodding and making 'uh-huh' sounds to the unsuspecting caller even as he did.

How do you rescue someone who doesn't even have the self-awareness to know how lost he is? I guess if I ever figure that out, I'd finally be able to pull off the ultimate salvation— my own.

I swallowed hard, then turned and unclenched my fist to reach for the door handle.

My fingers never touched the polished brass.

"Hello, Charma." His voice came low and soft, almost like a phantom's breath. He held back, mostly hidden in the dim light of the large marble-and-wood foyer just beyond the open door.

Though I could not see his eyes, I could just make out the glint of silver at the temples of his once thick, dark hair. Silver. Of course he'd age like that. Silver. No gray, no coarse yellow-snow-colored hair for him. Lucky bastard—life had always taken a special shine to Guy Chapman.

And heaven help me, I understood why. Even standing in his unseen presence made my heart race. My thoughts staggered drunkenly. The hair on the back of my neck prickled, and when I blinked, my eyes were moist with the threat of tears. Damn him.

I squinted—to try to get a better look, not to conceal my gut reaction.

Okay, a bit of both.

But I could make out only the suggestion of his form. Tall. Taller, even, than I had remembered him, which surprised me. Over the years I had built up this man into something quite sizable indeed, both in his stature and in the importance he'd played in the path my life took.

"Guess this visit is way overdue." He held out his hand.

I stared at the broad palm and long fingers and could not help but recall how they felt on my body. My heart beat in hard, heavy contractions that made my whole chest ache. And I recalled the last thing he had said to me standing in this very spot.

Suddenly retreat was the only thing on my mind.

"Won't you come in?"

"I'd...I'd rather not." I stepped back.

"I thought you had come to collect Miz—"

"I came for answers." I would not stand here like a child and let him speak my mother's name. Not after what he had done to her. To *me*. "Answers, Guy. That's all."

"Answers? About what?"

"About my aunts being evicted from the farm." There. If I kept focused, stayed away from all things personal, I could do this. I inched my chin up and narrowed my eyes until his shadowy form became a blur. "What do you know about that?"

He dropped his extended hand. "Don't ask, Charma. I have no desire to get involved in your family's affairs."

"Oh, really?" If he had said anything else, I might have backed away, run right down the stairs and all the way home with my tail between my legs. But to have the out-and-out gall to stand there and lie to my face? No, that would not stand. Not with me, not from him. "And when exactly did your *desire* wane, Guy? After you poured Mama's ashes into an urn? Do you think that when you wiped the dust of her remains off of your guilty hands you symbolically washed away any responsibility to my family for your actions? And even if you did, that hardly would absolve you of—"

"Damn it, Charma, this is neither the time nor the place. You want to rehash our personal history, you come inside and do it quietly, like we're a couple of adults." He cocked his head, and my memory supplied the exact tilt of his smile, the glint in his eyes as he added, low and laughing, "Or reasonable facsimiles."

"Reasonable? My home and my family are on the line here, Guy. The last thing I feel like being is..." *Here.* "Reasonable."

"Fair enough. That's one of the things I always loved about you, Charma. You never saw any use in hiding your honest feelings."

If I hadn't known better, I'd have thought he meant that as a compliment. I crossed my arms over my chest good and tight and fixed my gaze on the faint outline of his face. "And you hid everything, including the fact that you never had an honest feeling in your life."

"Bit harsh, don't you think?"

"Doesn't make it any less true."

His feet shifted on the old floor. No denial. No self-defense.

I exhaled and made a study of the weathered threshold between us. "I guess I don't know what's more foolish—my thinking I could turn to you for help and answers, or your thinking that just by saying so you can remove yourself from what has gone on in my family, from what is going on with them right now."

"Charma, I want to help you."

"Then tell me what you know," I whispered.

There was dead silence for a moment. Then the almost imperceptible rustle of his body moving, his shoulders rasping against the fabric of his shirt. He slid his hand into his jeans pocket. He jangled his keys. Finally, quietly, he said, "I can't."

We stood there at an impasse for a long, awkward minute. I could have asked him again, appealed to his sense of justice and honor, pleaded with him even for old times' sake, but I knew his reply would be the same. Just as I knew, down deep on a level I am not comfortable with taking too long a look at, that if he could, he really would have done something to come to my aid.

"That's it then?"

"Charma, I—"

"No, don't." I held up my hand to cut him off, amended it to a quick wave, then turned to head for the front steps. "Sorry to have bothered you."

"No bother." The door creaked, followed by the sound of his footsteps on the front porch.

I didn't want to do it, but I had to. How could I not? I turned my head just to see him once again.

My breath caught high in my chest. He wore his age like a comfortable pair of jeans, well broken in, worn almost threadbare in all the right spots, and all the more sexy for it. His hair *had* gone silver, and not just at the temples but in threads that tumbled throughout the coarse, dark waves.

Some folks say God is a man and so he is most kind to men as they age. Looking at Guy, I think God might just be a woman. Only a woman could understand that it takes time to make something truly awe-inspiring like a giant redwood, a fine wine or an honest-to-goodness real grown-up man.

He leaned one shoulder against a porch column and

tugged his tie loose at the collar as he gazed past me. "That your boyfriend?"

I glanced out to the curb, where Sterling still sat in his convertible. Having pivoted the rearview mirror completely toward the driver's side, he was gazing into it, flipping his collar up, then down, then up again.

"He's my, um..." *Lawyer? Backup boy toy? Pet?* I sighed. "He's none of your business. And please, don't feel you have to walk me to my car. I'm sure you have a cold body inside waiting for you."

"Now, you of all people should know, Charma," he drawled, all lazylike and coy as a snake coiling for the strike, "I haven't had a cold body waiting at home for me in over twenty years. Not since Bess and I broke up."

If he had taken the urn he'd stored my mother's ashes in and used it to bludgeon me in the head, it could not have hurt me more. And he knew it.

I did not turn to look at him. I just kept right on walking, calling back over my shoulder the single sentiment about Guy Chapman that had burned in my soul every day for the last twenty-plus years. "I hope you rot in hell."

6

I can't say exactly how we got to the Aunt Farm after that,
what roads we took or even what I said to Sterling along the
way. As to whether I observed proper manners in introduc-
ing the man to Minnie, Fawnie and Shug, I can assure you I
did not.

I also did not acknowledge with grace and gladness their
delight in telling me that Guy Chapman had called inquiring
as to my safe arrival. Nor was I particularly elated to learn that
they had invited him out to dinner. In fact, I believe when my
aunt Fawnie imparted this enchanting tidbit to me, with Minnie and Aunt Shug beaming beatifically at me, I told them if
anyone called me down to share a meal with that man, they'd
better sleep with one eye open, because retribution would be
forthcoming.

"I'll get you. I'll get you in your sleep when you least expect it," were, I believe, my exact words.

Aunt Fawnie pulled out all the stops, simpering and sulk-
ing, primping and pouting, and tossing out pathetic phrases
like, "We raised you better than this," and "Charma, you are

no longer at an age or in a situation where you can be so picky about turning away gentlemen callers."

The latter causing me to invite her to "bite my dimpled white ass" just before storming upstairs to the sanctity of my childhood bedroom.

I hardly think they missed the pleasure of my company.

In time I was called down to the evening meal.

I did not answer.

The phone rang a couple times, but if it was for me, no one came to get me. Fine. I had no intention of interacting with anyone until I figured out how to get a grip on myself again.

I wandered around my room, sorting through mementos and trying to find some kind of meaning in my being back here.

My Kokeshi doll beckoned me, a gift from Minnie's mother. Each of us girls had one of these simple painted wooden dolls to remind us that we held our own special place in the universe.

Mine was tiny. Just two small, rounded pieces of smooth wood with a red-and-white kimono painted on her body and an expression of serenity on her face. Minnie's Kokeshi was far more elaborate, and Bess had a tall, skinny one that she had draped with glittering necklaces and bracelets. Mine suited me, and it felt good to hold her in the palm of my hand again.

The Kokeshi, we had been taught, honored the souls of impoverished Japanese girl babies drowned because the family could not afford to feed them. Later, Bess tried to substantiate the story and found it was more likely the dolls were merely made to sell as souvenirs. By then it did not matter to us. As in all matters of faith, we had seized upon the deeper truth and would not be dissuaded by nitpicking details like facts. In our dolls we held a tangible reminder that no one else could direct our destinies for us.

It is a powerful thing to believe you control the fate of your own soul. More powerful still to face the fact that you have begun to ignore the responsibility of that blessing.

How had I wandered so far afield from the girl who had grown up in this room? From the winner of ribbons and trophies for speech contests and dance recitals? From the girl who had painted tiny five-dot daises on her vanity top—one flower for every boy she believed she had really, truly, passionately and achingly fallen in love with? A whole field of daises that ended in a bloodred blob of spilled nail polish obliterating the last flower she'd ever painted. The one she'd made for the last love she had thought she'd ever have—Guy Chapman.

Where was *that* girl?

I shut my eyes and, half in prayer, whispered, "And how do I get her back? Is it too late to be the woman that girl had always hoped to be? How do I... Where do I start?"

Only the sounds of the pond behind the house drifted upward into the open bedroom window.

Save me, Charma. The words from my dream—or had it really been a portent?—echoed in my thoughts. And suddenly I knew.

I was baptized in the church where four generations of Georges have committed themselves to faith and family. I confessed my sins, claimed my Redeemer, went under the water and came up whole and clean.

Dead to the old way. Arisen in the new. It is not an act or image I take lightly.

But here in this place where I had lived to the fullest, where

I had clung to my daddy's body even as the very life ebbed out of him, and where I been denied the same privilege with Mama—*this* was the one place I could recommit myself to the job of governing my own soul.

I set the Kokeshi back in its place, then tiptoed to the door, hoping to slip out unseen.

The draft from the hallway hit my skin. I thought of throwing something on over my nightgown. Any decent, reasonable person would. But the thing is, if you are on your way to perform a life altering, bold and empowering act, stopping to do the decent, reasonable thing negates the hell out it.

So I forged on, stepping lightly into the corridor.

"That you, Charmika?" Minnie invoked her mother's favorite nickname for me.

I froze in my tracks.

"Mommy and Aunt Fawnie have the boys down in the linen room," she called, then waited. When I didn't say anything, her voice grew more compelling. "Come in here and talk to me."

I knew exactly where to find her, of course. Across the hall. Down two doors. And step across the threshold right into 1967.

"Hi," she said, glancing up from a box of old romance novels she'd dragged from under her parade-float pink canopy bed.

"Hey," I said. I swear she looked all of six years old to me. Shy and innocent, but still wise beyond her years. And kind.

Minnie was born kind, and nothing in her life—so far— had succeeded in altering that. Not losing her daddy when she was young. Not growing up here among tough-talking women and tender-brained townfolk, either.

When she married Travis Raynes, the single most silent man I have ever met in my life, and moved to an isolated farm in Tennessee, her inner light could have dimmed. Instead, it grew stronger. She lost three babies but never lost faith. When she finally had her daughter, Abby, Min just poured every ounce of love for all the children she would never have into that one, wonderful child.

That this benevolent spirit took root and grew so strong here stands as a constant reminder to me of all this family is capable of, but so seldom achieves.

Sometimes I could just smack Minnie for that.

"Come on in." She picked up a paperback with the illustration of an angst-ridden nurse on the cover and began flipping through the yellowed pages.

I stayed put. "I heard the phone ring a little while ago. Anyone special?"

She nailed me with a discerning glance from the corner of her eye and laid the book back in the long flat box beside her. "Special?"

"Bess. I thought maybe she would have called and..." What? Confessed? Surrendered? We're talking Bess here. "I just thought Bess might have called."

"It was Abby." Minnie shoved the box of novels back beneath the ruffled bedskirt.

"Oh? How is she?"

"I don't know."

"You said you just talked to her."

"I said she called. But I'm not taking calls from anyone right now. I'm...I'm on retreat."

"Right. Retreat from telling me the truth, maybe. What's going on, Min?"

"I'll make you a deal. I won't press you for answers if you promise to do the same for me."

It was one of those offers I couldn't refuse. "So, where did you say Fawnie had the men?"

"Linen room." She pointed to the floor, indicating the room just below hers.

Fawnie, Shug and Mama loved linens. Table linens, bed linens, not to mention airing other people's "dirty linens" in public. So much so that they'd converted a small bedroom into a storage room for their treasured collection.

"Fawnie herded those poor fellows into the linen room to help her pick out some sheets to drape the mirrors—you know, because of her dying."

"And she wants to see what she's going to look like as a ghost?"

Minnie laughed. Then she held up a blue-eyed baby doll whose curly once-blond hair had been dyed with shoe polish—oxblood red—courtesy of a trip to Bess's private beauty salon. When Min spoke, she appeared to address the doll, not me. "I don't believe for one minute that you have forgotten *that* superstition."

Of course I hadn't. It was as old as the South itself, I daresay. The superstition went that if there was a dying person in the house, all the mirrors must be covered in order to prevent the soul, upon leaving the body, from accidentally getting trapped behind the silvered glass.

I don't know if this started because folks feared their relatives didn't know heaven from a hole in the wall or because most people round here were just naturally attracted to all things shiny and therefore more apt to lose sight of the bigger picture, even on their way to the Almighty. I only know that every time Aunt Fawnie gets a notion to up and die, the mirrors must be covered.

I do not wholly disapprove of this endeavor.

"Oh, I remember the tradition, all right. In fact, there are days I thought it might be smart to start practicing it well in advance of the Grim Reaper's arrival." I fluffed my hair and gave the soft padding under my chin a pat with the back of my knuckles. "Say, beginning in one's forties."

"Oh, please." Minnie thrust the doll into a black suitcase and shut it. "You still turn men's heads."

"Yeah, but only when I can get them in a hammerlock." I pantomimed clamping my arm around some poor man's neck and twisting it.

Minnie, whom age has made rounder, softer and even more glowing, snorted. "Says the woman dressed like a lingerie model and with a besotted boy toy *and* an ex-lover in the house at this very moment."

I shut my eyes and groaned between clenched teeth, realizing too late that she might take that the wrong way.

"This way, boys." The floor in the downstairs hall creaked with the halting gait of people following a stubborn fool determined to make her way around with just a prosthetic leg and a secondhand cane. The faint odor that always followed Miz Fawnette Faubus George—of stale cigarettes, fresh hair spray and eau de toilette—wafted upward. "Don't let them sheets drag on the floor."

"Oh, for... No more covering up, Fawnette." Shug spoke in her brassy mix of Japanese-English-with-Arkansas-overtones, loudly enough to make sure the first Mrs. Uncle Kel couldn't ignore her. "I swear. Looks like we're going to have the house painted. Why don't you just make a note to yourself—'Dear bossy old ghost, when you drop dead, don't look in the mirror.' It would save us a whole lot of trouble."

"Let's just get this last one in the hallway, Shug. Good Lord, I don't make fun of your traditions."

"Yes, you do."

"Only the stupid ones," Fawnie muttered.

Shug spat out something in Japanese, then added, "Let's get this over. My shows are starting soon."

"Don't listen to her, boys. Take your time and drape it properly. These sheets are special. I always use them for the mirrors because they fit just right. Guy, you remember how they go, from coming out here last winter after...well, you know."

Guy, you remember how they go from coming out here last winter after...

My cheeks blanched. The tears that rimmed my closed eyes felt cool and all the more out-of-place. Fawnie, Shug and Bess had carried out this very ritual on the night Mama passed away.

In my mind's eye I could see the three of them rambling through the darkened hallways. I could hear the whisper of crisp cotton sheets being dragged along the floor. The fluttering upward. Falling over each fixture. And all the while, Mama on the back porch engulfed by the night, rocking. Rocking as the life eased from her weary body.

I clenched my hands into impotent fists and pressed my lips tightly closed to keep from crying out.

"There, all covered, Miz Fawnette. Nothing more for you to worry about." It was Guy who spoke. The comfort in his voice, so frank and steadfast, eased my anxiety even from a floor away.

How unfair is life that I would find that kind of affirmation from a man that my heart would always link to fire and ashes, humiliation and betrayal? Standing here now, longing for the comfort only he could bring, I could almost forgive him everything.

Almost.

The imagery I'd used earlier, of him wiping away the dust of Mama's ashes to absolve him of his sins against me, filled my thoughts. How wonderful to wash away your past like that, how simple to start again. I had to get to the pond. Somehow, if I could complete my own ritual, then maybe...

"Minnie, I'm heading down the back steps." I retreated to the doorway, then paused. "Don't tell them where I am, okay?"

She shook her head and blinked heavily. "How could I tell them where you are? I don't think I know myself."

Her words followed me through the corridor. I could not escape them or the soft buzz of my aunts, Sterling and Guy talking in the foyer. Down the back steps I hurried, through the kitchen and then...

I found myself on the screened-in back porch.

The concrete stung my bare feet. A slight breeze stirred the leaves on the trees outside.

There was no light save the predictable patch of moonlight that illuminated the small, armless rocker facing outward, toward the pond. I froze. I curled my fingers against my throat. I couldn't breathe.

I closed my eyes, and that changed everything. That was how I took control. If I shut my eyes, it was no longer that I *couldn't* see anything but that I was *choosing* not to look.

So, I chose not to look.

Beyond the doorway lay the moonlit pond and salvation, mine for the claiming. But the only way out was through.

Blindly, I charged on, across the porch and out the rusty-hinged door, into the yard. I opened my eyes. The damp grass licked at my ankles and wet the hem of my gown, and I pressed on.

I raced around the side of the house, thudding down the well-trod path that ended at the low, rickety wooden dock.

The pond. The place where Bess had thrown me in—into its plant-choked waters where neither light nor sound not God himself could reach. If my father had not dived in after me...

I shut my eyes again and willed my thoughts to the task at hand. It was time to face my fears so that I could claim myself and somehow find the power to face Bess at last.

One step onto the floating raft of wood we called the dock set it bobbing.

I strangled back a gasp. Legs numb, I grabbed the post to steady myself and caught a glimpse of my reflection in the blackened pond.

This was abso-freaking-lutely nuts. A grown woman, jumping into a skanky old pond in her nightclothes? And to prove what?

I dug my fingernails into the soft wood of the post where the dock was secured. I hung my head. The water lapped beneath the sparsely slatted platform. The dock pitched slightly. I inhaled the muggy air and surrendered to my own shortcomings.

"What are you waiting for, Charma Deane? God Almighty to kick you in the butt?"

I jerked my head up. "Bess? Are you there?"

No answer but the sound of the water. Not the newborn heartbeat of my dream—*whoosh-whoosh, whoosh-whoosh*—but a thick and lifeless beating on the shore, *glub-blub*. And in retreat the sickening *sch-slurp* of water through the weeds and muck.

From the corner of my eye I saw the faint glow of lights from the house penetrating the night. Just the house. No person. And yet I did not feel alone.

"I swear to God, Bess Halloway, if you are lurking out there in the dark, you'd better show yourself or..."

Or what? What could I threaten *Bess* with?

Still no answer came.

Glub-blub sch-slurp. The dank warmth of the pond rose around me, yet I shivered, feeling suddenly naked. Emotionally, spiritually and physically.

"I swear to God, Bess." I started again, and again floundered, whispering to the stark but familiar grounds surrounding me, "I swear to God."

The dock rocked.

"I don't know if you're out there or if I am just placing you out there because ever since Mama died everything about *here* has become about *you* to me." I shut my eyes and shouted to the swaying grass, to the trees, to the very stars, as if they would carry my message to the one person I most needed to hear me. "You are the only human being on earth with that kind of power over me, and I hate you for that, you know it? Bess, I hate you!"

Night and silence absorbed my cry.

I exhaled a long, shuddering breath and leaned on the dock's post for support. "And damn it, Bess, it just *kills* me to hate you."

Isn't that the way it always was? Bess did whatever she pleased, went on about her life with no concern for anyone, gladly letting others suffer the consequences for her actions. I had lost my mother. I had lost something precious that tied me to this place and to my family. *I had lost my way and it was destroying me.*

"But you wouldn't understand that, because nothing destroys you, does it, Bess? You heartless bitch, I wish just once you'd find yourself on the receiving end of the kind of anguish you dish out." The air, dense with the odors of rotting vegetation and pond life, chafed at my already raw throat. "Dear God, I wish just once something would grip you by the very soul and squeeze until it wrung an honest emotion out of you, until you finally had to face the truth about yourself."

Then, at last—and I don't know if I heard this with my ears or felt it in the marrow of my bones—I finally received a reply.

"Careful what you pray for, Charma Deane. You just might get it."

The dock pitched.

"Bess?" Heartsick, half-dressed and just maybe half out of my mind, I braced myself straight-armed on the post.

From the drive came the sound of a car door opening and slamming shut again.

"Damn it, Bess, don't you dare run off now!"

A car engine started up.

Something between a cry of anguish and a howl of rage rose from my chest. After all this time I had my chance to confront Bess and she had cheated me out of it. Always on her terms. Never on mine.

I started to call out her name again but could only muster

a sob and a whisper, "Damn it, Bess, if you'd just once give me a reason to hope..."

"Charma? Are you out there?" Guy rounded the corner of the back porch, on the path toward the pond.

Beyond the house, tires crunched over the uneven drive. A set of taillights glowed red for an instant, then disappeared around the tall hedge wall.

My spirit took on a real and nearly overwhelming weight.

I stared at the weathered boards of the dock where Bess and Minnie and I had spent so many summer days sunning ourselves in pursuit of the perfect tan, the perfect look, the perfect afternoon. Secrets had been shared here. Hearts unburdened. Dreams unfurled.

Glub-blub. Sch-slurp.

Guy stopped where the ragged edge of the dock came to rest on an uneven chunk of concrete. He put one foot against a splintered plank, paused a moment, then said, soft as the ripples strumming over the muddy shoreline, "Come on inside, Charma. There's nothing for you out here."

Nothing for me out here. I recognized the truth of it even before he got all the words out.

I lowered my head and tried to look across the length of the pond. The water I had come to immerse myself in, to cleanse away my sorrow, to give me rebirth so I could begin my life again, now mocked me with its stench and murkiness.

Guy held his hand out to me.

I wanted to accept his comfort. I wanted to throw myself into his arms and hide there until the world made sense again.

But mostly I wanted...something I couldn't have. I wanted my family to be whole. I wanted to be young and to look at

the world with hope-filled eyes. I wanted Bess to stop whatever new malevolence she had set to unleash on us.

And I wanted my mother back.

I wanted... I wanted... God, it had to exist somewhere. It
could not be a cruel trick of life to get to this age, to lose so
much and in the face of every loss find nothing but an ache
at the center of my soul. What I wanted, Guy Chapman could
not give me.

I wanted peace.

7

The next morning the kitchen smelled of warmed-over sweet rolls and stale cigarette butts. Aunt Shug's perfectly preserved yellow dinette set glinted where the morning sun touched it like some holy artifact. The dozen or so pages of the *Orla Star and News* lay scattered around Minnie's plate and cascaded to the floor at her feet.

Dressed in an old T-shirt I'd found in my closet—the spoils of a college romance gone blissfully awry—and with my scrub pants rolled up to my knees, I gave a quick glance around the room to make sure Minnie was alone in there. The last thing I needed this early was a lecture on proper dress from a woman who wore a girdle and panty hose to hoe her garden, and from her Japanese cohort, who never left the house without an Atlanta Braves baseball cap covering her short white hair.

"All clear?" I asked in a loud whisper.

"Clear for now." Minnie, still in her cotton nightgown, pointed her bare toes to nudge out the vinyl-padded chair next to hers. "Sit yourself down and talk to me, girl. Start with the story about how Guy Chapman and that sweet young hunk of man meat of yours both ended up at our house for supper last night."

"He has a name," I said, getting hyperdefensive and avoiding her request all at once.

"And such a sexy one, too. Sterling. Nice. It suits him, don't you think?"

"Because he polishes up good? But no matter how fancy of a setting you put him in, he is never going to be the genuine article."

She pushed her chubby fingers through her thick, dark hair and laughed. The sun highlighted the roundness of her cheeks. The lines around her eyes and mouth deepened in the unforgiving light.

In girl math Minnie was thirty-two...thirty-four at most. It's a complex and constantly shifting system, but in Minnie's case the math is easy. Both Bess and I have reclaimed big chunks of our lives that we feel fate owes us for years invested in men who weren't worth the effort, time wasted on mindless family duties and that sort of thing. Minnie's rebate of years came in time off for good behavior and the fact that everyone knows that loving and being loved is essential to feeling forever young.

But Minnie was not a girl anymore. Intellectually, I knew that, but in my heart... In my heart I was totally pissed off, because acknowledging the reality of who Minnie had become made it all the harder for me to try to mold her into my vision of who I needed her to be.

"I don't know the boy well enough to make any kind of judgment," she said. "But I do know he went home in a huff."

"Did he?" I rubbed my temple with the heel of my hand, but that didn't assuage the dull throbbing that had begun behind my eye.

"He sure enough did. But not to worry, I don't expect it hurt anything—except maybe the young man's pride."

"Never underestimate the damage done when the only thing hurt is a man's pride." *A young man's pride.* I had almost said it that way, but stopped just in time. "Hurt male pride has left a long trail of stupidity and destruction in its wake."

"We moved on to talking about Guy now, or are we still on the topic of young Sterling?"

I reached behind me to the counter and tugged the half-empty pot from the coffeemaker. "Don't call him that."

"What?" She blinked her almond eyes at me, swirled the dregs of her coffee in one of Nana's delicate china cups, then held it out for me to refill.

"*Young* Sterling. Young, my ass."

"He *is* young, Charmika. Young, rich and more charming than a used-car salesman working on full commission. I certainly wouldn't have sent him home without so much as a good-night kiss if he were *my* lover."

"Oh, c'mon, Minnie. I might be staying here until this mess is resolved, but it's not my home. I can't just haul some guy up to my bed."

"Of course not. Not just *some* guy." She reached out and patted a strange set of keys resting atop a rich leather binder on the table. "Oh, by the way, he came back this morning."

"Guy?" I pressed the warm cup to my chest and tried to will my growing headache to abate. "Here?"

"Sterling." She held up the car keys and jingled them, flashing the distinctive Jaguar emblem.

I exhaled and took them from her, pressing the insignia into the palm of my hand.

"Why? Did you want it to be Guy?"

Found out. My pulse quickened and I tried to think up a lie. A good lie. A Bess-worthy lie.

Bess.

I put my head in my hands. "Oh, Minnie. I am such a fool."

"Because you're not sleeping with some too-slick, horny, overindulged *boy?*" She poured creamer into her coffee and plunked her foot up onto my knee. "Please, girl."

I gave her ankle a grateful squeeze and sighed. "What's wrong with me?"

"What's wrong with any of us? We're human." She said it as if that explained everything.

And I guess it probably did.

I rubbed my eyes. "You always could see right through me. I don't know why I ever even *try* to pull anything over on you."

"It's ridiculous. But you do it because you love me, and even though you know how important you are to me, you don't trust it. You don't trust anyone much. You're like Bess that way."

"I am nothing like Bess." I sat ramrod straight and hoped Minnie couldn't actually see my pulse pounding in my throat.

She gave me a sly look through half-lowered black lashes.

"What the hell is Bess thinking with this eviction crap, Minnie? What has she got up her sleeve?"

"Concealed weaponry?" She shrugged and took a sip of coffee. "I don't know. I didn't even hear about it until I got here yesterday."

I chucked Sterling's keys down on the tabletop and leaned forward, my curiosity definitely piqued. "You mean you didn't come because of the letter?"

"I haven't even seen *the letter,* girl. I came because…" She gazed down into her coffee cup as if it might hold the answers to the great mysteries of life, then set it down and shoved it aside. "I came for personal reasons and walked right into this hornet's nest. Right *out* of a hornet's nest and straight back into one. Always did have lousy timing."

"You want to talk about it?"

She shook her head, and I am ashamed to admit her reticence relieved me. Dealing with another family issue would just about have done me in. In fact, feeling as I did this morning, I'd just about do anything but face—

"'S'that you girls in there?" Aunt Fawnie's voice still had the rough-edged croakiness of early morning.

"Oh, shit." I shot up out of my chair. "Is it too late for us to duck out the back door?"

"In my nightgown?"

"Minami, I know you are awake. Don't you run off." From the sound of Shug's voice, the old gals were somewhere near the front door.

"I have things for you girls to do." Fawnie paused, probably to take a drag on her cigarette, then announced, "We got to get to work—now!"

"Work?" I mouthed the word more than said it, even though I knew my aunts couldn't have heard me unless I'd bellowed.

"The list," Minnie hissed.

"Shit."

"No." She laughed. "That's another list. One you're going to be on if she catches you here and you don't pitch in and help her with whatever nonsense she's got on her damn list today."

The list. It had been inscribed years ago on the yellowing pages of a Big Chief tablet and got dragged out at the first possible opportunity of every Death Watch we'd ever endured.

I could picture the title already, inscribed with indelible laundry marker in Aunt Fawnie's block lettering on the tablet's red cover. *Things That Have to Get Done Before I Die.*

Not a noble inventory of big dreams yet unrealized. No, ma'am. You would not find a single "climb Everest," "learn Italian" or "sleep with one impressive male specimen of each branch of the military (reservists don't count)" on *this* agenda.

This was the real deal. A list of things Fawnie wanted taken care of in preparation for the big-assed bountiful funeral of her dreams.

Those things don't plan themselves, you know. And now she had the added impetus of having to get it all done before Bess brought the sheriff in to toss the old gal out on her ass. With that threat buzzing around inside her bleached-blond beehive, Fawnie would be relentless.

I groaned. "You said Sterling was here already? Maybe we can grab him and use him as an excuse to get out of here— say we have to talk strategy or something?"

"Don't you hurt yourself rooting around in the attic for my old trunk, young man." Fawnie's cane rattled against the spindles of the front stairway.

Paper flapped.

Steady footsteps sounded overhead, then the groan of the rusty-hinged attic door swinging open.

"I have a lot of plans for you today, and it wouldn't do to have you incapacitated."

"Too late." Minnie shook her head. "She got Sterling."

I gripped the back of the chair. "I bet he never even saw it coming."

"Aunt Fawnie in the attic with the trunk." Minnie's dark

eyes sparked with fun even as her expression remained grim. "Just like when we used to play Clue right here at this very table."

"Yeah, until Bess took the weapons and used them to act out a murder-suicide pact between Barbie and Ken."

There she was again. Even when she wasn't in the room, Bess was here. I massaged my temple. "I don't know how much of this I can take."

"Then don't take it. Get out of here. I can cover for you for a few hours. Go."

"And do what?"

"I don't know. Drive around town. Get a Coke at Alpha Drugs. Cruise by the high school. Throw a penny in the bank fountain."

Minnie had just pretty much summed up the length and breadth of what there was to do on a summer morning in Orla, Arkansas.

But apparently she wasn't done. "Maybe go visit a friend...at Chapman's Funeral Home."

"No."

"Charma..."

"Charma! Minnie?"

"I'm dead in the water." Minnie flounced the hem of her nightgown with one hand and lifted her coffee cup with the other. "It's too late for me. Save yourself."

"I came out here with Sterling last night. I didn't bring my car."

Using one finger and without uttering a single word, she pushed Sterling's keys across the table in my direction.

"Technically, that would be stealing," I reminded her.

She raised one perfectly plucked eyebrow.

I clasped the keys in my fist. "And I always thought it would be Bess who'd finally drive me into a life of crime."

Minnie laughed.

I started to turn to go, then caught myself. "Wait, speaking of Bess—we haven't. We really need to talk about all the eviction bullshit."

"Later."

"Minnie? You in the kitchen? Charma Deane in there with you?" Shug's distinctive quick, shuffling footsteps, followed by the rolling thump and scuttle of Fawnette moving along with her cane and prosthetic leg, were aimed right at us. "Fawnette and I have a special project for that girl!"

Instinctively, Minnie and I each drew in a deep breath.

"I'll stay and appease them." My cousin tried to hurry me off with a frantic wave of her hand. "Take as long as you need, sugar. I, of all people, understand, and everything will still be here waiting for you when you get back."

I hit the door and took off toward Sterling's car, not sure if Min had meant that as a blessing or a curse.

And I didn't really bother to analyze it. I was free—for the moment. Free and riding around in a stolen vehicle. What the hell was a body supposed to do under those circumstances?

Couldn't go home. It's the first place anyone would look for me.

"Oh, hell!" The thought of people out looking for me turned my thoughts to Inez.

I rooted in my purse until I found my cell phone, and began punching buttons with my thumb while I tooled around the old familiar back roads, skirting the town proper. Sure enough, my new friend had filled my home answering machine and cell voice mail with pleas and bribes and, at one point, if I understood her right, an actual threat to the well-being of my aunt's assorted yard ornaments.

Her last words were the ones that stuck with me, though. "Charma, if I did anything to scare you off, if I pushed too hard or didn't push enough or whatever...I'm sorry. I can't help it. I'm a meddler. Where I come from, that's not considered a bad life choice. Where I come from, the women, we rely on each other. I want you to know that whatever is going on with you and that *loca revuelta* family of yours, you can rely on me."

"Thank you, Inez," I murmured over the *blee-eep* that signaled the voice mail had ended. "Good to think I can rely on *someone*. 'Cause I'm sure not going to find any help in my *loca revuelta* family."

What had Bess set in motion with this awful plan of hers? And what did she hope to gain from it all? If the answer was that she'd wanted to drive me over the edge, then she was well on her way.

And I had to decide if I would let her off, or if I'd get proactive on her ass and *do* something about it.

I punched another button on the phone.

"Yes?"

"Sterling! Thank heavens you had your cell phone on you." Heavens my ass, the man never went anywhere without the damn thing. "Don't let on it's me, okay? Can you talk? Are you busy?"

"Of course I'm busy. Your aunts have seen to that. You took my car and left me here at their mercy."

"I am so sorry about that." Empty words. I had run off without a second thought for Sterling's feelings, and I'd do it again under the same circumstances. We both knew that.

"Aunt Fawnie isn't driving you crazy, is she? I know how irritating she can be and—"

"Get your butt back here, Charma."

His sudden commanding tone startled me. "Sterling, I am so sorry about the car, but I—"

"Now."

"Fine. That suits me just fine. I'll swing by and honk to pick you up, and then you and I can go over to your office and discuss—"

"I'm not going anywhere."

"You can't be serious." I mustered up an airy, flirtatious laugh that fell like a stone in the already heavy conversation.

"I can be. I am." Fawnie and Shug squabbled in the background; he called out something indistinct and they quieted. "Look, I have to go now. I have work to do."

"Work? *What* work?" A petulant five-year-old would have sounded more mature at this point. "Hauling trunks down from my aunts' attic?"

"No. Legal work. Your aunt Fawnie has hired me to help her get her estate in order."

"You're going to play lawyer for Fawnette?"

"Not playing here, Charma." His tone had a well-deserved indignant edge.

Talk around town said that Sterling had never done a lick of real work in his entire career. Oh, he'd filed a few papers and gone over documents and given best-guess advice over the phone—but always and only to members of his own well-heeled family. A lot of folks joked that Sterling's idea of preparing briefs was draping his tighty-whities in a handy place so he could make a quick exit after a night of habeas corpus.

But it was damn snotty of me to all but throw it—his lack

of a career, not his tighty-whitie-related exploits—in his face like that.

"I'm not *playing* at being your aunt's counsel, here. I sincerely like the old gal. I want to help her." The quiet kindness of his tone shifted to amusement when he added, "Besides, I can't live off my family's money forever."

"So you're going to live off mine?" I really never *do* shut my mouth when I should.

For several seconds nothing but a hard silence came in answer. Then Sterling spoke, deep and low, each word measured and packed with meaning. "I am going to help a sweet, lonely, frightened old woman who deserves better than her self-absorbed nieces have shown her these last desperate five months."

Lonely. Frightened. My first thought was that he could have been speaking about me. My second and more profound thought was that he was trying to tell me that not everything was *about* me.

I shut my eyes and sighed. "How long is all this going to take?"

"I can't say for sure. Why? You trying to figure how you can keep running and hiding from your responsibilities until I'm done?"

"I've not run away. I'm not hiding." I had and I was. And once again my choices made me ask myself who I had become and what I planned to do about it. My mind tried to put the pieces of the last twenty-four hours together, to try to find the right path to take. I'd started out so sure of myself yesterday, and now...

And now, just like last night on the patio when I'd been confronted with Mama's rocker, the only way out was through.

"In fact, I am handling personal responsibilities at this very moment."

"Doing what?"

"Well, I..." This was it. Now or never. I either outted myself as a big fat liar or did what I had said I'd never do. I gripped the phone so tightly my hand trembled, and I gritted my teeth. "I'm headed to Chapman and Son's Funeral Home to...to...to collect my mother's ashes."

"Well, it's about damn time. When you're done with that, get your 'ashes' back here and join the living again, Charma. There's still a lot you have to do."

8

"The lady is asking too much, Guy." An unfamiliar male voice carried out from the room beyond the back porch.

I'd come around to the back this time, hoping to keep my resolve never to enter Chapman's front doors, and also to get the element of surprise on my side. It hadn't been easy, either, circling around the block in a swanky convertible to slip through the back alley. But I'd done it. Marched boldly up the back walk without setting off any dogs barking or letting the old metal gate creak to alert anyone of my arrival. Now my hand froze, midknock. Had I come at a bad time?

Guy laughed. Good and loud.

His laugh had always been his best feature.

No. Not even I am liar enough to try to sell that load of horse manure. But the man did have a good laugh, especially for someone having grown up in a family that regarded a sense of humor as a character flaw.

"You know, Dathan, that lady doesn't much *ask* for anything," Guy said. "She just tells you the way it's going to be and expects you to get on board her bandwagon—or get run over by it."

I *had* come at a bad time. A few minutes sooner and I'd have heard who the heck they were talking about!

"Asking or telling, she's expecting too much," the strange man said. "One poorly played decision on our part now and this whole thing could go under, sink like a stone."

Bad timing be damned. How could a person hear something like that and not *have* to find out more?

I knocked quickly.

"It's open, Rebecca."

The invitation wasn't for me, but I took it all the same.

"Hi," I shouted, all light and cheery and with all the brashness of a bake sale mom trying to sell bourbon balls to Baptists. "Hello? I hope it's okay for me to come through the back like this."

"Charma!" Guy stood straight. He had been leaning against the counter. In his red Arkansas Razorback T-shirt and crisp blue jeans, he looked even more casually sexy and rumpled than I could have imagined.

Suddenly I wished I had taken the time to do more than slap on some mascara and lip gloss.

"Charma?" A man with skin as dark as the coffee in his stoneware mug sat at the kitchen table staring right at me. Dressed in a starched white shirt, black tie and pants, he wore his youth in other ways. Small gold loop earrings and a gleaming head recently shaved played against the stiffness of his attire. Also, he clearly lacked the life experience to hide his surprise, which bordered on dismay. He couldn't keep the edge of trepidation from his tone when he glanced at Guy and whispered, "This is Charma? *The* Charma? *Your* Charma?"

"*Your* Charma?" I folded my arms and cocked my head at Guy.

He didn't deny a thing, just stood there, smiling. "We thought you were Dathan's wife."

"Rebecca. I heard." I'd come here to assert myself—why not start on the spot? I held my hand out to the man at the table. "I'm Charma Deane George Parker, and you are…?"

"Dathan Daniels." His hand had swallowed mine, but he kept his touch so light I hardly felt a thing before he withdrew and picked up his mug again.

Guy shifted his weight, glanced at the floor, then cleared his throat. "Dathan is my—"

"I drive the hearse." He took a sip of coffee, and his wide golden wedding band winked with warm light.

Guy stepped forward.

Dathan did not look at him but simply stood and smoothed his tie down the front of his shirt. "And I have work to do."

"Oh?" In some settings you can pack a lot of question into a single syllable.

"No, no one died." He shook his head. "Just two days until Memorial Day, you know. We have a lot to get done before the ceremonies."

"Ah, yes, the *ceremonies,*" I said. What I had *wanted* to say was "Oh, hell, the ceremonies." With all that had gone on I'd forgotten all about the hoopla that accompanied the holiday around here.

Aunt Fawnie would insist we attend at least one memorial service. With her own ever-impending death hanging over us and the added bonus angst of her impending eviction by her own beloved niece, Fawnie would want to make sure everyone saw her putting on a brave front and thinking of others before herself. "I suppose it will be an all-day event again this year?"

"Parade through town in the morning, service and refreshments at the cemetery at noon, family reunions and church suppers the rest of the day," Guy confirmed.

"Nothing like a little cookies and punch with the dearly departed before knotting up the 'ties that bind' with everyone else." I smiled, albeit weakly.

"That's the way it is around here." Dathan shrugged. "Guess folks don't take death as a viable excuse for not keeping up the social responsibilities of a relationship."

Was that a condemnation or praise?

"If you'll excuse me." The young man took a step backward. "Nice meeting you, Mrs. Parker."

"Call me Charma, please."

He nodded and smiled, but not a charming, happy smile. There was worry in this man's dark eyes, and it put a soft buzz in his voice as he echoed my name, "Charma."

"Dathan, could you...?" Guy jerked his head to one side.

"Already on my way." He took the tone of a colleague or perhaps collaborator, not that of someone who just "drives the hearse" speaking to the man who owned the whole business.

It was a small thing to notice. Not important in the big scheme of things, but it stood out in my mind. Something was up here.

"Charma?"

"Something is up here, Guy. Don't try to deny it."

"I'm glad you came by." He smiled that great smile of his that showed just a flash of his white teeth and made his eyes go dark and enigmatic.

"Don't change the subject," I said, when what I wanted to

do was plead with him, "Don't lie to me," or should that have been "Don't lie to me—again"?

I wet my lips and took a nonchalant stance. "What's going to sink like a stone? Are you in trouble? Not that I care, of course."

"'Course not. Why would you?"

"Just that I overheard Dathan say some woman was making demands. One thing I know something about in this life, it's demanding women and how to handle them."

"Demanding women, my ass!" A raspy feminine voice rang out from the next room. "Who? Old Fawnie? Shug?"

"Bess!" I whipped around just as my oldest cousin swept past Dathan and anchored her feet at the edge of the kitchen floor.

"I'm sorry, Guy." Dathan stood at her shoulder. "Ms. Halloway insisted on coming on in."

She stood there in a shapeless dress of some gauzy, exotic fabric. Even in this heat she wore long sleeves, pushed up to the elbow, and managed to look cool and lean and most definitely untouchable. Her lips curved, but I wouldn't have called it a smile. No light reflected in her dark eyes. She had tied her hair back in a scarf so that only a few black tendrils fell around her gaunt cheekbones.

At the sight of her standing there, I felt...nothing. And everything.

In a split second I was a child again, immersed in fear and darkness and incomprehensible loss. I was a teenager who thought Bess hung the moon. I was a young woman standing alone in the moment she learned that the man she loved and the cousin she adored had run off together. I was the essence of myself boiled down to a cardboard character in Bess's paperback novel, words and actions attributed to me and mine that had no rooting in reality. And I was myself sitting in my son's brand-spanking-new home with Christmas decorations still glittering around me when Guy called to say that this woman who stood before me now had held my mama as she slipped from this life, had sent her body to be cremated and had never once picked up the phone to tell me what she had done or why.

"It's all right, Dathan." Guy moved between Bess and me like a referee getting ready to run down the rules before a no-holds-barred cage match. "Why don't you ladies come into the—"

"You certainly have got your nerve." I ignored both the men and narrowed all my energy on to Bess. "What the hell do you think you are doing here?"

"What does anyone do at a place like Chapman's?" She shifted her feet, and her oversize clothes moved about her body like curtains wafting in a gentle breeze. "I'm making burial arrangements."

Memorial Day. Of course. The perfect time to stage a coup and get back in the family's good graces. *Why sure, I'm yanking the homestead out from under two helpless old ladies, but look how much I love y'all and what a lovely tribute I've arranged for the family.*

No. Not if I could help it. "I thought Mama requested there be no service for her."

"Not for your mother."

"Then if you think you can get on the good side of Aunt Fawnie by pretending to organize some gargantuan funeral to appeal to her and that silly Death Watch mentality of hers..."

"Aunt Fawnie will outlive us all." She shook her head.

"I haven't come on family business, Charma. It's personal."

Guy edged forward, his hand on the hearse driver's back. "Dathan, why don't you and I—"

"Stay," Bess commanded.

"Yes, you should stay, because I sure as hell don't plan to. This is not over, Bess." I had come to finally deal with my mother's ashes—and to get the inside scoop on what my cousin was up to. And she had stopped me cold. Whether that was her intent or not, she had once again gotten the better of my plans to be the family hero, the savior.

And that royally pissed me off.

Enough to make me say something I never dreamed I would say, and knew deep to the center of my being I could not back up. "Whatever you have planned, expect a fight on your hands. You won't win this, Bess. You will not win. Not this time."

I spun around, my emotions vibrating just below the surface. If I could just reach the door...

"Charma." Guy reached out, but his fingers only grazed my arm.

"Go ahead and run off, Charma Deane." The hoarseness relented to an oily bravado in Bess's words. "You never had any real fight in you, anyway."

Pride stopped me in my tracks. I've always had far more pride than I had common sense, and it made me say things I almost always instantly regretted, such as, "I'm not running anywhere."

"You honestly think you have the strength to stand there and hear what I have to say?"

No! My mind screamed it. My heart pounded it. My legs wanted to turn and carry me out of there and away from all of this forever. I squared my shoulders, lifted my chin and said, "Yes."

Bess looked at Guy.

He shook his head.

Dathan retreated a step across the threshold into the next room.

I held my backbone rigid as the staff of Moses. I held my tongue and, as hard as it was to do, I held my cousin's gaze without once wavering. "Tell me the truth, Bess. I can handle it. Why are you really here?"

"I'm dying, Charma. And I'm here to make my funeral arrangements."

"Liar!" I shoved Bess backward with both hands. I'd done it without thinking, but in the aftermath, I had to admit, it felt damn good.

Dathan moved in behind Bess and steadied her on her feet.

Guy grabbed my right arm. Maybe he thought I'd take advantage of Dathan holding Bess like that, and haul off and slug the living daylights out of her. God have mercy, I almost had the courage to do it right then, too.

"I thought you had outdone yourself in spitefulness when you helped Mama die at home alone, then had her body cremated before I even knew she was gone. But *this?* Feigning some terminal illness is an all-time low, even for you, Bess."

For the first time I could ever recall, her cool, dark eyes did not meet my gaze.

Bess could look anyone square in the face and lie. Parent or preacher, lover or landlord, cop or cousin, she could spit fire, split hairs or spin a sob story that would break your heart right in two. Not a word of it would be honest or sincere, but she'd never waver. She'd never so much as blink.

But when Bess avoided eye contact, she did it for one reason and one reason alone—to hide the thing she feared most. The truth.

My stomach lurched. I tried to will her to look at me, and when that did not work, I resorted to the lowest form of goading in the George family repertoire. "This stunt is... is...positively Aunt Fawnie-esque."

She peered my way at last, her eyes no more than slits. "You don't have to go *that* far."

"Don't you dare talk to me about what goes too far." She'd almost had me there. I had almost believed. It wasn't enough that she betrayed me by keeping me from Mama's deathbed, now she had to make a mockery of it all for nothing more than a grab for false sympathy. Bile rose in the back of my throat. "You finally pulled something so ugly that you fear you've fallen out of everyone's good graces and it galls you. So you cooked up this story to make a play on the family's emotions. *That's* going too far, Bess. It's manipulative. It's malicious. It is an action without one last shred of mercy."

"And the worst part is—" she stepped forward and at last leveled her gaze at mine "—it's true."

"True that you lied?"

"True that I'm dying."

I looked to Guy.

"Cancer," he said softly, but without hesitation.

Nobody I knew said that word without hesitation. Most of them said things like "the big C," as if couching the very ugliness of it in a benign—pun intended—euphemism robbed the disease of its power. I knew this because we'd dealt with the disease before.

My eyes went instantly to the scar at the base of Bess's

throat, where she had had a malignant melanoma removed nearly fours years earlier.

"You beat cancer." And once Bess had defeated something, it would never dare rear its head again. Right?

"It came back," she whispered.

"No." It didn't. It *couldn't*.

"Charma, I know you're angry at me."

"Angry doesn't begin to cover it." I was trembling and so confused. Bess had cheated me one too many times for me to just blindly accept this. I couldn't. Because believing her meant the unimaginable.

I turned to Guy. "She's the demanding woman, isn't she?"

He glanced downward, then rubbed his fingertips over the back of his neck.

Looking beyond Guy's left shoulder, I honed in on Dathan. "She's the demanding woman. The one who wants y'all to do something that you know in your heart is too risky. Did she ask you to play along with this farce of hers? Was that it?"

"No." Guy stepped forward at last and took me by the shoulders.

I hated to admit it even to myself, but that's what I wanted. I wanted him to move in and take charge so I wouldn't have to deal with this...this...

"Charma, stop this nonsense," he said softly.

Nonsense? Hardly the word I was looking for. I stiffened under his grasp.

"You need to take a deep breath and—"

"Don't you tell me what I need to do, Guy." I pulled away from the support he offered. "Dathan described Bess to a tee when he said, "She's asking too much. Too much is always the jumping off point for my cousin. She doesn't *know* anything less."

I spun on my heel and charged out of there with my head high and my mind reeling. The back door slammed behind me, then the screen door.

Despite the clouds, the glare of midday stung my eyes but I fought back any soothing tears.

Bess...dying... Bess... It's a lie. My feet landed hard on the sidewalk intensifying the throbbing in my head.

It's a lie. Like the time when she pushed me into the pond, knowing I feared the water with all my being. She's throwing me into something just as frightful now, something I am just as powerless to save myself from. And this time I don't have a daddy to dive in and rescue me. I don't have anyone I can rely on for that. This time, if I surrender to her trickery, I will go under and never come up again.

At last I made it to the back gate. My fingers shook too hard to undo the latch. The dull metal slipped from my grasp and fell shut time and again. Consumed with blind rage, I kicked the gate and spat out a curse.

"Charma, come back into the house." Guy fitted his hand to the small of my back.

Guy had never been, nor could he ever be, my rescuer. He was as bad as Bess. Worse. From Bess I had always known what to expect, but Guy? His betrayals had always blindsided me. I could not afford to accept his comfort, not unless I was prepared to pay with my heart.

I jerked backward with my elbow to keep him at bay.

He sidestepped the jab, then slid his hand around my waist and clutched me closer.

I tried to pull away.

He stood firm, my back to his chest, his face resting against my hair.

Lord, it had been so long since I'd had a man's arms around me, a real man's arms. Guy's arms. I had missed it more than I could ever express in words or even cogent thoughts.

"It's okay, Charma," he whispered.

"It is not." The words gurgled in the back of my throat.

"I know," he said.

And I knew he did know.

I leaned back on him and lost all semblance of composure. I did not just cry, I sobbed. I did not just sniffle, I snorted.

He handed me a soft white cotton handkerchief.

A woman of another generation would have thought it simply as a conventional gentleman's gesture, but it only served to remind me of Guy's line of work. I mean, who the hell carries a white linen handkerchief these days?

Old men and undertakers, that's who. If I could have stopped sniveling long enough, I'd have asked him if he'd gotten the idea in some oversize reference book: *The Moron's Guide to Being a Mortician.* "Always carry fresh white hankies to hand to distraught relatives of the deceased."

The deceased. That had an instantly sobering effect. Deceased, to cease to exist.

I raised my head, looked out on the grating normalcy of the quiet neighborhood and whispered, "How long have you known?"

"She discussed it with me when she made your mother's arrangements."

"That long?"

"She knew about the cancer returning then and wanted to

seek...well, all that's for her to tell you. Don't you want to go back in and ask her yourself?"

God-a-mercy, was he nuts? I shut my eyes. "No."

"She needs you to be strong for the rest of the family, Charma."

He *was* nuts. He'd have to be to think that I had it in me to deal with Bess dying coupled with what she was about to do to my aunts. "Me?"

"She says you are the only one who can do it."

"She lies, Guy." I took a deep breath. "She would only have said something like that if she wanted something."

"She does."

"I knew it."

"She wants you to get everyone else ready. She hasn't told anyone in your family yet. She told me she wanted you to hear it first so that when she's ready to tell the family, there will be one person around to hold things together."

"And you believed her?"

The nod of his head said yes, but doubt clouded his eyes.

"I see." I reached for the gate latch again, this time with a far more steady hand. The metal clanked as it flew open. I started to walk through, then paused and looked back at him. "When did she tell you that?"

"Today. She showed up about an hour ago. Before that I hadn't seen her since..."

"Spare me the details." I held up my hand. "But I wouldn't mind if you did answer me one question."

"Anything."

I gave him my best "yeah, right, buddy" look—and having raised two rambunctious sons practically on my own, I have honed that look to steely-eyed perfection. I leaned against the open gate for support. "Fine. Answer me this. If Bess has gone to all this trouble to get to me to insure there is one person around to hold our family together, why is she doing everything in her power to tear that family apart?"

He gave no answer.

I hadn't really expected one.

I gave a quick nod—something between a "Well, you think about that, why don't you?" and a goodbye—then turned and made my way down the walk.

9

The scuffing of my shoes over pavement.

The clunk and wham of the car door opening and shutting again.

The jangle of keys.

The comforting click of the safety belt fastening into place.

I tried to keep my mind on the everyday actions, the mundane. The things that grounded me in the moment and kept me from thinking about what had just transpired. For now I had only one purpose—to get out of here. To get as far away from Chapman's and Mama's ashes and all thoughts about...

"Bess!"

I jerked my head around to confront the person I had just glimpsed in my rearview mirror. "I'm warning you, Bess. Get out from behind this car before I give in to my darker impulses and back it straight over you."

"You wouldn't dare."

I stabbed the key in the ignition and shouted above the rev of the engine, "Don't tempt me."

"But, Charma, hon, that's exactly what I have come here to do."

"Tempt me? To what? Murder you?"

"That would be sort of superfluous, don't you think?"

I hated her both for using a word like *superfluous* with such style and ease and for reminding me of just how pointless and probably petty my wish to murder a dying woman was.

"Maybe *tempt* isn't the right word." She folded her arms and cocked her head. "*Push*. That's better. I've come to give you a much needed push."

I shivered and cursed in the same instant.

"What's the matter? Someone walking over your grave?" she asked.

"Shove it, Bess."

"Shove, push, whatever it takes, Charma. And you can clench your jaw and shoot daggers with your eyes all you want, we both know you are never going to out-stubborn me, so you might as well hear me out."

"All right. Say your piece." I gripped the wheel and gunned the motor again. "But talk fast."

"First, I have a confession to make."

"After the life you've led? I'd suspect you have a boatload of confessions to make."

"Well, this particular one is about Guy."

"That particular one, I've heard a million times already. You were young...*ish*."

She prickled at that addition.

Bull's-eye. "Guy had cold feet, you had... I don't know, what? Ice water in your veins?"

She looked away, if only for a second.

Another direct hit.

I smiled, just a little. "You both got caught up in a moment of careless abandon. The two of you realized your mistake almost immediately. Purportedly within hours of returning from what was supposed to be *my* honeymoon."

She did have the good form to fake a wince, and opened her mouth to say something.

I'd be damned if I'd give her the chance to water down with her justifications the story that had become a part of our personal litany over the ensuing twenty-some years. "But you and Guy were both too proud and too pigheaded to admit to the world you'd been wrong, much less that you'd *done* wrong. Done wrong to the one person who loved you both more than life itself."

God, why did I say that last part? I'd have taken it back if I only could, but it hung in the air between us, all barbed and tangled and ugly. All the times this dreadful tale had been spun out over the years, the phrase "done wrong to the one person who loved you both more than life itself" had never been a part of it. Because Bess had always told it.

I pressed my chilled fingertips to my collarbone. To hell with her. I had said nothing but the truth. To hell with her feelings and her need to confess her sins. I couldn't bear her guilt and maintain my fury, too. And at this point my rage at Bess was the only thing keeping me from caving into a pile of sobs and sorrow.

"Charma," she said softly.

"Even though you two lived in the same house for three years, you never really shared a life, much less a great love." I recited it like a child spooling out a memory piece at Sunday school, hoping to get a Bible bookmark for her effort. Flawlessly, emphasis placed to please the listener and with no real conviction on my part, I finished up, "The two of you were never happy together and so on and so on and so on. Is that the gist of it?"

"You know it is. But that's not the confession I'm talking about."

Here it comes. With the witnesses gone, I would finally learn why she had come to Orla and what she was up to with her wicked eviction notice. Funny, but suddenly I didn't want to know. A lie I could protect myself against, but the truth?

"It's about Guy, about why I came to see him today."

"You said you wanted to make funeral arrangements." I looked at her all squinty-eyed and accusatory, but underneath that a powerful hope welled up. "You telling me that's not really the case?"

"No. I didn't actually come here to make my own funeral arrangements."

Relief. Then anger. Relief again. Then, as always, the smart-ass remark. "Too bad. Because I'm going to have to kill you now."

She moved at last to the passenger's side of the car, placing both hands on the door to lean in and say, "Don't bother. Time will take care of that. I *am* dying, Charma."

You are not. I bit my lip and blinked to stay the swell of tears and keep me from saying anything I might regret. Okay, correction, keep me from saying something I might have thrown back in my face later.

"But what brought me here today was something else. I wanted to pump Guy for information about you."

"What? Why, you dirty rotten sneak. Going behind my back to someone that we share such a cruel personal history with to try to get some dirt on me?"

"I know. I know." She glanced down, touched her tongue to the middle of her upper lip, then cocked her head to study me. "So why are you at Chapman's today, Charma?"

Trapped, I fell back on the avenue of last resort. I blurted out the truth. "Same reason as you. I hoped to get Guy to rat you out."

Bess laughed.

If she had done anything else, pitched a fit, cussed me out, even broken into a piss-poor act bemoaning her fate, I'd have pulled away and driven off without backward glance. But Bess when she laughs...

I turned the car off and squeezed my eyes shut.

"At least *I* had the pretext of planning a funeral. What possible excuse could you have used?"

I rubbed my forehead, the tonic of Bess's laughter fading as I forced myself to answer. "Picking up Mama's ashes."

"You mean you still haven't—"

I shook my head and raised my hand to cut her off. "I cannot do this here. I cannot do this now. I cannot do this...at all."

"This is ridiculous, Charma. Get out of the car so we can talk."

"You aren't the boss of me, Bess. You want to talk, you get *in* the car."

She popped open the door and dropped into the seat.

"I only said that because I never dreamed you'd actually do it," I muttered.

"Drive," she said.

"Not until you buckle up."

"Why? Because I might end up dead if I don't?"

"Buckle up or shut up."

She laid her head back. "Jeez. Why does everything have to be a battle between us, Charma?"

"We've had good times, too," I protested, and then felt childish for having done it.

I glanced down the alley at the backside of one of Orla's lovely old neighborhoods. I wondered if Bess felt any connection at all to places like this. If she felt any sense of loyalty to the people here, any respect for their way of life, any gratitude for the escape that they had provided her simply by existing.

Nothing Bess had ever done indicated she did. Not that idiotic book, not the things she had said about the town on her publicity tours and certainly not her scheme to come here and usurp the George family home right out from under Fawnie and Shug.

And even so... I turned to my cousin, a gaunt and gray reflection of the person I had never *not* known.

"We're family," I said softly. "As long as the battles don't end in bloodshed, it's just our way of showing how much we..." *Love each other.* My mind completed the sentence one way, but I could not make myself give the feeling voice. I cleared my throat and wimped out with a non-specific, "...how much our lives are intertwined."

Click.

The buckle slid into place.

I started the car and began to back out of the drive.

"Nice." Bess ran her hand over the leather dash. "You buy this with some of the money from Aunt Dinah's estate?"

Bitch. I didn't have to tell her I hadn't touched a cent of Mama's estate, and I *wouldn't* tell her. To say it out loud would show my inability to get on with my life, my weakness. One never shows weakness to Bess. In fact, given the chance, if one has even the slightest shred of instinct for self-preservation, one puffs oneself up and shows Bess nothing but claws. "I didn't buy this car at all. I stole it."

"You?" She lifted an almost invisible eyebrow. "*Stole* a car?"

"Okay. It belongs to a friend. But he didn't give me permission to use it."

"This friend—any chance he'll call the police on your ass?"

"Sterling? Are you kidding?" It came out before I could stop it, so I embellished. "He's a powerful attorney, though. He doesn't have to call the law. He can make my life a living hell all on his own."

"You're a regular outlaw, Charma Deane, a bona fide buck-wild heathen if I ever saw one."

"Don't use *that* word around me, thank you very much."

"That word? The *F* word? I didn't use the *F* word, you idiot. I said bona fide buck-wild he—"

"*That* word." I pulled out of the drive and headed toward nowhere in particular.

"*Heathen?* Oh, shit, when are you people ever going to get over that? The literary world got over it entirely within ten months after it came out, so why can't you?"

"You know why."

She rolled her head to one side and said something I couldn't hear. Probably the *F* word. Coupled with the now forbidden *H* word.

We drove in silence for a moment before she ran her bony fingers along the edge of the lowered window. "So this friend, obviously a man of good taste. Good-looking, too?"

"Like those things matter to you."

"Fair enough, I'll ask about what does matter. The man is obviously well heeled. Is he also well hung?"

I scrunched down in the seat, my arms braced straight against the steering wheel, and muttered, "Shut up."

"Oh." She nodded and raised her face to let the air blow through her once glorious black hair. "Too bad. At least he has this nifty convertible to compensate."

I laughed. I couldn't help it. I'd wondered the same thing when Sterling bought the overpriced showpiece. "Okay, so we're off and driving in the compensation-mobile, where do you want to go?"

"Let's go pitch pennies into the bank fountain."

"You kidding? You used to give me and Minnie so much crap when we asked you to take us to do that."

"You two were snot-nosed eleven-year-olds. While I was a sophisticated woman of the world at sixteen. What would it have looked like?"

"You never gave a damn what things looked like to the world."

"To the world? No. But to you and Minnie? I couldn't blow my cover and let you think I actually cherished doing stupid stuff like that."

"Really?"

"Really. It's one of those rare good memories for me. Let's go to the fountain. I need you to take me there, Charma."

Save me, Charma. The cry from my dream formed full and clear in my ears. I lifted my face to the wind, made a left and did exactly what Bess asked of me, knowing full well doing as Bess asked had proved more than one person's undoing.

10

"Do you believe in portents, Bess?"

"What?"

"You know—dreams, visions, omens, signs? Dreams, I guess, mostly. The kind that..." It all sounded too stupid to say aloud.

I pulled into a space in front of the long, sleek bank with gold-tinted windows and a modern art marble mosaic and waterfalls-style fountain in front. The architectural style had caused quite a stir when they built it in the early sixties. I know this not because I remember it, but because all these years later, people are just now getting over it. The addition of a bronze monument to the town's war dead out front added on a few years back went a long way toward assuaging the ruffled feathers of the traditionalists.

Compromise. Some people think it's a nasty word, but whole communities flounder and fail for the lack of it. Families, too.

"Look, Bess, I just had this...this dream is all. I was standing by the pond and someone kept calling for me to save them. And now you show up and say—"

"Are you out of your mind? You sound battier than old Fawnie." She clutched the handle with both hands and leaned her whole body against the padded door to push it open. "Grab your purse, we're going to need change—a whole lot of it."

"Change?" I obediently lunged back in the car to snag my shapeless summer bag. "For what?"

"To make wishes, damn it. That's what people do here, isn't it? Throw in a coin and whisper their deepest hopes to the heavens?" She turned and looked back at me. For a moment I thought she looked like a paper doll dressed in real doll clothes, the world surrounding her more substantial and multidimensional than Bess herself.

She's already begun to fade away from us. I swallowed hard and moved up the long, low concrete steps toward her, my hand thrust into the change pocket of my bag to fish out coins.

"Here." I reached out, the clump of cash jingling softly in my relaxed fist. One shiny new dime escaped my grasp and bounced off the sidewalk and rolled away.

She cupped her palm under my hand and accepted the offering. "Got any more? I have a lot of wishing to do."

We touched. Her gaze sank into mine.

Lord, she seemed so frail. Her once olive skin had turned ashen, and her black eyes, deep within their sockets, stared out above dark half-moons tipped on their sides. The simple act of breathing seemed to make her entire body tremble. I feared that if I embraced her, she would break into a million bits in my arms.

"You okay?" she asked, her voice as craggy as Aunt Fawnie's the morning after her poker nights with Shug and Mama—

when she'd finished off a second pack of smokes and a pint of sloe gin.

"I'm okay." And even as I got it out, the tears began again.

"Oh, shit. Don't you start," she said. "Wipe your nose."

I obeyed dutifully, swiping under my eyes the spotless white hankie Guy had handed me earlier, then finishing up with a sinus-clearing honk.

"Better now?" she asked.

"No." I shook my head and sniffled into the cloth again.

"Well then, *get* better, and fast. Time is no longer my friend—not that me and time were ever all that close." She peered back over her shoulder and frowned. "Especially after I noticed it celebrating each birthday by dragging my ass down another inch toward my ankles."

"Don't." I reached out, but not to hug her. Bess and I, we did not hug, or kiss one another on the cheek, or even stand side by side and pat each other on the back. It wasn't our way. But I had to reach out to her now. So I caught her sleeve in my hand and balled the fabric in my damp, curled fingers. "Don't try to make light of all this. I can't stand it."

"Too bad." She shook her head. The scarf holding her now dull, coarse black hair in a ponytail rustled softly. "But the one dying gets to set the tone for the big event. That's God's rules, Charma, not mine."

I couldn't help smiling, just a little. "Since when do you go by God's rules?"

"Since I realized I couldn't circumvent them." She held my gaze for only a second, then looked toward the water, which gurgled and splashed into a white marble pool. "Anyway, I do not want this to get maudlin."

"Why not?" I gave her sleeve a shake. "You *lo-ove* maudlin."

She smiled, sort of. "Well, then…messy. I don't want this to get messy. I want to keep it quiet for as long as possible, and I do not want Mom and Dad or the boys and their families to know until it's over. That's why I need you, Charma Deane."

"To do *what?*"

"To keep my dying a secret from my family."

The dank summer air pressed down on me. My mind swam. Had she just asked me to do to her parents and brothers what she had done to me? How like Bess to take something so anguishing, something that you didn't think could get any worse, then to add a sadistic personal twist and make it so.

"No," I whispered. "Don't. Please do not ask that of me, Bess."

"I'm not asking you to do anything evil. Just to help me simplify things."

"Simplify? In other words, to sweep the harsh reality of it all away?" I buried my fingers more deeply into her sleeve and gave her arm a tiny yank, as if that would somehow startle her to her senses. "To metaphorically run ahead of you, throwing open the windows and chasing all the potentially painful human emotions out of the room?"

She set her jaw, and her perfectly lined eyes did not blink. "Is that too much to ask?"

"Yes." The word crumbled in my mouth as if everything inside of me had dried up to dust. I blinked and no tears came. How could she ask this of me? How could she?

But asking how or why Bess did anything was a waste of

breath, and I knew it. I dropped my arm and shook my head. "You always ask too much, Bess. You're playing by God's rules now. Not even you can command a tidy little death for yourself."

"Oh, but this isn't for *myself.*" She waved her hand to dismiss the idea entirely. "Lord, no, Charma. I plan to suck every last drop of drama and pathos out of this as possible. I say let there be prayer vigils and keening, rending of clothing and so much gnashing of teeth that we have to keep a dentist on call 24/7."

"But you said you didn't want things to get messy."

"For my mother," she whispered, almost inaudibly.

"Oh." Her mother. My aunt Ruth. However misguided, Bess wanted to do this to protect her mother. I was at once touched and infuriated. How dare she determine the way everyone would deal with this? How dare she cut off the people who loved her? And in the last days that they would have to give and receive that love ever again.

"Bess, I—"

"C'mon." She jerked her head slightly and made her way to the water's edge.

I paused, realized I could not say these things to Bess, not here, not yet, and followed.

We stood there watching the trickle of crystal clear water for a minute or two before Bess pinched a nickel out of the heap and threw it.

Splish. The water rippled out from the spot where it had gone under.

I plucked up a penny and simply held it between my thumb and forefinger. "Please don't ask me to do this, Bess, not even for Aunt Ruth's sake."

She snatched the penny away. Maybe she thought if I threw

it in after what I'd said, my wish might come true, and she had to prevent it.

Or maybe she just wanted all the wishes for herself.

"Don't you understand, Charma? You have to. I don't want my mom, or my dad and brothers, for that matter, but especially my mom, to have to go through the ugly, awful process of watching me die. Hell, she had enough trials standing by and seeing how I lived."

The wind picked up. I think, in the distance, I heard a rumble of thunder.

"Besides—" Bess sent the copper coin skimming over the quiet water. Then, for the first time in forever, she took my hand in hers "—you have to do this, Charma. You promised me. We promised each other."

We had. A blood oath made nearly thirty years ago.

At the time of her death, my grandmother had held sway over all the George family women. The born-Georges are often characterized by our fervent spirituality, strong wills and a uniquely feminine physical presence. Big hearts, big mouths and big butts. We obeyed her implicitly. The married-ins, with their various and sundry vices, avarices and an almost mystical quality to dominate everything around them, had big hair, big tits and big plans. The married-ins seemed ever at war with the iron-fisted matriarch.

That was why Nana Abbra had deeded the Aunt Farm to her daughter, Ruth. Fawnie and Shug hadn't realized it, but Mama had to have known. It was Nana's last little vindictive dig to show everyone in town who would forever remain the real queen bee of the George family.

Poor Nana. She had always underestimated her daughters-in-law. It was at the hands of the widows whom she had bad-mouthed and bamboozled that Nana was laid to rest. She went to meet her maker wearing a bathrobe, streetwalker-red lipstick, her once beautiful silver braids done over into an old-lady-blue poodle hairdo, and clutching a bottle of Japanese plum wine to her ample bosom.

God rest her soul.

"Remember? At Nana's funeral?" Bess asked. "I cut our fingers and we made a vow. Do you remember it?"

I nodded.

"Live without limits," she began for me. "Love without questions."

I nodded.

"Laugh without apologies." She gave my hand a squeeze. "And whichever one of us dies first..."

A tear slipped down my cheek. I could not look at her.

She tucked my hand under her arm and gazed at the flowing waters, or perhaps beyond, at the image of the two of us reflected in the golden windows. "Whichever one dies first, the surviving cousin will move mountains to get to Chapman and Sons Funeral Home first to do the other's clothes, hair and makeup. Right?"

"Right," I croaked.

"Because, honestly, it doesn't matter how extraordinary a life you lead…" She exhaled, tipped her head and pressed the back of her hand to the loose skin under her pointed chin. "Unless you look great in your coffin, all that people will remember is that you got sent off to heaven looking like hell."

I laughed. A real laugh. Then swept my knuckles along my own softening jawline.

She reached over and took my hand, still fisted around the coins, and turned me to face her.

Her fingers had grown delicate as dry bones and were cool to the touch. I could see the veins through the tissue-thin skin of her exposed forearm. And yet beneath the place where my thumb skimmed her skeletal wrist, her pulse still beat hard and strong. Any argument I had about the nature of that old vow evaporated.

"If you don't stick this out with me, who will be there to make sure I don't get buried in something ghastly like pink silk and pearls?" she asked.

"I won't just sit by and watch you give up." My gaze retraced her pulse points, wrists, neck, even the blue veins that now showed at her temples.

"God's rules," she reminded me. "Not mine."

"I don't believe that for one minute, Bess. You always play by your own rules, even if you have to make it look like you're following someone else's rules just to keep them in the game." An observation born of experience, not a bitter accusation.

She knew it, too. I could see that she did.

She made no righteous protest, no forceful offer of proof to the contrary, not even a derisive snort to pooh-pooh my opinion.

Her own rules, even if she had to make it look like she was following someone else's rules just to keep them in the game. I exhaled long and low and finally met her gaze. "This is why you sent the eviction notice, isn't it?"

"Actually, yes." *Plop. Splish.* Another coin went sailing, then sinking.

"I knew it."

Poor Bess. She had spent so many years alienating the people who loved her. Now that she needed us desperately, pride and fear prevented her from coming to us to ask for our forgiveness and support. So she'd made up this elaborate game to get us to play along. But by her rules. Always *her* rules.

And it had worked. She had me. I was in on the game fully, wholly, irrevocably. And as soon as Minnie, Shug and Fawnie heard the news, they would be, too.

"You went through all those ridiculous machinations." I shook my head. "When all you had to do... Bess, we're family. No matter what happens, whenever one of us needs the others, that's it. We're there. You didn't have to go through that awful charade of kicking Fawnie and Shug out of their home."

"Oh, that was no charade, Charma." No light shone in her eyes. "I fully intend to throw the old ladies out."

"Wh-what?"

"The Aunt Farm belongs to me. Nana Abbra willed it to my mother, and my mother gave it to me. It's mine, Charma. I want it. And in thirty days I will have it."

I could not read her emotions except to say they were raw and naked and ugly. And they terrified me.

I stepped back. "Then I can't help you, Bess. You can't take away the only home I've ever known, hurt the people who mean the world to me, then expect me to keep your secrets and God knows what else in return."

"Oh, yes, I can, Charma." She cocked her arm and pitched the remaining coins into the pool, spattering droplets of water on her long, flowing clothes and colorless face. Then she turned and, without wiping the water from her cheek, looked at me. "I'm done. I have a room at the Wycliff Hotel. I can walk there from here. We'll talk again soon, of course."

"You can't just walk away like that, Bess. You owe me some kind of explanation."

"All in due time." She eased herself slowly down each step. "Remember now, don't tell anyone about our visit."

"You can't make me do a damn thing I don't want to." Could she? I searched my mind for anything she could use against me to get her way. Nothing. But then she'd never had to use anything but my love and trust to set me up for whatever hurt she wanted to send me.

I watched her making her way toward the sidewalk, every step a deliberate effort.

I sat down on the edge of the fountain to keep myself from running after her, to guide her, to help her, to do whatever she needed at this time when she needed me most.

Oh, God, she could still make me do anything she wanted, and I knew it. No matter what went on between us, I loved Bess. Loved her like my own flesh. Not independent and separate from me, but a part of me, a piece of the whole of my life. If she died...

My heart pounded hard. So hard it seemed my pulse came not in the regular ebb and flow of daily life but in erratic convulsions. I floundered, mentally, then forced myself to latch on to the one thing that could keep it all from overwhelming me. "I won't be pushed in over my head, Bess. I'm stronger than that now. If you want me to help you, you are going to have to—"

She stopped and turned and looked me straight in the eye.

I swallowed and pressed my lips shut.

She nodded, swept her hair and the scarf holding it off her shoulder, then put her back to me and kept walking.

11

"I swan, girls. It's Decoration Day. You knew we'd go walking the graves. You should have worn better shoes for it."

"Walking the graves is my family's euphemism for checking out the sites to make sure everybody is tucked in where they belong and putting their best foot, uh, headstone forward," I whispered to Inez, who had invited herself to this traditional family outing when I'd called her and, without ever explaining why, broken down and cried like a baby.

Inez could never resist a baby, not even the middle-aged kind.

"Don't apologize. I'm having a ball." Inez tossed her head, sending her earrings dancing. "Your aunts are...what's the word?"

"Certifiable?"

"Fabulous."

Inez had dressed not for paying respect to the dearly departed but for a party guaranteed to wake the dead. If Minnie or I had shown up looking like that, Fawnie and Shug would have thrown a conniption. Inez? They fussed over her like she was the second coming of Tallulah Bankhead.

"Always wear orange, honey. I don't care what people say. Orange is your color!" and "New Jersey? You got this in New Jersey? I didn't know they had anything this nice in *New Jersey!* Promise me next time you go back, you'll get me one just like it."

Yeah, right. Like Fawnie would flounce into the Wednesday Afternoon Women's Cultural Society wearing something from a warehouse club in New Jersey.

I hoped Inez did send the two-faced phony an outfit. Fawnie was on Death Watch, after all, and we might just need something to bury her in.

Not that I was jealous of Inez. I'm too mature to get green-eyed over a few harmless compliments. It's just that I had worked up a really good pout over not wanting to come here today, and Inez and her plastic jewelry had stolen my thunder. After the news about Bess, I didn't have much thunder in me, so I took it doubly hard.

Of course, it didn't help that it wasn't Inez's size six Barbie-style high-heeled slides that had gotten stuck in the mud and slowed us all down.

"C'mon, hurry. Don't be so pokey." Shug adjusted her straw hat, waved Min and me onward, then went back to helping Fawnie handle the uneven ground. "We got to go by your daddy's grave before the ceremony starts."

"We're right behind you." Minnie braced her hand against my shoulder to steady herself while she whacked one tangerine-and-cherry espadrille against a tree to get a blob of dark mud off the side. "Remind me to start wearing all-terrain hiking boots whenever we go out with those two."

"I'm thinking of renting full body armor." Like that would offer any true protection. Not that my current chosen safeguard—silence—had done much to shield me from reality, either.

Two full days to let the news brew inside me, and I hadn't found the courage to tell anyone about Bess yet. Maybe I thought that, by keeping the news inside me, it would snuff itself out like a candle deprived of air. Or maybe if I just gave it some time, just gave Bess some time, she'd...

I grabbed Minnie's wrist to support her. Or was I trying to make her support me?

She slid her shoe back on, flipped her hair back and smiled. "There. All better."

From this cemetery to God's to-do list, I wanted to say. Instead, I took a deep breath of the damp earth and the aroma of chicken frying for the neighboring church's dinner on the grounds. "Minnie, there's something we—"

"Gather, y'all. Gather!" A few yards away, Fawnie paused and held her hand up with such enthusiasm that it made her wobble on her one good leg.

Shug, Sterling and Inez all stepped up to catch her should she totter off her prosthetic pedestal. Which she never would, not in front of anyone who might take some pleasure in her doing it, at least.

We'd wanted to bring a wheelchair for her, but she said it wouldn't go with her outfit. What she meant was it wouldn't go with her objective, which was to make everyone in sight see her as a brave figure struggling against the fate God had handed her. Besides, she'd recently upgraded from the old push-style chair, and when the cemetery superintendent prohibited her new mode of transportation for safety reasons, Fawnie decided to play the poor pitiable amputee to the hilt.

And it worked. All eyes stayed glued to Fawnie, and more than a few tongues wagged at the sheer nerve of her performance.

She didn't care.

"Now, y'all, come in close and listen up." Inez had loaned her one of her spare pairs of big round sunglasses and a bright head scarf. She looked for all the world like a Hollywood tour guide directing her charges. "Now that woman there—" Fawnie jabbed one bony finger at an ornate marble stone "—never married."

"It's true." Shug used a well-placed swerve of her hips to wedge her way between Sterling and Fawnie. "She was a quiet one, lived in a room over the meat market. Went off to Alabama in 19...was it 72?"

"Earlier." The bubble of stiff blond hair trembled with a persistent shake. "Right around the time Kel died."

"That's right. That's right." Shug patted Fawnie's forearm in a gesture that spoke so much about the two of them. She left her darker hand resting on the pale, aged-spotted skin. "When she moved back here, she bring a carrot-top baby she claimed belonged to her dead sister. Only she never said she had a sister before that. And the man who run the meat market—"

"The *married* man who ran the meat market," Fawnie embellished.

"Yeah, the *married* man who run the meat market." Shug wagged her finger. "Full head—red hair."

Fawnie narrowed her eyes first at Sterling, then at Inez. "You can imagine how folks around here took to that."

Inez cackled.

Sterling's watered-down smile practically screamed *Must maintain look of empathy.*

"Didn't matter to us where that child come from, though. We—"

"Didn't matter one iota to us." Fawnie leapt in to concur before Shug had even finished her sentence. "We had her right on out to the house and let her stay as long as she needed."

"She was welcome in our home till her dying day."

"Till her dying day," Fawnie echoed, bowing her head for the proper dramatic effect.

...welcome in our home till her dying day.

Oh, Bess. The slow, consistent ache that had started the second Bess proclaimed her intentions now swelled to fill every part of me. My head throbbed. My heart hurt. My very consciousness grew tiny thorns that tore at my every thought and emotion. *If you wanted to live out the last of your life at the Aunt Farm, Bess, all you had to do was ask. They could never have turned you away. You didn't have to—*

I pressed the heel of my hand to my temple. "Min, can we—"

"Did we know her?" Minnie peered at the unfamiliar name on the stone.

The rest of the group had moved on to an ill-kempt plot.

"That man there used to beat his wife." Even without nursing a long-ashed butt, Fawnie still spoke in that familiar drag-lag-expel rhythm. "Had an unfortunate accident at the kitchen table one night."

"Hmm." Sterling caught my eye and winked. "What happened? Did he eat his own cooking?"

"Don't be foolish." Fawnie coughed.

"Yeah, don't be foolish." Shug smacked him lightly on the arm and grinned. "He was cut open, throat to thingamabob, with a Civil War bayonet."

Inez gasped, muttered something in Spanish and crossed herself.

Shug caught a glimpse and must have liked what she saw. She sputtered out a Japanese word that I readily recognized as not being of the holy variety, then did her own mangled version of making the sign of the cross.

"A *bayonet?*" Minnie picked her way toward her mother along the lush green path among the graves. "Mommy, that hardly sounds like an acci—"

But Fawnie and Shug had already gone on to the next grave site.

"Now this one—" Fawnie spread her hands out to indicate a tall gray tree stump form with names carved on every knot-hole "—this one here is a *real* interesting story."

Sterling slipped behind me. "Do your aunts know how everyone in this cemetery met their maker?"

"It's a gift." I glanced back at the man who had set up a makeshift law office in the kitchen of my family home. "Some people never forget a line of poetry. Others know baseball statistics. Fawnette and Shug collect death stories."

"Ah." He nodded, probably filing that away to use as another means of ingratiating himself to my aunts. Not that he had to try very hard to do that.

Ever since he'd showed up, the pair had done everything they could to get a kind smile or, better yet, a playful flirtation out of Sterling. It wasn't about him, of course, it was about one of them grabbing some attention, however fleeting, and depriving the other of having it. They couldn't have been more obvious if they had dressed up like a chicken and a moon maiden and held up hand-printed signs à la *Let's Make a Deal. Pick me!*

"...never did find his head." The older of the pair placed her hand on Sterling's arm, gave it a pat, then laughed as if only the two of them were in on the joke.

Shug knocked Fawnie's hand away, nodding. "And *that* should be a lesson to us all."

"Amen!" Minnie raised her face to the heavens, her eyes shut.

"You know what the hell she's talking about?" I whispered.

"No idea." Min spoke from the corner of her mouth. "But if it involves keeping your head, then I'm for it."

The tinkle of slender gold bracelets called attention to the fact that Fawnie had stopped and put her hands on her angular hips. "Are y'all listening to me, or am I flapping my gums just to hear my own voice?"

"Does it matter?" Shug's own silver bracelet, thick with charms for every event in her life, jingled, too, as she waved off her old friend's surliness. "You gonna keep yakking anyway."

"Well, maybe I'll just stop yakking."

"Oh, yeah, that's gonna happen. Only time you stop yakking, Fawnette, is when you in the ground with the rest of them. And then you probably be a ghost hanging around here trying to tell everyone they should have listened to you while you was alive." Shug tipped her softly padded chin up and, nose crinkled, gave the practically silent laugh she always saved for when she was thoroughly pleased with herself.

"Well, pardon me for trying to impart a little local history to the young folks."

"Oh, don't pout. Gives you wrinkles." Shug laughed again, then took Fawnie's arm. A gentle tug and they both started toward the large plot surrounded by an iron fence at the back of the cemetery. "Come introduce the family to Inez and Sterling."

"Sterling." Fawnette corrected Shug's rendition, which came out sounding more like "Stirring."

"That's what I said."

"She did." Sterling stood up for her. "And I'd be proud and honored for you two to tell me all about your dearly departed loved ones."

"Good. We start with that damn Nana Abbra." Shug jerked her thumb at the towering white marble monolith with roses, a cross and a sweeping scroll carved on the front bearing the name George.

The family plot.

A chill crept over me.

"No," I whispered.

I could not go through the slightly askew wrought-iron gate that separated the past from the present.

It had been a long time since I'd come here out of anything but obligation to Mama and my aunts. A *long* time, certainly, since anyone was laid to rest in this pretentious little piece of prime Orla real estate.

How long would it be? I had to ask myself, hanging back a few yards while the others went on gabbing as if nothing would ever change, as if it had not already irrevocably changed. *How long before we stand here again? This time to bury Bess?*

I couldn't move. I didn't even think I could speak until I pulled Minnie back and said, "Min, wait. I need to talk to you."

"You don't have to say a thing. Mommy and Fawnie are so clueless. I know you don't want to go in there."

"You do?"

"Sure. What with Aunt Dinah not even having a resting place, much less one with the family."

Actually, I hadn't thought about that. Great. Now I was paralyzed with fear, anger *and* remorse.

"I don't want to go, either," Min confessed.

"You don't?"

"And watch Mommy and Aunt Fawnie playing to a brand-new audience, each trying to outdo the other over who was hated more by Nana and loved more by Daddy? No, thank you." Minnie's mouth set in a grim line. "I've had enough choosing sides and dealing with the fallout of hurt feelings and unexpected consequences in my lifetime. I came here to get away from having to do any more of it."

That was the first allusion Minnie had made to what had sent her into hiding in the sanctuary of our childhood home. A good and loving person would have wrapped her arms around Minnie then. She would have asked, "What's wrong?" and "How can I help?" She would have moved heaven and earth to lift the burden off her cousin's shoulders and ease the hurt away in whatever way she could.

"Good. Let's not go with them then." I did not have the luxury of loving empathy. Bess had snatched that away from me just as surely as she had snatched away my wishing coins. I wanted to kill her for that. And worse, for me and all the others I would drag along with me, I wanted to *save* her.

That's what ate at me the most. Despite everything, I still wanted more than life itself to save the woman who wanted to destroy my family. I guess I should have felt the same way about Min and whatever was plaguing her, but, really, short of anything life threatening, Bess's situation had to come first. Besides, if Min needed saving, she'd ask and I'd oblige.

She had to know that.

Didn't she?

"Min, about this thing, whatever it was that brought you here, is it...huge?"

Her eyebrows crimped down over her dark eyes and she blinked slowly. "Huge?"

I laced my arm in hers and inched closer, like we were ten-year-olds again. "World-cracking-open-to-the-core-if-you-don't-deal-with-it-immediately huge?"

She blinked again, then looked off toward the two women regaling Sterling and Inez with who knows what kinds of stories. The leaves from a nearby tree cast her face in dappled sunlight. She tilted her head. "It's not life and death, if that's what you're asking."

I am. Life and death. Anything less would have to wait, if at all possible. "Will this...problem of yours...will it be resolved soon?"

"Soon?" She faced me, her eyes narrowed in concern. "How soon?"

"Like, I don't know." I sort of shrugged. "Like...this afternoon?"

I guess I'd inadvertently put her at ease, because she smiled then and asked, "What? You on a deadline?"

I took a deep breath. "Actually, yes, I am on a deadline." Literally. "I have to solve any and all outstanding family issues as soon as possible."

She leaned in close. "Why?"

I shut my eyes. "So I can drop something truly monumental on everyone."

"Oh."

Scared that if I said another word I'd just blurt it all out in a horrid, ugly mess, I pressed my lips shut and shifted my shoes in the plush grass.

"Let's you and I go sit on that mourners' bench." Minnie tipped her head toward a concrete slab resting on the backs of two kneeling cherubs.

The idea of being upheld by angels appealed mightily to me at the moment, so I nodded and followed her.

We sat, and finally she fitted her arm snug around my shoulder. "What's wrong? Are you okay, Charma?"

"Me? I'm fine." And for the first time in a long time, I meant that.

Strangely, my revelation about needing to try to save Bess had pulled me into this weird, focused calm. The proverbial eye of the hurricane, I suppose. It gave me a strength and perspective lacking these last few months. I wound my arm around Min's waist and gave her a squeeze. She felt softer than I ever remembered her, and still smelled of the cherry lip balm she never went anywhere without. "But what about you? Are you okay, Min?"

She dropped her arm from around me and shook her head. "It's just one of those mother and daughter things."

I looked out at Aunt Shug bending down to straighten the small flag on Uncle Kel's grave, while never letting go of Fawnie's frail hand.

"No. Not her." Her eyes followed my gaze. "The other mother-daughter dynamic."

"Abby?"

She nodded. "That's why I'm not taking phone calls from her or her daddy. I just don't know what I might say to them."

"About?"

"Don't ask, Charmika. Please."

"Okay. But if you can't talk to me about this, you really should talk to Abby. That's the only way you two can resolve your problem."

"Abby and I don't have the problem. *I* have the problem. It's me. I *am* the problem." She looked heavenward a moment, tucked her hair behind her ear, then forced a smile. "Listen, I just think that until I work through my own stuff, I can't talk to *anyone*. I don't want to say something I'll regret."

"Lord, how did you grow up in the exact same household with me and turn out so damn wise? You know, if the rest of the women in this family followed that not-saying-anything-they-might-regret rule? Nothing but silence. Years and years of deathly silence."

"Oh, I screw things up plenty, don't worry about that." Min rubbed my back lightly. "Funny, I thought that by this age we'd have an instinct for what to do about almost anything. That we'd feel..."

"Smarter? Braver?"

"Like the grown-ups." She raised her open hand in the direction of the two women signaling the groundskeeper over to tend to the troublesome gate. "Look at them. There stand the most ridiculously fearless women I have ever known. I can't imagine either of them facing any problem and not knowing exactly what to do. And your mama was just like them."

"She was. So why aren't I more like her?"

"Who says you're not?"

"I do."

"I think you're selling yourself short there. But what I think doesn't matter. If you really believe that, if you want to be more like Aunt Dinah, then do it, Charma. Start today."

"It's not that easy."

"Screw easy. No one promised life would be easy. If it's what you want…if that's who you want to be, then why waste another minute?"

"Damn, Minnie. I think maybe you *are* a grown-up."

"I have my flashes." She leaned her head on my shoulder and sighed. "Travis says I ought to take something for them."

"Travis speaks?" I laughed lightly.

"When it matters, he does. Maybe some of that rubbed off on me. I would never have spoken to you about being more like Aunt Dinah if I didn't think you needed to hear it."

"Hmm." Doubt and gratitude in a single syllable.

She slipped her hand in mine, just like when we were children at the edge of the pond. "You can do it, Charma. You can do anything if you set your mind to it."

Jump, Charma. Jump out past your fears. Daddy's words took on gigantic proportions, filling my every thought, emotion and sensation. And still I hesitated. Too bad I didn't have Bess around to give me a—

"Oh, God, Minnie. I get this now. You're right."

"I am?" She sat up, her eyes searching mine. "I mean, I *am*. It's definitely time for you to take charge of your life, Charma, and do what you have to do."

I squared my shoulders and fixed my gaze on the family plot. "Exactly."

"So, what *exactly* are you going to do?"

"Not me, Min, *us*."

"*Us?*"

"Yup. The two of us. From this moment on, like it or not, we're going to be the grown-ups."

"Do we have a secret handshake?"

"We don't need no stinking handshake." I smiled. "We're in this together till the bitter...no, I refuse to accept that. It won't be bitter, we won't let it."

"What won't be bitter?"

"The end," I said.

"Charma, talk sense."

"Too late for that now, Min. The time of reason has passed. Now comes the time of doing what my mama—and *your* mama and Aunt Fawnie—would have done. What they did for that poor woman from Alabama and who knows how many other women who needed safe harbor."

"And that would be?"

I scanned our surroundings, and just for a moment my eyes met Guy's. He cocked his head, gave me a slow, smart-ass smile.

Suddenly I not only knew what I had to do, I knew who I could trust to help me accomplish it. I stood and pulled Minnie up beside me. "You and I are going to go get Bess and bring her home."

"How?"

I glanced back at Guy, returned his smile in kind and asked my cousin, "You ever ride in a hearse?"

12

"A hearse?" Bess stopped short just inside the Wycliff's tall, narrow door. Her eyes fixed on the gleaming golden behemoth now waiting at the curb.

The wind picked up. The hotel's tattered burgundy awning flapped overhead.

"It's not just a hearse." Min battled Bess's wheeled suitcase over the threshold. "It's a 1974 end-loading Cotner-Bevington Oldsmobile with landau roof and stained-glass viewing windows."

"She found the owner's manual inside." I craned my neck to talk around all our purses and Bess's makeup bag piled in my arms. "Read it out loud to me the whole way over. Guess that was easier than actually talking."

"Hmm." Bess leaned against the hotel door, her fingers curled around the brass handle.

"If it helps, it was never put into service as a funeral car." Minnie wrestled with the case one-handed, gave up, used both hands and walked backward, which made it easier for her to talk to us, anyway. "*This* is the hearse Guy totaled. You know, one day after his daddy had it delivered and two days before Guy was legally able to drive any car at all, much less this thing?"

"I figured as much." Bess hung on to the open door long past the time we needed her to hold it for us.

The cool lobby air wafted out, bringing with it a distinct and familiar smell. Old newspapers, floor polish and peppermint.

"Being here again puts me in mind of the afternoons Nana Abbra brought us girls here for tea and culture." I hugged the bags close and sighed.

"I remember that!" One wheel on Bess's suitcase squawked and rattled. Minnie kicked at it to set it straight again. "How Mommy and Aunt Dinah would get us all done up in frilly dresses and fancy tights, and Aunt Fawnie would douse us with perfume on the way out the door. How our Sunday shoes echoed in the lobby and how the staff used to serve us Coke in our teacups and wink because we thought Nana didn't know. Wasn't life simple and lovely then?"

"Your mommy and Aunt Dinah dressed you up in frilly dresses to make Nana think they weren't raising a pack of heathens."

"Language," I reminded Bess.

She mouthed the word at me in bold exaggeration, then turned back to Min. "They put you in fancy tights to hide your skinned knees and Fawnie doused you with perfume to cover up the smell of her smoke. Furthermore, the real reason Nana Abbra brought you here was to pump you for dirt on your mothers. Seems the only thing simple back then was you two."

"Simple and *lovely*." Minnie batted her almond eyes like some cheap coquette.

"Simple and lovely," Bess conceded, but she did not physically move an inch.

"Are you coming?" I tried to calculate what I'd say if she suddenly refused. I did have her luggage and makeup bag to hold hostage, and looking at her, I figured I could probably do a fireman's carry and get her as far as the front seat. If push came to shove.

And with Bess it usually did.

"I'm coming." Bess fiddled with the scrunchie holding back her hair. "I said I'd come with you and I will. I was just thinking."

"About what?

"That...'74 Costner-Bentley."

"Cotner-Bevington," Minnie called out, having almost reached the darn thing at last.

"Whatever." Bess tossed off a dismissive wave. "I wonder if you know, Charma, that after he and his friends tore the shit out of that...that thing, darn near broke his father's bank account, not to mention the old man's heart, Guy spent the better part of twenty years trying to get it back into perfect working order."

I stopped partway between my two cousins and turned only my head toward Bess. "You say that like it has some deeper meaning."

"Man invests nearly half his lifetime trying to put right an impulsive mistake of his youth." She drew in a ragged breath. "It *does* have a deeper meaning. Even more so that he just handed the keys over to you."

"He did no such thing. He told Dathan where to find the keys and let him hand the keys to me."

"*You* being the X factor in the whole equation. No way

would he have done that for another living soul. In fact, if he hadn't figured his tearing away from the old gals and the Memorial Day service in his shiny black hearse would have caused a scene, he'd be the one driving you to get me at this very moment, and you know it."

I had no illusions. Whatever Guy did at this point had more to do with Bess's dying than with anything he and I might have shared a million forgotten years ago. I had to believe that. Otherwise...otherwise I didn't know what the hell I would do, and that uncertainty scared the hell out of me. "Some people would say *you* are the X factor, Bess. Not me."

"Some people don't have a clue what they are talking about, do they? Though I doubt a lack of any real knowledge ever stopped anyone around here from going right on talking about the object of their ignorance."

"Or writing about it." *Shit, yeah, I said it.* I *had* to say it.

"Water under the bridge, Charma," Min called out. "Let it go."

Bess opened her mouth.

"Both of you." Min's tone brooked no argument. "Now are we going to stand here all day melting, or are we going to jump in this baby and go?"

"Go," Bess said. "I just wanted Charma to take a moment to consider the significance of the gesture. People usually do things for a reason. They aren't always smart things, and they don't always accomplish what the person had hoped, granted. But sometimes, if you look beneath the surface, beneath the most obvious—"

"It's nothing, I tell ya." I stood firm. "Guy lent me a hearse built more than three decades ago. It's not like it's a...a..."

"Spanking new Jaguar convertible?" Minnie offered, a wickedly innocent smile playing at her lips.

I raised my chin. "Well, yeah."

"No comparison." Bess tipped her head back to rest it against the door. Her eyelids fluttered, then shut entirely. "That convertible is nothing more than a young man's plea for attention, a masquerade, an aerodynamic rolling penis with global positioning software and antilock brakes at best."

"Well, thank you very much, Bess." I pushed my fingertips against my temple. "You just made an obscene version of that weenie-shaped hot dog car pop into my head."

"With that adorable Sterling at the wheel!" Minnie chimed in.

"Shut up, both of you. This is not the big deal you're making it. It's transportation. It's not a manifestation of Guy's regret or the automotive equivalent of a love token from him to me." I strode on up to where Minnie waited, dumped my load on top of hers, then returned to help Bess down the walkway. "It's just your standard gold-tone big-ass butt-ugly seventies-style Oldsmobile hearse, okay?"

"*Olds*-mobile?" Bess finally stepped from the doorway, slinging her lightweight, butter-colored sweater around her neck like a cape as she did. "Bit optimistic considering its function, don't you think?"

She smiled.

Okay, she didn't *smile*. But she didn't smile in the way Bess does when most people *would* smile.

I considered it a minor victory.

It didn't lift the weight of the world off my back, but it did lighten my load enough that I could joke, "So what would you call it—a Deads-mobile?"

"It's a *hearse*." Bess had stopped not smiling, and moved on to her trademark superior smirk. "You're taking me back to the Aunt Farm in a lousy hearse."

"Why not?" I asked, not backing down an inch. "I thought maybe you could use the practice riding in one."

She narrowed her eyes, but not before I caught a glimpse of the old fire in her.

God, it was like...like water in the desert, that look. Bess was still here, still with us, still alive.

There was still hope.

She lowered her head and may have even laughed. "You are one truly twisted individual."

"Flattery won't save you now, sister." I pushed past her and opened the driver's side door. "You still have to sit on the hump in the middle."

Bess sucked her cheeks in, or perhaps she actually had grown so gaunt and weak that the very act of drawing a deep breath made her face go skeletal. She stepped forward. Her ankle buckled.

I lunged out to offer my arm for support.

She got her footing and batted me away.

Another breath, another step.

Her black-and-floral summer dress hung heavy from her shoulders, the hem just brushing the tops of her canvas shoes with every movement. Though I could not see her legs, I imagined them skinny as matchsticks.

Sunlight bounced off her dark hair, creating a halo effect here and there. If it warmed her, she did not let it show, just kept on moving forward.

Breath. Step. Breath.

If she falls, I thought, I will just pick up her crumpled

body and carry her. I'll carry her all the way home if I have to. And I'll take care of her. Always.

Step. Breath.

Sweat trickled down the back of my neck. My head swam. My clothes stuck to every curve and hollow of my body. I pulled at my collar.

The terrible heat did not seem to bother Bess.

Here I was, wishing I could crawl out of my own skin, and she didn't even remove her sweater. The empty sleeves dangled down her front like an exhausted child catching a piggyback ride.

She looked old. So old.

She lifted her head and met my gaze.

I did not reach for her again, just opened my hand and hoped she'd sense in that gesture everything I was willing to give her, everything I would do, all that I would sacrifice if only...

"Geez, Bess, that case was heavy." Minnie tossed the other bags in the back and swung the door shut. "What you got in it?"

"My life," she called out before stopping directly in front of me to whisper, "Does she know?"

I shook my head.

"Your life? In a single suitcase?" Minnie stopped beside the passenger door. Her face glistened. She shaded her eyes. "Bullshit."

"No, I got rid of that." Bess let out something between a laugh and a shudder, then looked first at me, then at Min. "Funny thing, this past year, I found out that once I culled all the bullshit out of my life, there really wasn't very much left over."

I touched her back.

She sighed. And I swear she let herself rest against my damp palm. If only for a moment.

"Not very much of substance, anyway." She got in the car and slid to the center of the seat, finishing, "Just what you put in the back there, and a few boxes and a trunk in a self-storage unit on the far side of town."

"Great. We can pick those up before we go out to the farm."

"I'd rather leave them, if you don't mind."

"Well, I do mind." I got in and slammed the door. "We have wheels. We have room. We have time. Lord knows when we'll have all three of those at our fingertips again."

"Lord knows." It was more a breath than a whisper.

Minnie plopped down on the other side of Bess. "Lord knows what?"

"What crawled up Charma Deane's butt to make her so damn *proactive* all of a sudden."

"Proactive?" I asked, starting the hearse.

"She means bossy." Min whipped her hair around with one hand and began twisting it into a knot at the back of her head.

Bess shifted in her seat. "Actually, I meant—"

"Actually, she meant who the hell died and made you the freakin' Queen of Sheba?" Min poked a pencil through the tight coil of silver-laced black hair.

I laughed. "I know it's been a long time since we three have been together, but, jeez, Bess, how could you have forgotten it's Minnie's sacred role to act as interpreter-peacemaker between you and me?"

"Oh, I haven't forgotten. If you'd think for yourself a minute, you'd know that."

Her secret. She had not wanted anyone to know. Not even

Min. Now I knew why. She did not want her words edited or reshaped to blunt their effect. And she damn sure didn't want a peacemaker.

"Buckle up," I said.

"Why? Because we might have a wreck and I might be killed?"

"Yes. And because Guy spent half his lifetime putting this baby back into mint condition, and I'd hate to return it to him with your guts splattered all over the inside because the hearse stopped for a bunny and you didn't."

"Why do I think Guy would get over that?" She slid the buckle into place.

"Damn bunnies," Minnie muttered. "If any cross our path, I say just run over the little bastards."

I rolled my eyes.

"You better buckle up, too, Min." Bess wriggled to free the belt lodged between them. "No one would get over it if *you* got splattered all over the inside of hearse."

I pulled out onto the street and took the long back way.

"Where is everyone?" Bess asked. "The town looks deserted."

"It's the holiday." I took a right. "Nobody celebrates it at home in Orla. Guess they figure why stay put and stare out your window in hopes you'll witness something shocking, titillating or gruesome, when you could go out to a family reunion and be sure of it?"

"Hmm." Bess rubbed the back of her neck.

"This is where you're supposed to make a disparaging remark about—" I cut through a narrow alley to miss the crowd heading toward the noon potluck at the VFW "—what did you call it in your trashy whore book?"

"I did not write a—"

"A swamp of a small town where whatever doesn't keep moving gets sucked under into the lifeless muck," I deadpanned. "Or words to that effect."

"I resent your calling my book trash."

We came bumping out of the alley, and I turned the wheel toward home. "Yeah, well, we resent you trashing our family in your book."

"Trashy whore book," Minnie corrected, then turned to Bess, putting on an air of seriousness that the topic definitely did not deserve. "Or TWB, as we in the immediate family took to calling it."

Bess groaned and laid her head back.

Minnie studied Bess's profile, the mock somberness of her expression falling away to reveal sober concern.

"Not that everyone begrudged your literary effort, Bess." I rushed to fill the silence and distract Minnie. "Mama personally checked your book out of the library each and every time a new copy came in."

"Aunt Dinah?"

"Yes," I said. Hundreds of people around town had loved Bess's book. All that awful stuff about the George family?— hell, they ate it up. Why couldn't I have used one of *them* as an example instead of Mama? Two subjects that I wanted to avoid with Bess in the entire universe of things to talk about, and I go and bring one of them up myself. Did I say two subjects? *Mama. Guy. Bess dying...* Three subjects.

Oh, and *the book.* Four.

And her kicking the aunts out on their skinny old asses.

"Aunt Dinah checked out my book?"

Mention of Mama's name drew me back from what was stacking up to be a pretty sizable list of off-limit topics.

"Yes, she did," I said in my best end-of-discussion tone.

Bess rubbed one of her sweater's sleeves between her palms. "Every time a new one came in?"

"Yeah." Min's gaze followed Bess's every movement, and that preoccupation colored her tone. "They had to keep replacing it, you see, because someone kept checking it out, then losing it."

"Let me guess—Aunt Dinah?"

Maybe Mama didn't like you as much as your keeping her to yourself in her last days makes you think she liked you, six-year-old Charma asserted silently. Meanwhile, the older but not necessarily more mature version did this deliberate shrug thing and rubbed salt into the presumed wound. "Lost it in the dishwasher, in the bathtub. Once on vacation she even lost it in the Atlantic Ocean."

"Really?"

"Yes, *really*." Bess was the boyfriend-stealing, nasty-book-writing, mama-cremating liar here. How dare she take that high-and-mighty tone with me? "As a general rule Mama could not abide book burning, but book drowning..."

"Bess, are you all right?" Min's words seemed to come from someplace faraway. Some place cold and unsafe.

"I'm fine," Bess murmured, folding herself smaller into the place between us.

"I don't think you are," Min said. "When I first saw you, I chalked it up to the dingy light in the hotel. But now that I'm seeing you in broad daylight..."

"Hearse light," Bess corrected. "Nobody looks good in hearse light."

"Yeah, but *you* look like you're riding in the wrong part of the hearse."

"Min!" I hit the brakes.

That threw us forward all together, and it took a second to settle back in our seats, just enough time to leave a conspicuous break in the conversation.

Bess glared at me.

"I swear I didn't say a word."

"Who has to say anything? Bess shows up in Orla to make a heartless grab for the farm, she drops some big-ass secret on Charma and, most telling of all, when we show up out of the blue to force her to come stay with us, she does it. No excuses. No questions. No hurling a Kokeshi at our heads in an attempt to put our eyes out."

"Have I not apologized enough for that?" Bess hunched down low, her arms locked across her body. "Damn it, Minnie, who knew a stupid wooden doll could do that much damage?"

Min clicked her tongue and pointed to the scar that still crossed her eyebrow.

I laughed under my breath and started driving again.

"The point is, Bess, Charma doesn't have to tell me a damn thing. She shouldn't have to. Whatever this is, whatever is wrong with you, I should hear it from *you*."

"Prepare to be disappointed."

"I'm prepared for a whole lot worse than disappointment, sugar." Min reached out. Her plump tawny-colored fingers made a startling contrast to the grayish pallor of Bess's rail-thin arm. "A whole heck of a lot worse."

Nothing. Bess did not move or speak. Gave no response at all.

Min leaned forward to talk to me over our cousin. "It's the cancer again, isn't it?"

Bess shot me a look that once would have shriveled me to dust.

"Bone," I said softly.

"Okay." Min nodded in a way that made me think she had no idea she was nodding. She wet her lips. Tears welled in her eyes.

I blinked and a warm trickle rolled down my cheek. There is that old blessing: May you be so close that when one cries, the other tastes salt. That was Min and me.

And Bess, if she'd let herself be a part of it again.

Let herself, be damned. She *would* be a part of it. And we would be a part of her down to her very last breath. That's what we faced now, and there was no use pretending otherwise anymore.

"She opted out of traditional treatment." When my voice wavered, I paused. Even with more than two days to think about it, saying it out loud carried a power I could not have prepared myself for. It made it...true. "She went in for something alternative in Mexico, instead."

"I see. And?"

I shook my head.

Min shut her eyes and whispered, "Shit, Bess."

"I'll try, Min." Bess scrunched up her face and balled her hands into fists. "But couldn't I just pee my pants instead? At my age that takes almost no effort at all. Hell, I'm literally one good sneeze or a coughing fit away from Noah launching the Ark."

Silence.

A whole damn hearse filled to overbrimming with silence.

Then I laughed.

Bess followed.

After a minute, Min joined in.

What a sight we must have made. Three idiot women crammed into the front seat of a vintage hearse laughing so hard the whole thing shook. *Laughing.* Not because something was so funny, but because it was so damn serious and what the hell else could we do?

"We have to stop now, or Charma will have to explain the giant wet spot on the front seat," Bess said.

"You wouldn't dare," I said.

"I could sit in your lap if you want to protect the seat, but then we'd both have wet spots to explain."

"I can hear it now. Charma running into the house hollering, 'Bess peed my pants!'"

Bess covered her face. "Shut up, Min, or I swear I'll pee yours, too."

"Girl, you have no decorum at all, do you?" Min wiped her eyes. "Peeing in other people's pants! I swanee."

"I can't help it." Bess stopped to draw in a slow, deep breath, then let it out all in one rush. "Look at how I was raised."

"You were raised just fine," I told her, deciding not to point out that, because of Uncle Chuck's work with the State Department, Bess alone had grown up in a world of culture, protocol and diplomacy. "You just chose all on your own to act like—"

"A heathen." She forced the word in.

"I told you that's a dirty word around me." I eased the hearse back into gear and it started to move again. "I was *going* to say asshole."

"I like heathen better." Min gave her shoulders a smug little wriggle. "It reminds me of when we were girls and just about every time we got up to anything daring or dangerous or the least bit interesting, Nana would holler at us."

"Y'all don't act any better than a pack of heathens." Bess and Min shouted it together in a booming Nana Abbra tone.

"'Member the time you sassed her back, Bess? When you said—"

"How the hell do you know what a pack of heathens acts like?" Bess demanded, as if she'd just asked the question yesterday.

"Man, if Nana could have caught you, you wouldn't have sat down for a week." Min stared into space a moment, then turned her upper body toward Bess and me. "I always thought whoever they were, those heathens sure did have a lot more fun than us Baptists."

"Hmm." Bess and I had the same response. Maybe because while Min had stayed true to the tenets of her faith even back then, we had done our share of exploring the heathen side of life. And liked it.

"So, what do we do now?" I asked as we approached the road that would take us out to the Aunt Farm.

"Only one thing we can do." Bess sat up straight. "Joyride."

"Joyride? In a hearse?" Min's eyes grew wide.

I glanced at Min, so brave in her attempt not to break down over the awful news. Then at Bess, so worn and thin and yet so hard and determined to see her plans carried out.

What had I set into motion today? What would come of bringing the three of us together again, and of taking Bess back into the very home she vowed she would take away from us?

"Yes, a joyride. In a hearse. Really. Can you think of anything more fitting?" Bess asked.

"Because of your condition?" Min murmured.

"Hell, no, because of *our* condition. We're heathen girls!

And we're running in our pack. Let's go out and do something to make Nana proud."

"I think I already have," I said softly, imagining how delighted my grandmother would have been to know that Fawnie and Shug might just get thrown out of her house for good—and that her granddaughters would be the cause.

13

"That makes eight, ma'am." A redheaded boy in a blue shirt and khaki pants handed a second carrier loaded with extra-large drinking cups through the drive-up window. "You sure you don't want anything else?"

"No. These cups of ice will do just fine, thank—"

"Yes, thanks!" Bess practically crawled into my lap to get a good look at the poor kid as, laying the old Arkansas twang on thicker than flies on roadkill, she said, "You've saved our skins today. Hell, forget our skins—what you really saved was our *noses!* Our AC gave out twenty minutes ago, and that body in the back? *Pheuw-ee,* it's beginning to stank!"

"Body?" The kid's freckled face went ghostly white.

"Let's get this ice where it can do the most good." Bess squirmed around in her seat and shook one of the cups so that it sounded as if she'd begun flinging the contents into the back of the hearse. "Gun it, honey! We gotta get this stiff to Bug-tussel before sundown."

I had two choices at the point. Hold up the entire line while

I attempted to explain the situation—perhaps starting with describing Bess as an escaped mental patient—or smile meekly at the kid, shrug and hit the gas.

The engine growled.

The tires squealed.

Minnie giggled so hard that she toppled one of the cups onto the floorboard.

And that poor boy leaned so far out the window watching us take off that the next driver pulling up nicked the kid in the ear with his side mirror.

I tapped the brakes as we passed the Stop sign, then roared off into the street.

The cup on the floorboard pitched and rolled, spewing bits of ice against my bare ankle.

"Get that cleaned up, Min," I snapped, more out of frustration at my complete loss of control over the situation than out of any real anger at her.

"It's only ice." Bess situated a drink carrier securely in the open space behind us.

"Yeah. It's only ice," Min echoed.

"Don't you two dare double-team me." I wanted Minnie firmly on my side. Always. Bess's very presence threatened that, something I hadn't considered before making this a two-woman rescue operation. "Get this ice cleared away."

"Ease up, will you?" Bess settled back down and refastened her safety belt. "It's like someone yanked your tension wires— all the way from your flash-frozen anklebone to your rage-induced red-hot cheeks."

"My *what?*"

"These." Bess tapped the angular bone below her eye. "What? Did you think I meant the other cheeks?"

I made a sharp turn to take a shortcut, which shows you right there the kind of state I was in. A shortcut to where? I had no idea where we were headed. Bess had thrown a monkey wrench into the whole operation.

And I had to monkey wrench it right back from her. Even if I had to use a real wrench—and/or real monkeys—to do it.

Min rose up from floorboard cleaning duty, rolled down the window and threw some ice out. "What other cheeks?"

"Charma thought I accused her of having red-hot raging butt cheeks."

All innocence and sweetness, almond eyes blinked my way. "Well, she does."

Make that a monkey wrench for two. "Minnie!"

"You *do*, Charmika." She flicked the last piece of half-melted shaved ice at me. "Whenever Guy Chapman is around."

Bess tsked insincerely, quite unconvincing in her disdain. "And I thought you were bumping uglies with convertible-compensation man."

"Stop it!" Control. That was my goal. Start with directing the conversation, then on to total cousin domination. "No more talk about raging butts or bumping boy toys. You got that?"

Min brushed droplets of ice water out of Bess's ponytail. "Have you seen the boy toy?"

"The car?"

"No, the actual boy."

"He's a man," I growled.

"Cute?" Bess placed her head next to Min's and shot me a look from the corner of her eye.

"Just *darling*." Min giggled. "Moved here not too long ago from Atlanta. Old money."

"Oh, the best kind." Bess rubbed her hands together. "Family?"

"Estranged from them but not from their financial assets."

Bess patted her palm against her chest. "Be still, my heart."

"And he's a lawyer."

Bess shrugged. "Nobody's perfect."

"Yeah." Min sighed and pressed her shoulders back. "He's no Guy Chapman, but I wouldn't kick him out of bed."

"Careful, Min, you're telling this to two women who *have* kicked Guy Chapman out of bed." Bess turned toward me.

I could feel her gaze searching my profile. I clenched my jaw.

"Though in all honesty, I suppose I should say I didn't kick him so much as I didn't stop him when he wanted out. Charma?"

"I didn't kick anybody, Bess, and you know it. Though I personally did feel a bit gut-kicked when Guy left me for that no-good backstabbing tramp he ran off with—you remember her, don't you, Bess?"

"Just barely," she said softly.

Our eyes met and I believed her. This was not the same woman who had betrayed me on my wedding day.

She winced out a smile, then looked away.

No, not the same woman. *This* was a whole new woman, one capable of betraying me and my family in whole new, never before imagined ways. If I allowed it.

If I didn't allow it—if I finally stood up to her and forced her to deal with the reality of who she was and how much we would love her if she let us...

Shit. I had gone nuts. Honestly. Soap-opera-talking, angst-ridden, women's-movie-channel-sentiment-spewing nuts. And that had to stop.

"Okay, no more talk about Sterling, Guy, beds or butt cheeks. Just tell me why, Bess, did you have us buy eight bucket-size cups of nothing but ice?"

"Not to worry, I have a plan, cousin."

"That's when I worry the most, *cousin.* When you have a *plan.*" Even more so when I couldn't figure out that plan and come up with whatever counterattack it might warrant.

"Relax, will you? And point this hearse toward the nearest liquor store."

"Why?"

"Glug. Glug. Glug." She raised her hand and tipped back her head.

"Should you be doing that?"

"What?" Bess's frail fingers disappeared under the mass of her scarf and tied-back hair. "You think I might get a crick in my neck?"

"Not that." Minnie threw her own head back. "Drinking. Do you think you should be drinking? In your condition and all?"

"If you can't drink when you're in my condition, when the hell can you?"

"It doesn't matter either way. We're not going to find an open liquor store in Orla on Memorial Day, anyway."

"Okay then, how long before the old gals and crew head back to the house?"

"Let's see…the service would last half an hour." I did a mental walk-through of the events I expected would take place at the cemetery in our absence. "Then they'd want to trot Sterling around like a prize-winning pig to show off to all their closest and oldest friends. Flaunt. Flaunt. Catty remark. Hissy fit. Choosing up sides. Dredging up old grudges. Threats made. Wigs pulled askew, maybe even off. Cooler heads—no pun intended—prevail. Let's see…then kiss, kiss, all is well. They should make it back to the house in…"

Bess and Min exchanged glances.

"What? You envy me my life here, don't you?" I rushed in with a quip before either of them could confront me with their honest opinions. "Living life on the edge…of nowhere. Running with hell's aged. Scoffing in the face of convention."

Bess narrowed one eye at me. "Convention?"

"Mostly Shriners."

"Shriners' convention?" She rolled her eyes.

"Okay, maybe not a whole convention, but Orla has its share of Shriners. And let me tell you, you don't know jack about scoffing until one of those jerks picks you up for a date. I mean, have you *seen* those teeny clown cars they drive?"

Instead of the chuckle I'd hoped for, Bess shook her head. Her expression went grim, even more grim than you'd expect from a woman taking what she knew would not be her first ride in a funeral car. "Charma, it doesn't have to be this way."

"You'd think not." I did not let down my guard, or my glib air. "But those Shriners really are attached to those cars."

"Screw the Shriners, Charma!" Bess shouted.

Minnie rounded her lips and rolled her eyes in mocking innocence. A few decades ago she might have chanted, "Charma got in trouble."

"I'm not talking about clown cars or crazy aunts or the nonexistent dating scene in this swamp of a town. I'm talking about your life now." Bess pushed her fingers into her hair at the temples, almost covering her ears. She bowed her head. "Your life, Charma, does not have to center around Orla and the Aunt Farm. You don't have to stay here. With your skills, not to mention your inheritance, you could go anywhere, do anything. Charma, you're a free woman. Or at least you will be once I take over—"

"For your information, Bess, I have already screwed a Shriner." Like hell Bess was taking anything over for me. And how dare she, anyway. How dare she presume I wanted anything different from my limited, lousy, hellhole life. How dare she tell me what to do and where to go. I'd tell her where to go, but given her diagnosis and the life she had led, I feared she might be headed there already. "And just for the record, he proved your car-as-compensation theory wrong."

Bess slid her fingers down the sides of her face to her neck and groaned. "Just tell me when you expect Fawnie and Shug to get home."

"Well, let's figure an hour for the normal stuff."

"Normal being a very loose description," Min interjected.

"Then we'd have to allow extra for all the time they will milk sympathy from everyone over Min and me taking off and leaving them in the care of a lawyer and a stranger from New Jersey."

"You have no idea when they'll get back there, do you?" Bess droned.

"None whatsoever," I confessed.

Min shifted the cup from one hand to the other, then flexed her freed fingers. "Why do you ask, Bess?"

Bess put her back to me. "Because surely ol' Fawnie has a secret stash somewhere out there."

"Aunt Fawnie doesn't have anything but that nasty sloe gin crap," I said, quick and hard, just the way I wanted to end this line of discussion.

"And she only keeps that on hand for medicinal purposes."

When Min raised one finger to add emphasis, she looked just like her mother. "Fawnie figures anything tastes that awful can't be sinful."

Bess slumped down. "Since when did the old bat care what was sinful?"

"Since God pushed her down the stairs," I muttered.

"And to think I worry sometimes that God and I won't get along." Bess laughed. "Well, if that's all we've got, I say sloe gin fizzes for everyone."

"Bess, you can't—"

"It's okay, Charma, Min will go in and get it. Like when we were kids, remember?"

"I remember you always coming up with things for me to do and then disappearing when the shit hit the fan." Min narrowed her eyes at Bess, but that didn't hide the care and concern in her expression as she added in almost a whisper, "That's what I remember."

"She's telling you to do your own dirty work." I took on Min's traditional role as interpreter in a stupid attempt to steer things my way. "And I'm telling you that you can't boss us around anymore. You can't make us do your bidding because you're the cool one, the older one, the worldly one."

"How about because I'm the half-dead one?" She feigned a childlike pout.

"You'll have to look more pitiful than that to get to me," I warned her.

"How could I look *more* pitiful?" She played it up big, a spark of humor in her dark, dark eyes. "I'm already in a hearse."

"Okay." Min caved. "Where does Fawnie hide the stuff?"

"The old standbys?" Bess poked her bone-thin fingers up

to count them off. "Behind the encyclopedias? Out in the garden shed? Under the bathroom sink?"

"Her artificial leg," I drawled, helpful as ever.

"Ri-i-ight." Bess laughed, did a little head wobble to indicate a drunken Fawnie, then acted along as she said, "And whenever she feels the need of a little sin-free sippage, she whips that sucker off and glug, glug, glug."

"Of course." I guided the hearse onto a rutted rural road and kept my eyes peeled for wildlife—of both the animal and the party animal variety. "That makes perfect sense, doesn't it? In this family, instead of getting water on the knee—we'd get gin."

"Got me there." Bess elbowed me lightly. "So, where does the old soul keep the stuff, really?"

"I told you. Her leg. In Grandpa's old silver hip flask. Strapped on with tape."

"You're lying." Bess leaned back in the seat.

I gave my head a quick shake. "If I'm lying, I'm dying."

"Shouldn't that be my line?"

She intended it for a joke, but I didn't respond. Making the last turn down the road that would lead us home had drained the humor right out of me.

"Don't fight, you two." Min flattened her hand against the passenger window. "Look, we're almost there."

"What? No! Turn around!" Bess lunged to grab the dash. She whipped her head back and forth as if she had only now realized where we were. "I didn't really mean for us to go out to the farm so soon. Not if there isn't any booze there."

"I can't turn around." I couldn't. Between the narrowness of the familiar road and the wideness of the unfamiliar vehicle—not to mention my own stubborn determination not to let Bess get her way—I had no intention of trying to navigate anything so treacherous. "Where would we go, anyway?"

Bess grabbed my arm. "How about your house?"

I gripped the wheel.

"Charma sold her house." Min settled the cup on the floor between her feet at last and began rubbing her hands together, presumably to get some warmth back into them. "Right after Aunt Dinah—"

"Died." I shoved the word in before Min could gloss it over with some ridiculous euphemism.

"But you'd lived in that house for fifteen years." Bess stared at me, and when I didn't respond, turned to Min. "To just suddenly up and leave it."

"Market was hot. Boys had grown up and gone." *I'd all but turned into a ghost haunting the shambles of my own life.* No need to share that tidbit with anyone. "What did I need a house for, anyway?"

"I didn't know."

"How could you?" I'd slowed the car to a crawl, making it easy to give her my consummate eat-shit-and-die look—only I didn't really mean it. "You couldn't be bothered to pick up a phone, not even when it mattered most."

When was that? When Dinah died? Or when I found out my cancer had returned? Or maybe when I realized I wouldn't beat it this time?

She didn't ask for specifics, but then she didn't have to, because we both knew it wouldn't change anything now. "If I had called, would you have talked to me?"

I kept my eyes straight ahead.

"I thought not. So don't get pissy with me for not calling." She reached behind her to get one of the cups of ice, lifted the lid, then took a long, labored swallow of the liquid inside. "So. You sold the house."

"It just felt too...small all of a sudden."

She nodded. "Where'd you move?"

"I rented one of those places across from the high school, you know the ones."

"Yeah. Sure." She didn't even ask how an efficiency apartment could suit me when a four-bedroom house had grown too small. "Closer to work, then?"

"I quit my job. Or rather, it quit me. No funding for a full-time school nurse with my seniority anymore, and since I didn't really need the money..."

"Charma always was such a softie." Hand still on the window, Min shook her head, and a tendril of hair slipped from her makeshift chignon. "Y'all think it's me, but she's just as bad."

"What are you doing now?" Bess asked.

"Pulling into the farm."

"No, for work. What are you doing with your life?"

I eased the hearse slowly to the right, keeping its nose straight to avoid getting the paint scratched by the overgrown hedges that flanked the first few feet of the curving, quarter-mile drive.

"Charma?"

"We're almost there."

"She's studying to be a midwife." Min beamed. "Isn't that just perfect?"

"I'm not studying to be a midwife, I'm just in transition."

Bess took another sip. "Was that supposed to be funny? Midwife? Transition?"

"Believe me, there's nothing funny about it."

"Thank God," she whispered. "I've just about had it with the bad puns for one day. I'm worn down."

"You look it, too. Worn down the last of the dog-gnawed bones, drug out from under the porch and gnawed on again." I used a phrase borrowed from a woman who routinely passed through the doors of the Aunt Farm in her short respites between abusive lovers. It had long ago become an endearing family expression. One Bess had twisted and used to make George matrons sound like backwoods bimbos. "Not quite the homecoming you'd have written for yourself if you'd added this chapter to your nasty little mem-noir."

"Shove it, Charma," she muttered.

"I love you, too, sunshine," I muttered right back at her, and shut the engine off. "We're here."

This was it. I had finagled and cajoled, bypassed and out-and-out bullied my way to this point. I had won. Now what?

Take Bess inside.

Get her comfy in a room.

Wait for her to die.

To die or evict my aunts, whichever came first.

What a hollow victory.

I glanced at Minnie, who had already climbed out and had begun to help Bess ease across the seat.

No. Not hollow. Bess needed us and we had her with us. That was a victory.

A small one.

The first of many. One after another they would add up, until it all came together. Bess, the house, the aunts. One by one I would win each small battle, and like a million drops of rain it would all add up to a potent reservoir where I could finally throw myself in and—

"Put this hearse in reverse, Charma Deane Parker." Sterling pounded on the hood with one fist to underscore his fury. "And haul your ass out of here."

14

Poor Sterling. He had no idea who or what he was up against.

"Be a dear and get the bags from the back of the hearse, 'kay?" I dropped the keys into his palm, patted his tight, smooth cheek and walked right on by him to join my cousins making their way up the walk.

I'd done it. I might one day regret what I'd done. But I had made my move and carried it through. I had, in essence, done what my father had asked of me just before he died—been bold and fierce and had jumped out beyond my fear.

Bess glanced back over her shoulder. Maybe it was a trick of the sunlight. Or maybe she was just flushed with exhilaration at the chance to get in a dig at her nemesis, but she looked warmer, somehow, more vibrant, more *there*.

"Bring what's left of the ice in those cups along, too, sweet thang," Bess cooed at him. "We're having a little celebration. And you're invited."

"Sorry, but I have to decline that invitation." Sterling moved quickly and quietly and placed himself directly in Bess's path.

"Too bad." She took another step even after he had cut her off, placing herself a little too close to a man she knew only by my connection to him and his questionable motives for car ownership. "You don't know what you're missing."

"Maybe not, but I know what *you're* missing, Ms. Halloway."

"That's just a rumor." She raised her eyebrows and cocked her head. "I actually do have a heart."

Sterling's eyes went hard, but not too hard. He wanted to throw some smart remark in her face. You could see it all over him, from the cocky tilt of his lips to the way his lean body loomed large over Bess's frail form.

I swallowed and wished I'd brought one of the ice cups with me.

Sterling's white cotton shirt stuck to his shoulders in the heat. You could practically hear the sweat trickle down his spine.

In the end he had enough grace, good manners and legal training to keep calm if not cool. "What you're missing, Ms. Halloway, is the chance to get yourself a toehold on this property. Leave. Now."

Leave? How dare he bark out a demand like that. I was the one in charge here, after all. "Sterling, stop—"

Bess cut me off with a raised hand. "I can handle this, Charma. My name is on the deed to this house, Mr...?"

"Mayhouse. Sterling Mayhouse."

"Sterling." She nodded and wet her lips, then held out her hand. "Bess."

He took her hand in his and for a moment they both just stood there.

I should have made my move then. Should have seized back

my admittedly tenuous hold on the events of the day. But before I could wedge myself between the two combatants and demand my proper due, Min pressed up close behind me.

"Do you think she's still strong enough to bend his arm behind his back and throw him to the ground like she used to do us?" Min whispered, loudly enough for everyone to hear.

"She can try." Sterling's gaze never faltered from Bess's eyes, but his mouth did betray him with just the hint of a grin.

"Careful what you wish for, Sterling, honey. You might get it," Bess murmured.

"I could say the same to you...Bess."

Bess took a long, ragged breath, then tilted her head ever so slightly to concede his point.

Wow.

Two minutes.

I was dumbfounded.

Sterling had known Bess all of two minutes and he'd already accomplished something I don't think I ever did—he'd humbled her. Just barely, but still...

"You know, legally, it's my house," she finally said to him. "We both know I *will* get through that door. Why quibble over when?"

"Because *legally* it's the two Mrs. George's home. They have every lawful and moral right to it, at least for the next twenty-four days, and I've advised them not to surrender so much as a square inch of it for your possession. After all, possession is nine-tenths of the law. But then I think you knew that old saying, didn't you?"

"Because I am, myself, *old?*"

"Because you are, yourself, no fool." It carried all the weight and worth of a real compliment. Sterling, for all his youth and vapid charm, clearly had a healthy respect—perhaps even ad-miration—for the woman he was up against.

Poor foolish boy. I laid my hand on the tense muscle of his upper arm. "Sterling, let's not—"

He brushed me aside.

"You may have found a way around your cousins' defenses, Ms. Halloway." He pronounced her last name slowly and surely, as if he had some chance of setting the boundaries be-tween them and holding that line. "But you won't get past me."

"Oh, no?" Bess smiled—the way a dog "smiles" just before it bites.

Brushed aside. *Me*. Well, if he thought he'd ever get into my bed now...

"Don't waste your time with him, Bess." I cupped Bess's elbow in my palm. "Let's just—"

"Back off, Charma." She jerked herself loose and fixed her whole Bess-ness on the man blocking her way. "And just what lengths are you prepared to go in order to do to keep me from going into my own house, sweet thang?"

"Whatever it takes." Sterling stood firm. "*I* will never back down from you, Ms. Halloway. You can count on that."

He held Bess's gaze for one second. Two...three...

"Never make promises to a lady you don't intend to keep," Bess said, her tone low and breathy.

"I never would. But that doesn't apply here, does it?"

"Because it's not in the strictest legal terms a promise?"

"No, because you're no lady."

"Enough!"

Both of them looked at me and blinked.

"First Bess tries to wrestle away what little power I had to direct the day's events, and now Sterling wants to muscle in?" I marched forward, up onto the porch. "I won't have it, I tell you."

"But he has such nice muscles." Min followed my lead up the front steps, curling her arm in a bodybuilder pose as she did.

"You're not helping, Min," I grumbled, even as I nailed Sterling with a red-hot glare. "And that crack about *I* will never back down, what was that supposed to mean?"

Sterling opened his mouth, coming toward me.

I held up my hand to stop him on the first step, and said, "Charma will back down but *I* won't, that's what it meant. Well, now it's a point of honor—" and perhaps my last stab at maintaining my hold over anything "—to prove you wrong."

"Huh." Bess managed a couple of the old wooden steps without any apparent struggle. She even found enough strength to give Sterling's shoulder a nudge as she swept past.

"Don't you get so high and mighty, Miss Possession Is Nine-Tenths of the Law." I placed myself between her and the door. "I'm not one-hundred-percent sure what needs to happen next."

Sterling leaned forward to put his lips next to Bess's ear. "Huh to you, too."

"But I can tell you both this—from this point forward, neither one of you yells jump until I say how high."

"Wha...?" Min tipped her head.

Sterling looked at the ground to hide his amusement.

Bess folded her arms and issued the challenge. "Jump, Charma."

"Don't you think I won't." I raised my head and shot mental daggers at her.

"That's all I ask," she said softly.

What the hell was that supposed to mean? I didn't really want to know, which was good, because I had no illusions that Bess would tell me. So I took a deep breath, a moment to compose myself, and was ready to take things in hand again.

"That act don't mean nothing to me, Mrs. George." The high ceilings and hardwoods created the perfect echo chamber for carrying the Puerto-Rican-by-way-of-Jersey accent down the hall, through the screen door and out onto the porch. "I have been a nurse for thirty years. I know how to handle your kind, *dama vieja, mala y loca.*"

"My friend Inez." I shot a preemptive answer at Bess, assuming she'd wonder more about a stranger spouting Spanish in the house than someone calling one of our aunts...well, *anything.*

"Don't you fool with this lady, Fawnie." Shug's voice lagged Inez's in volume but made up for it in barbed vigor. "She been a nurse almost as long as you been a nut! *And* she got your leg!"

Min whipped her head around so fast it knocked her hair loose from its knot. "Oh my gosh, the leg is off!"

"She can keep it." You could practically hear Fawnie suck cigarette smoke deep into her lungs, then flick the butt into a potted plant. "I move faster on this thing, anyway."

I shut my eyes. "And the chase is on."

A blond blur on wheels whirred through the foyer.

Two dark-haired shapes followed behind, one shouting in Japanese, the other in Spanish. And I didn't have to understand either language to know that neither Inez nor Shug was reciting Bible verses at the fleeing, one-legged Fawnie.

"This is new." Bess peered around Sterling to the chaos

playing out on the other side of the tarnished door screen. "What's going on?"

"Couple months ago Fawnie decided the prosthetic leg and cane combo slowed her down too much, so she got herself one of those electric scooters they advertise during daytime TV." I rubbed the back of my neck, but that didn't ease the tight twisting of muscles working up from my shoulder blade to my skull. "Now when she decides to go on a tear about something she's motorized."

Min paused from letting her hair down—or was she putting it back up? Even the most innocuous things suddenly seemed so unclear and complicated. "Mama said she hides the key."

I applied more pressure to the tender muscle. "And then tells Fawnie just where she puts it every time, in case she forgets."

Min shook her head. "And you said in the cemetery that you wished we were more like them."

"I didn't say that," I protested. "*You* said that."

Bess placed her hand on my back in a show of comfort and let her weight fall lightly against me. She had obviously gotten tired but did not want to show that weakness in front of Sterling. "You really have your hands full with these two, Charma."

"Hands?" I anchored my feet firmly and pressed my body toward hers to lend some physical support. The step we stood on creaked. "Hell, I don't even stick my toe in the water around here. We talk on the phone daily, several times a day, in fact, but until your little eviction stunt I hadn't come out here on any kind of regular basis since Mama died."

"I can understand the pain this place holds for you,

Charma." Sterling spoke directly to Bess, not to me. "Seems like it's a family trait, this not-so-much-as-sticking-a-toe-in to see how your aunts are doing."

Min, the peacemaker, rushed in. "Well, up until five months ago, nobody needed to stick anything anywhere."

We all looked at her.

Her smile trembled. She shrugged. "Aunt Dinah always had a way of keeping things around here under control."

"Aunt Dinah had a way of keeping *everything* under control *everywhere*." Bess pulled away from me then, sliding her hand away slowly as she added, "Right up until the end."

"Subtlety was never your strong suit, Bess." I moved up to the next step and looked back down at her. "But the fact that Mama became the queen of all control queens does not absolve you of your part in her death."

"You make it sound like I held a pillow over her face, Charma."

"As far as I'm concerned, you did. And Daddy's." She opened her mouth, her whole face scrunched up as if she wanted to refute it all—or sneeze. I didn't allow her the satisfaction of either one. "Hell, for all I know, given the time and the opportunity, you might have eventually wiped out our entire family line."

She exhaled in one hard, long breath, and her whole body seemed to grow smaller. She lifted her face, her dark eyes cloudy, and asked hoarsely, "Then why bring me out here?"

Because I could not let you die alone.

Because if I don't save you...

If I don't find you...

Reach you...

If I don't make some sense out of your life and the choices

you've made, then I don't have any hope of making sense out of my own.

And most of all—

Because I love you.

Despite everything, I did love her.

But I couldn't any more have said it then than I could have forgiven her for her hand in my father's drowning or her callousness about my mother's death.

"Why, Charma? Surely you have some explanation for your actions." Bess sank to the step and sat there, looking back at me over her shoulder. "At least admit it was all *your* idea."

"Of course it was Charma's idea." Sterling kept his eyes trained on Bess. "It's just like her. She wants to help everyone, with the possible exception of herself. Of course she fell prey to your plan. You knew she would."

"What plan?" I asked, not sure I wanted to know.

"Don't you get it, Charma?" He turned his eyes in my general direction but never broke eye contact with Bess. "If you let her take up residence in this house, you don't stand a chance of staving off the eviction."

"Oh." I should have known that. And I suppose now that I did know, that knowledge should have influenced my decision. But how could it?

Bess was dying.

She belonged in our home.

She belonged with people who loved her unconditionally.

It was that easy.

If in the end it cost us that home, well...it was just a house.

But family...

"Don't y'all try to stop me." A whiff of smoke and perfume breezed through the screen. Over the whir of her electric scooter, Fawnie hollered, "You know half the town's down at the VFW talking about how this family ain't nothing but a bunch of heathens and lunatics, and I gotta get down there and join them."

Bess glanced up at me, then at Min.

Min returned her look, then focused on me.

It was one of those moments. I could jump in with abandon or be swallowed up by the tide of circumstances far beyond my control.

"Heathens, maybe, but we are not lunatics," I hollered in Fawnie's general direction, knowing she'd scooted on already. "Well, not that anyone could prove. You still want to come and stay with us, Bess?"

Bess looked up at me for what seemed forever, then finally bowed her head, nodding almost imperceptibly.

"Okay," I said softly.

"I knew you'd make the right choice." Min drew me into a quick hug, then jerked her thumb toward the doorway and asked Sterling, "What got Fawnie all worked up, anyway?"

"There was an...incident at the cemetery."

"Oh, poor Sterling." Still laughing, Minnie reached out and planted a quick, mommylike kiss on the man's flushed cheek. "There is always an incident at the cemetery. That's the only place Fawnie gets to rub elbows and butt heads with her best friends in the world."

"If they are best friends, then why do they butt heads?" he asked logically.

"Don't try to figure it out." I patted his arm, realizing that gesture, too, had a decidedly mommy-esque vibe to it. "Orla is a small town where people have known each other roughly since Methuselah wore knee pants. These folks have been getting up in one another's business all that time, too. Used to be instead of one big incident on national holidays, Fawnie and her friends spread dozens of tiny episodes out over the course of a year. People hardly paid any heed to a fallout in the flats section of Faymar's Boot-ique or a dig over doughnuts at the Daughters of the Confederacy. Not even the occasional butt-whoopin', hair-pulling no-holds-barred wrestling match down at the Piggly Wiggly."

"Mrs. George!" Inez trotted out her best no-nonsense tone.

"What?" Two voices filled to overflowing with nothing but nonsense came back at her.

"Not you. You! Scooter lady. If you ever want to walk again you better put that thing into reverse and get back in this kitchen."

"Better do it, Fawnie. She's got your foot in the garbage disposal. She goin' to turn it on."

"The hell she is! That's a two-hundred-dollar shoe on that foot."

Beep. Beep. Beep. The electronic warning went off as Fawnie backed into the kitchen.

I bumped Bess's back with one knee. "Sure you want to move in here?"

"She most certainly *does* want to move in here, Charma." Sterling took the last two steps all at once and placed his hand against the front door. "But it's not going to happen."

"Aw, look how he still thinks he can tell you what to do, Charmika." Min pressed her hands together. To anyone who didn't know her it might have looked like just the sweetest gesture, but I knew that girl had had her fill, and that if Sterling had any sense at all, he'd haul butt. "Isn't he cute?"

I came up beside Min and crossed my arms. "He's just darling."

"He's so cute I could just eat him up." Bess bared her teeth, then held out her hand and let Min pull her to her feet.

"Sterling, if I wanted to let a man order me around—" I placed my hand firmly on top of his and met his gaze without blinking "—I'd be driving across the country in a second-hand RV with Boyd Parker."

Sterling didn't budge. "Wouldn't that be a little awkward, sharing the place with your ex and his new child bride?"

"Ooooh." Min shut her eyes and hunched her shoulders.

"I like this man." Bess pushed back her hair and shoved her sleeves up past her elbows.

"I don't know, Sterling." I held my ground. "Fawnie and Shug managed to both be married to Uncle Kel at the same time. Maybe it's a George family tradition."

"Or a family illness," he said, his eyes pleading with me to come to my senses before things went too far.

"I swear. Standing there in the doorway all grit and determination like that?" I moved in close enough to let him see in my eyes that he had lost this war. "You almost looked like a fully growed man, Sterling."

His arm slackened just a bit.

I grabbed the handle and flung open the door. "Min, take Bess inside."

"I think you're a yummy fully growed man." Bess rubbed Sterling's ear as she moved inside. "If that helps."

"I am sure you're just filled to the brim with concern for how you can help me, Ms. Halloway."

Min and Bess slipped over the threshold.

"Charma." Sterling curved his hand around my upper arm

and tucked me in so close that the buttons on his crisp white shirt pressed into my shoulder. "I can't let you do this."

"Sterling." I met his gaze. Be strong, I told myself, for Bess. "You can't stop me."

He opened his mouth, I assumed to argue—or worse, to rattle off some legalese that meant he could, indeed, stop me from bringing Bess home to die.

"Sterling..." I wet my lips. "Please."

His gaze fell to my lips.

I thought for a second he would kiss me, hard and passionate and angry. I thought he would grip my arm tight and beg me to stop acting like an injured child, and trust him. I thought he'd ask me to come home with him and let us pound out our differences between damp, disarranged sheets.

"Bess? Oh, girl..." A crash that sounded like something had dropped on the kitchen floor followed Shug's quiet words.

"Praise the Lord, it's Bess!" Fawnie paused. I don't know if she did it to actually pray, to wrap Bess into a welcoming embrace or to put out her cigarette. "Look here, Inez. This is Bess. Our Bess is come home."

"I..." I pushed away from him and ducked inside the open screen door. "I have to go."

He nodded. His Adam's apple bobbed. He took a deep breath, gave a glance out at the driveway, then back into the dim light of the house. Finally he commanded my gaze and, without blinking, whispered, "Just remember I warned you. You are going to regret this sooner and more vehemently than even you can imagine."

15

Fawnie's signature perfume—if you can call the smell of hair spray, stale smoke and too much toilet water a perfume— wafted into the kitchen a full four seconds ahead of her. The tip of her cane thumped softly on the old floor next. She did not follow it right away.

I debated jumping up out of my chair to offer my help, but knew it would only get me swatted away, maybe even cursed at.

Lucky me—a natural helper born into a family so mule-headed in their independence they'd rather fall on their faces than take someone's hand for support. I lifted my head and looked from the doorway to the hall, which led either down to Bess's bedroom or out to the back porch, where Mama had spent her last hours without once asking for her only child to come to her. Fawnie, Bess, even my own mother had all pushed me away and closed me out at the time when they should have needed me the most.

No wonder I became a school nurse—one of the few nursing jobs where I could rely on a fair amount of resistance and downright rejection on a regular basis. I don't have the life experience for anything else.

Oooh. Good argument. I reached for a pen to scribble it down so I could bring it out next time Inez pushed the midwife idea at me. But the only paper handy at the table this morning would have to come from Fawnie's death-list tablet.

And since I didn't particularly care to find myself chased around by the old gal on her scooter while she tried to bean me with her cane for touching her things, I decided to commit the thought to memory. And in doing so pretty much kissed it goodbye.

"I seen Minnie and Shug out on the front porch swing reading the paper and talking. You're here, and I'm getting in there. That accounts for most of us." Fawnie finally came shuffling into the room dressed for breakfast in more finery than most women wear to a cocktail party. Of course, no one has ever figured out what Fawnette puts in her "special" morning tomato juice, so maybe there's a correlation. "Is Bess up yet?"

"No." I swirled some cream into my freshly poured coffee and clanked the spoon around to keep my hands busy and avoid the urge to grab my aunt and steady her. "Not yet."

"Why, that girl!" She used her cane to drag out a chair, the metal legs screeching in protest. "I have half a mind—"

"'Nuff said, Aunt Fawnie." I planted my foot just so to make the chair safe for her to plop into, raised my cup of coffee in salute to the sentiment, then added, before I took a sip, "Leave Bess alone."

"If you girls loll around in bed all day, how will I ever get anything done?"

"I don't know—work *around* us?"

"Show a little respect, young lady." She nudged the chair again, braced one hand against the chrome side of the yellow-topped table and started to lower herself to sit. "Behave or I'll boot you right out of this house. I will."

"Boot me out? With one leg? You'd fall on your skinny old butt." Instinctively I leaned forward, ready to catch her should she lose her balance.

She made it. The old chair cushion and Aunt Fawnie both gave out a threadbare sigh.

I grinned at her and covered my concern with more teasing. "Then *you'd* be the one lolling in bed all day."

"Well, you're safe then. Only because I don't have time to waste nursing a wounded tailbone." She cackled, stopped to cough, then pulled out a hankie and blew her nose. "You should act more tender toward me, lamb. I count on your tenderness most of all. What with the trouble with the house and...you know."

I stiffened. "And what?"

She reached across me and slid the scruffy Big Chief tablet the length of the table. "And this."

Things That Have to Get Done Before I Die.

I skimmed my fingertips over the bold black lettering. Irritating and idiotic as I found it, I had to admit Fawnie had something I didn't. A plan.

I had no idea what I needed to do now that I had Bess in the house. My current list wouldn't take up a page in a tablet, much less the entire thing. *My* plan I could have scribbled on to the back of a gas station receipt: *Pray for a miracle.*

"Time we got down to business on this, don't you think?" Fawnie flicked open the tablet's cover.

"Already on it," I murmured, even as an impromptu plea ran through my being. *Dear God, give us that miracle. If that's not to be, then just give me a shove in the right direction—or into the path of an oncoming train, whichever gets me out of this with the least amount of mess and pain.*

"What's that, girl?" Fawnie paused with a pair of jeweled reading glasses lifted halfway to her face.

"Um, number one," I read obediently from the list.

"Oh, good, let's get on to this right away."

"Repaint trim, shutters, steps and *whole outside of house?*" I propped my elbows on the table and ducked my head to catch her eyes. "The whole outside of the house, Aunt Fawnie?"

"Why not? Before I go, I aim to see this place restored back to the way God intended the fine homes of the right people to look. Rose-pink with white trim, gray steps and black gloss shutters."

I considered asking her to recite chapter and verse where the Good Book said God had intended that, but feared she might actually come up with something that might make sense. The prospect made my head hurt. "Okay, moving on. Number two. Fix the broken sidewalk out back where the toilet landed."

"You know that story, don't you?"

I nodded. "Mama must have told it to me a dozen times."

It happened before I was even born. Nana had gotten a notion to completely remodel the old-fashioned upstairs bathroom. And she had decreed that her sons would be the ones to do it for her. Mama said it was Nana Abbra's way of getting Daddy and Uncle Kel away from their wives for a project she expected would take a month of Sundays. But Daddy and Uncle Kel figured they'd knock it off in a single Saturday afternoon. Even if it meant tossing a toilet out the window.

"All but ruined themselves for their husbandly duties that day, you know."

"Hauling the tub downstairs, right?" I added, quick to keep Fawnie's train of thought from taking a side trip into husbandly duty-ville. Not that she'd go into detail, she was too much of a lady still for that, but even the polite terms she'd use to couch her complaints gave me the creeps.

"Oh yeah, I thought they'd never get it downstairs without pulling something vital out of whack. Then your daddy come up with the bright idea of wearing your Nana's old-fashioned lace up girdle like a truss, and they were on their way." Fawnie lowered her glasses down low on her nose and gazed in the general direction of the back window. "You never heard such language, lamb."

I didn't have to follow her line of vision to know she meant the claw-footed bathtub that still sat exactly where they had put it down in the backyard all those years ago.

"And that was just your grandmother," she concluded.

I laughed out loud. Daddy and Kel done up in women's undergarments carrying a bathtub out of the house while Nana Abbra cussed a blue streak? No wonder people talked about this family. "I wish I'd known Daddy when he was young. Or at all."

"Them boys." She shook her head, laughed, then reached for the newly opened packet of cigarettes on the table. "They was something back then, I tell you."

"Boys?" I started to laugh again, then realized that my father and his younger brother would have been closer to my son's age back then than to mine. Boys, indeed.

"Your daddy got Kel up to it, you know." She drew out a cigarette and rolled it slowly between her fingers. "I swanee, Kelvin didn't have the smarts God gave a biscuit."

It was the catch in her voice when she spoke of her husband that got to me. Even more than forty years after his death, after all the hurts and humiliations she'd suffered because of that man, Fawnie still had it bad for Kel.

I wondered if, when I reached Fawnie's age, I'd look back on some man in my life that way. Certainly not my ex-husband, Boyd. But maybe...

No maybe about it.

Guy.

Even now, I suspected, when I spoke of the man who'd jilted me with my own cousin, my voice had that infamous Fawnie tremble. I pressed my lips together and curled my fingers into a tight fist.

When the women in my family loved someone, neither time nor heartbreak nor even death seemed to diminish it.

Was that a good thing? I didn't know. But the very notion of it both comforted and scared the hell out of me.

"He was a handsome one, that Kel." Fawnie raised the cigarette to her lips, then fumbled for the lighter. She stroked her thumb down it time and again without success, then rested her shaking hand on the table a moment and said, "Not half as handsome as your daddy, but with a much more gentle nature. That had a powerful appeal."

"I don't really remember Uncle Kel all that well, Aunt Fawnie." *Except the fiasco at his funeral.* I eased the lighter from her arthritic fingers.

"You don't?"

"Honestly, I don't even remember much about Daddy, either." *Save the sight of him in the pond the day he died.* "Except for all the stories my mother told about him."

I flicked the lighter and held the flame out for her.

She rested her hand on mine, lit up, gave me a thank-you pat, then leaned back in her chair and inhaled. Even as the stream of smoke blew through her lips, she managed to croak, "That damn Dinah. Couldn't get a word out of her about herself, but get her to talking about your daddy? Whew! You couldn't hardly shut her up."

"She really loved him?" What I'd intended as a simple statement of fact came out sounding peculiar, almost like a question.

"Shoot, yeah, she loved him all right." A drag, a moment holding in the smoke, an exhale and a glance away before she added, "I guess."

I hunched my shoulders and knotted my hands in my lap. "You *guess?*"

Fawnie picked a tobacco flake from her coral-painted lips. "Your mama always was an odd duck. And in this bunch, that's saying something, child."

I offered the obligatory smile.

"I believe she loved your daddy. People who fought as mean and laughed as hard and found so many excuses to go off alone together as those two did had to have loved one another."

I rested my arms on the table and leaned toward her. "But?"

The quick shake of her head made her hairdo wobble. "Dinah was the most contented widow-woman I ever knew. She loved your daddy. But she didn't need him. And she didn't miss him. Not as long as she had his money in the bank, the use of his house and a good story to tell on him."

Wow. No one had ever said anything quite so brutal—or

so absolutely on the mark—about my mother to me in my entire life. I didn't know whether to jump up and hug Fawnie's neck or wring it.

I mean, she'd said the words. They were out there. From this point on, we couldn't go back to playing like my mother was something we'd now both acknowledged she wasn't.

Oh, wait. This was Fawnie. She could do anything she damn well pleased.

In a sudden rush of anxiety I had to make her tell me more before she up and changed her mind—or worse, changed *my* mind. "Go on, Aunt Fawnie. You were saying that Mama didn't need my daddy, just his name and money?"

"She needed those things," Fawnie finished. "Not for their material blessing, you understand. Though, Lord knows Dinah *loved* her material blessings."

I nodded and scooted to the edge of my chair.

"But those things—the house, the money, the stories— Dinah needed those to shelter her, to keep her safe. To keep everyone else..." She raised her arm, her palm turned out as if she'd pressed it flat against an unseen wall. "You know?"

"I know," I said softly. I knew that wall well. Too well.

I had memorized my mother. The lilt of her accent, the huskiness of her deep, genuine laughter, the smell of her hair, the softness of her skin. I could imitate for you to this day the face she made in the mirror when she put on mascara. I could show you exactly which of the trees beyond the drive Mama hit the night she used a double-barreled shotgun to discourage a certain man from calling. I could go to her room right now and pull out her favorite scarf, gloves, earrings and handbag by touch alone, I knew them that well.

But I could not tell you what she wore the night she died.

Or why she found it necessary to keep that wall around her, even after she had left the house, the money, the stories and me behind.

Reaching out, I closed Fawnie's hand in both of mine, breaking through my mother's invisible wall for both of us.

"Damn it, Dinah," Fawnie whispered.

I shut my eyes and swallowed as best I could around the lump in my throat.

"Damn it, Mama." I echoed Fawnie's sentiment. "Everyone thought she shared those great stories to bring people closer, but she really used them to keep everyone away. Just like they thought she opened her house to unfortunate women out of the goodness of her heart, when really it just kept one person—" me "—from getting close."

"It done a lot of good for a lot of people, lamb. Does it really matter why she did it?"

Yes, I wanted to say. *It matters to me.* Instead, I pushed down my pain and jumped out beyond my darkest fear to ask, "Do you know why, Aunt Fawnie?"

She shook her head and squinted her eyes, the cigarette at her lips. But she didn't inhale. She just held it there a moment, then dropped her hand to flick ashes into a used breakfast plate. "It happened after your daddy died. She changed. I guess it would change a person, that kind of thing. Having to make that kind of choice. After that she was...well, you know how she was."

"Choice?"

"You know, about your daddy." Fawnie laid the cigarette aside, lowered her head and covered her eyes with one age-spotted hand.

"About...Daddy?" My heart hammered in my chest. Startling new concepts and long-submerged memories swam in my mind. What choice had Mama made? What really happened that awful day? "Aunt Fawnie, I don't understand."

"Don't fret it, lamb." She blew her nose, tucked her hankie down her dress front, then picked up the cigarette again. "I never understand nothing around here, lamb. Except my calling and my place in this family. If the good Lord hadn't set that out for me, I probably wouldn't understand that, either."

Fawnie code for: We're not talking about Dinah now, we're talking about *me* and my precious death list. The chance to learn more had passed.

"One thing for sure, I never understood what got into those two that day." She tapped her painted fingernail beside the second project on the list.

"What got into them was Grandpa's private stock bourbon."

She laughed. "I'd deny it if I didn't miss that private stock so much my own self. My, we were wicked in those days—and full of life."

"Full of life and bourbon."

"And bourbon." She stubbed out her cigarette, nodding. "Hopefully, whoever we get in to paint and help us out with a few other modest chores on the list won't have them same tendencies."

"Modest chores?" I glanced over the remainder of page one and shook my head. "Aunt Fawnie, if you can't die until all *this* stuff gets done, you're going to live forever."

"I'll have to live forever if I plan on waiting around for that Bess to drag her high-and-mighty hind end out of bed." She reached for the packet again.

I opened my mouth to defend Bess, but it was Min's voice that filled the quiet air.

"Leave Bess alone, Mommy."

"Why? She not leaving us alone." Shug's short, quick foot-steps reverberated lightly down the hallway. "Unless you count throwing us out on the street as leaving us alone. Leaving us alone to starve and die."

Min strode into the kitchen. She tossed the newspaper onto the table and started to refill her coffee cup. "That is not going to happen."

"Why? 'Cause you going to take us into your house?" Shug whisked off her beloved baseball cap and took a swipe at Min's behind with it. "You're not even *at* your house."

"Off-limits, Mom." Min sidestepped the cap, her white nightgown rustling around her bare legs. "You are not going to turn a rant about Bess into an attempt to pry into my personal life."

"Pry? Pry?" She fitted the cap back on and worked it down low over her eyes. "I don't pry. I *don't* pry. If I pry, I know something. I don't know nothing. I don't know why you don't talk to your husband. I don't know why you don't talk to my grandchild. I don't know why you bring that Bess here after Sterling tells you not to and then let her stay in bed all day like she own the place."

"I do own it." Bess stood in the doorway, bathrobed, bare-foot and belligerent.

And for all her bellyaching about *that Bess* only moment's ago, Shug was the first one to pull out a kitchen chair and say, "Sit here, sugar."

Shug slipped her arm around Bess's waist. They made quite

the contrast. Tall, slender Bess in her colorless robe with her long dark hair tangled against her pale skin, and sun-bronzed Shug in her bright blue jogging suit, her short white "hat hair" sticking out in spikes just under Bess's chin. The sweet-tempered woman who came halfway across the world to marry into our family and the bitchiest born-George woman alive, who wouldn't even pick up a phone to speak to our family—unless it was to cause trouble.

"You okay now?" Shug wrangled the chair close enough for Bess to grab the back of it in both hands. "Sit. Sit and put your feet up, if you want."

I expected Bess to offer to put her feet up—up Shug's ass if the old woman didn't back off. But she didn't. She didn't curse or make a smart remark or even flinch away.

That's when it hit me.

Shug knew.

I don't know how or when she found out but...

I caught my aunt's gaze for a split second, just long enough to confirm it.

Then she looked away.

She knew. It should have made things easier, but all I could think was—now it's all of us keeping the secret from Fawnie. Lord help me, I was so sick of keeping secrets.

And on the heels of my aunt's candor about my mother...

"Can I pour you a cup of Mommy's atomic lava java?" Min lifted the coffeepot high, unleashing the aroma of Shug's superstrong brew into the room.

"No. Not coffee. Not coffee." Shug swatted at Min's upraised hand. "Juice. Better for her."

"Make it my morning special," Fawnie croaked around the cigarette between her lips.

Bess situated herself delicately, as if she feared the chair was made of broken glass—or that she was.

Shug dived into the fridge.

Bess stretched across the table. "What you smoking these days, Aunt Fawnie?"

"I don't know. Some long skinny sons of bitches."

"She say she likes her smokes like she likes her men." Shug chuckled low as she poured the thick red juice into a small clear glass. "And I say that's why we always find her boyfriends thrown in the gutter with lipstick on their butts."

"Mommy!"

"What?" Shug set the drink in front of Bess.

Bess held her hand out. "Can you spare me one?"

Fawnie pushed the cellophane wrapped packet toward Bess, then tapped it with two mocha-frost painted nails. "Them things'll kill ya, you know."

Bess didn't acknowledge the warning, but when she reached out to take the offering, her hand brushed Fawnie's and their gazes met.

Fawnie knew.

Okay, that might be giving the old gal a little too much credit, but she suspected something, that much was clear.

Shug knew. I knew. Min knew and Fawnie suspected.

And not a damn one of us was going to say a word about it. Because Bess had decreed it so.

Her rules.

Always.

Well, to hell with that. I stood. "Since we're all here—"

"Shouldn't you be returning a hearse?" Bess scowled at me.

Let her scowl. I'd come this far, and I wasn't going to slink away now. "C'mon, y'all. If we ever hope to share this house,

to find a way of peaceful coexistence in order to face whatever lies ahead together—"

"Point of order." Bess raised her hand. "I didn't sign up for
the house sharing. My plan involves single occupation of this
dwelling, and therefore I do not care to have myself included
in this peaceful coexistence program."

"Bite me," Min said.

"Interpreting for me again?" Bess asked.

"Editing." Min hopped up on the kitchen counter and let
her legs dangle. "I'd think as a writer you'd know never to use
ten words to convey a thought when two will do."

Bess bowed her head, then turned to me, her hand still
raised. "I'd like to amend my statement. Bite me."

"Cute." I moved over to stand by Min, leaned back against
her and dug my elbow into her thigh to warn her off further
interruptions. "But cute doesn't cut it around here anymore."

"Is that why you're not sleeping with Sterling Mayhouse?"
Bess finally picked up the juice Shug had given her, but she
didn't raise it to her lips.

"Screw Sterling," I snapped.

"I'll put it on my list." Bess met my gaze, her expression
only half-teasing.

My *Things That Have to Get Done Before I Die* list. As soon
as the thought popped into my head, the urgency of the moment faded. Why the hell shouldn't Bess get to play things by
her own rules, at least for a while longer?

"Okay." I sighed. "Y'all do whatever you want to do. I'm
going to take a shower, then take the hearse back to Chapman's.
Maybe when I get back, we can all sit down and have a talk."

"The time for talk has passed." Fawnie's hand landed on
the open tablet. "Now's the time for work."

"Damn right." Bess sniffed at the tomato concoction, then held it up to the light for a better inspection. "Let's get to work today and get this house packed up so I can move in."

"This isn't moving work, child. It's death work."

"Death?" Bess lowered her drink, but not all the way to the table.

I could feel Min tense up behind me and I'm sure she felt my whole body clench. Maybe all that honesty about my mother had gotten Fawnette on a roll. Maybe for all my worry about keeping secrets from her, she would, at last, be the only one among us brave enough to say what we all had on our minds.

"Yes, *death.*" Fawnie's bracelets clinked from the sudden movement of her putting her hands on her hips. "On account of your killing me with all this eviction crappola."

"Fawnie." I breathed her name as much as spoke it, and shut my eyes.

"Oh, that." Bess smiled, gave a curt nod, slid a cigarette between her fingers, then picked up her glass and started eyeing it again. "Very well, carry on with that by all means."

"I will. These things don't plan themselves, you know." She sent the lighter sailing across the sunny yellow Formica at Bess. "And no use trying to figure out what's in that stuff, just drink it up so we can get on with our work. Our death work."

"Moving work, death work, tomato, tom-ah-to. I'm for anything that leaves this place cleared out and ready for me to move in." Bess raised the glass in salute, then drank the mixture down in one hard gulp.

Her rules.

Well, we'd just see about that.

"I don't care what y'all do while I'm gone, but when I get

back from Chapman's," I said, taking advantage of the moment to make a great exit, "we *will* talk."

I can't be sure, but I believe I heard Aunt Fawnie bark out "bite me" as I walked away.

16

"Welcome to Chapman's, how can I—" Guy stopped a few feet out of the front office.

It was like I'd passed through a time portal.

Twenty years.

Gone.

An entire lifetime washed away.

I felt lighter, somehow. And cleansed of all the grubby, nit-picky details of who did what to whom and why.

Just like that. Just by walking through that door—the door I had walked through the night before Guy and I were supposed to get married. I felt nineteen again.

Nineteen and come to tell the man I loved with all my heart that I thought we should postpone our wedding. Indefinitely.

"Hello, Charma Deane." He finished slipping into his suit jacket, then stood there, just looking at me. No expectation in his eyes. No residual resentment over what had passed between us. Just a gentle reminder of what he had said to me all those years ago. "If you ever change your mind, Charma, walk back through that door and I'll be here."

Of course, he wasn't there the next day when I came back to tell him I'd changed my mind. He wasn't there—here—for me ever again. Until now.

"Hello, Guy," I said softly.

"You look nice."

"I look stupid." I pulled off the sparkly scrunchie that Shug had used to catch up my hair, and shook my head. I pressed my hand to my lips to wipe away the thick, sweet gloss Aunt Fawnie had insisted I wear. If I could have slipped off the silly ruffled sundress I had borrowed from Min and stood before this man naked, I'd have done it. Not to offer him my body, but to offer him, after all these years, my apology. To show I had come at last without guile or deceit. With nothing more to hide.

"Never expected to see you come through that door again."

"I never expected to." I glanced back at the practically ancient silver bell still swinging gently. I should not have done this. I should have called him to come pick up his damn hearse, then hidden in my room when he came by. "Not *this* door. But I couldn't come around to the back, because I have the hearse and the alley looked pretty narrow."

"It is." He smiled. Not a mortician's smile—a man's.

"I thought so," I murmured.

Run, Charma, run. I had to get out of here. Away from Guy and the feelings he awakened in me. I'd survived these past few months on nothing but hurt, anger and fumes of all the higher emotions burned up with my mama. And this man played a vital role in all of that. I must not let myself forget that. I must never forget.

"Glad you did, though." He edged closer to me.

I could smell the hint of cedar from his closet lingering on his jacket. If I had lifted my hand, I could have traced every line on his face with my fingertips. Lines that had not been there the last time I had stood with him in this exact place.

The cutting pain I had expected at that memory did not come. Only a glancing sadness. They say getting older does that, eases the old heartaches, maybe sometimes even erases them.

So much had happened. So much water under the bridge. A lifetime of stories written now in fine lines on our no-longer-youthful faces. And yet...

"Glad I did what?" I asked before I let myself finish that far-too-dangerous thought.

"Came through that door. You don't know how many times in this last year since I've been back I heard that bell, looked up and hoped..."

"Don't, Guy." I shut my eyes. If he started talking about hope and all the time that had passed, I might do something crazy—like listen to him and believe. "I only came to return the hearse."

"Really?" He inched in closer still and curved his fingers under my chin.

"Uh-hmm." I started to nod, then froze. The movement produced the effect of him stroking my skin.

Guy, touching me in a way that was impulsively innocent and insanely intimate all at once. I wet my lips and nodded again.

"Too bad." His gaze drifted to my mouth. "Because I don't give a damn about that hearse, Charma."

"You lie like a rug," I whispered.

"Huh-uh." He brushed his thumb over the corner of my upturned lips. "Not to you."

"Since when?"

"Since you walked through that door." He swept my hair back off my shoulder. "Because I know you'd never have crossed that threshold unless you were ready to trust me again. And there is nothing in this world that I want more than to be worthy of that trust, Charma. *Nothing*."

He moved his mouth over mine.

I inhaled, taking the very breath from him. We hadn't been so close in more than twenty years, but it all felt so familiar, so natural, so...

"Wow!"

"That the one he jilted?"

"Shut up!"

I couldn't have jumped back faster if we'd been doused by water like two dogs going at it in the yard.

Guy clenched his jaw and straightened away from me.

A young man with spiked blond hair peeked out the office door. He raised his hand in hello.

I did likewise, saying to Guy through my smile, "I don't believe I know him."

"New guy. Sales. Dathan brought him on board."

"Dathan?" My hand dropped to my side. "Why would the self-described 'guy who drives the hearse' be hiring salespeople?"

Guy took my arm again and moved me back a step, out of visual range. "We had a lot of turnover last year."

Turnover. Tidy word for the total upheaval his family business had gone through. "Yeah, I heard about your brother."

Guy nodded. "Thanks for not throwing it in my face that I got what I deserved."

"Why?" I folded my arms, only a tiny bit peeved that my own sentimentality over the moment had prevented me from making the connection and tossing out a flip remark about Guy's karma coming to bite him in the ass. Of course, as long as I draw a breath, it's never too late for a flip remark. "Were you engaged to marry the embalmer he ran off with?"

"No. But I had spent a long time building a life without roots. Working my way up the sales ladder at one place, moving on and upward to a new company, a new town. A year or two later, doing it all again. I had pretty much planned my life around *not* coming back to Orla. I certainly never planned to run a funeral home. My brother changed my plans for me like that." He snapped his fingers. "The stupid, selfish—"

"Hi." Another face appeared at the doorway, this time a lovely dark-skinned woman with her hair pulled up high into a cascade of spiral curls.

"Y'all go on with the meeting, Rebecca. Charma and I were just, uh—"

"You were going to see that I get home," I prompted, wanting keenly to spare him any embarrassment.

"I'm going to drive Charma home."

Rebecca nodded and shut the door.

"No, I meant..." One day I would not do this. I would not rush in to the rescue. I would think of myself first, of the consequences of my actions, and recall that running headlong to save someone else always came with a price. "If you have to stay, Guy, I can always call Min to come and get me."

"If I *had* to stay, Charma—" he grasped my arm lightly, opened the front door and ushered me out onto the wide, shaded porch "—I'd put a bullet through my brain."

In all the possible scenarios I had played out in my mind

about seeing Guy today, not once had the words "put a bullet through my brain" come into play. What do you say to a statement like that?

"Have you had lunch yet?" It's probably not a textbook response to the whole bullet thing. It certainly didn't help me get away from Guy. But it would buy me time. Time away from the reality of Bess and the work at the house, and time to find out what the hell was going on in Guy's life.

Not that I cared.

"Because I was thinking if you haven't had lunch, we could maybe get a couple barbecue sandwiches at the Crossroads Market."

"Why, Charma Deane, you asking me out on a date?"

"No!" Was I?

"I think you are." He moved in even closer than when we'd been interrupted.

"No," I whispered, torn between wanting him to take me in his arms and kiss me senseless, and the fear that I was just that—totally senseless and unable to stop myself from doing something I would ultimately regret. "I was just...hungry."

"I know the feeling." He lowered his head.

I guess I should feel guilty that I placed both my hands flat on his midsection and pushed with all my might. But I don't. Besides, the look on his face was too good when I clucked my tongue and said, "I mean *hungry* hungry, you old fool."

He raked his finger back through his dark, silver-touched hair. "Really?"

What? Was he nuts? No, not really. Had he not felt that spark between us? Didn't he want to drag me upstairs, throw me on the bed and stay there until we'd worked through twenty years' worth of loss and longing between the sheets?

But one of us had to act the grown-up. "Just lunch, and then you can take me back to the farm."

"If that's what you want."

It wasn't. In fact, I'd left my car at my apartment when Inez dragged me out of bed at an ungodly hour to attend the birth of RoryAnne's baby. Having Guy take me out to the farm would prove damn inconvenient. The only thing worse would be having Guy drive me to my apartment.

I couldn't bear to have the man see the way I lived now. A year ago, maybe. When I still had my every-small-town-girl's dream house. When my dressertop overflowed with my date book, my jewelry and my official school name badge with my whole title spilled across it big as life. My den wall told my personal history in silver-framed photos, from my first son's birth to my last vacation with my mother. Oh, and when I still had at least one tall, hairy, big-footed boy under my roof to show what I had done with my life. Well, maybe I'd have allowed Guy in then. But not now.

"Actually, Guy, now that I think of it, maybe this is a bad idea."

"What? Your coming here? Me taking you home? Lunch?"

Us nearly kissing? Interesting how he hadn't included that in the list.

"All of it." I made a circular gesture with both hands. "Let me just call Min."

"You don't have to do that, Charma. You can have use of the hearse for as long as you need it."

"I don't need it, Guy. I have my own car."

"No, you have what used to be a car. Now it's a piece of crap." He moved to the railing and leaned against it. The hot breeze that caught a wayward curl of his hair swept along the hem of my dress as he said, "What did you do? Give your real car to one of your kids?"

I cocked my head. "How'd you know that?"

"I know *you*, Charma. You never put your own needs first. That's what makes it so easy for people to take advantage of you."

"Yeah, but I didn't come here to talk about Bess." I laughed like I thought that was damn clever.

He nodded, all solemnlike.

"I also didn't come here for a free personality evaluation." I moved toward the front steps, took in the view of the manicured lawn, pristine walkway and the faded grace of the fine homes beyond. I turned to him. "I just wondered how you knew I had kids?"

"You do. Two, right? Boys? Bess's mom forwarded her the announcements for the first one."

Of course, he and Bess were still together then. Though not happy, she had always rushed to add in her well-crafted story of it all. And who was I to mess with such a polished presentation?

"And your second son—well, it's a small town. Everyone knows your business, and for some reason they all seem anxious to share it with me."

What? What had people told him? I wanted to stand there and demand information. But if I did that, we might as well go to lunch together; then he'd want to drive me to the farm, or worse, home, and...no wonder I felt dizzy and confused all the time. My life had become an endless round of musical chairs. And if I didn't play things just right, I'd definitely fall on my ass.

I motioned toward the vehicle waiting by the curb. "You really don't mind if I keep the monster awhile longer?"

He looked out at it.

Sunlight glinted off the seventies-posh golden exterior.

"I really don't mind," he said, no discernable emotion in his tone.

"Okay. That's probably for the best then. We, uh, we sort of spilled some ice and water on the floorboard, and I really ought to run it by the car wash and use the wet vac to get it up before it molds."

"You do what you have to do, Charma." Again, no inflection gave away his feelings.

"You're not mad about the spill?"

"Why would I be?"

I leaned back against one of the huge columns at the top of the steps. "Because word around this all-too-small town is that you have a special attachment to that hearse. That you put a lot of work into restoring it, putting it back exactly the way it was."

"That I did. And it taught me a very important lesson."

I pulled my shoulders up as if that might better brace me for what he would say. "What's that, Guy?"

He gave the hearse one more glance, then turned and walked toward me. "That nothing can ever be put back exactly the way it was. No matter how hard you try. No matter how much you want it to be made whole and unspoiled again."

"No, I don't suppose it can."

He reached out to touch my cheek with one finger. "Doesn't mean it can't still be something good, something worthwhile."

"I have to go." I moved down the steps like Cinderella fleeing for her life.

"Charma?"

I stopped on the walk. Checked to make sure I still had on both my shoes, then took a deep breath. I didn't say anything, but I didn't have to.

Guy said it all—everything I hoped and everything I feared. "If you ever decide to come through that door again, I'll be waiting."

17

I did not cry until I got almost home. Almost to the farm, that is. Oh, who the hell was I kidding?

Home.

The lumbering patchwork of gothic Southern mansion, gingerbread-decked Victorian and sturdy Arkansas farmhouse with its chipped paint, patched roof and sagging windows, every one of them framing a memory, was home. That apartment I had rented in a fit of self-pity, what was that but a storage unit for all my foolishness?

A place where I could warehouse my stuff, my feelings, my very self, until I found a better use for them all.

I laid my head on the hearse's steering wheel and murmured, half in prayer, half in self-admonishment, "God, I have been such a mess. I *am* such a mess. But I don't want to be. I *can't* be. How can I hope to be of help to anyone else when I can't even..."

I couldn't finish that sentence. Not honestly. I had no idea what I needed to do make my life right again, to make myself whole, to—

I raised my head and caught a glimpse of the tall grass swaying by the edge of the pond.

"To direct the destiny of my own soul," I whispered.

I opened the door and sat there, my gaze fixed on the dock thrusting out into the dark, weed-choked water.

That was the answer, of course.

To go under and lose myself.

I shut my eyes.

To die to the old ways and leave them behind.

Birds and bugs chirped and clicked and buzzed and beat their wings. The leaves rustled. The dust infused the dank air. I drew it in.

To wash away the past and be reborn.

I listened for the water's thrum against the shore but heard only the hard, steady rhythm of my own heart.

Jump, Charma!

"Yes," I whispered. "That's what I have to do."

It would take a show, of course.

If I hopped out of Guy's reconstructed memorial-to-past-regrets hearse, walked down to the pond and threw myself into the water? My family would have been more receptive to my fulfilling that age-on-my-bare-ass-jumping-in-the-ocean threat I made to Fawnie. At least with that there would be a big to-do. Internet fame. Media attention and sympathy from around the world.

But jumping unprovoked into a skanky pond fully clothed?

That, everyone would consider just plain nuts.

Stark raving lunacy? Well, bless your heart, you can't help that.

But just plain nuts? That wouldn't *do*. Not for a George.

No, some old ways refuse to die. You can't even beat them

with a stick into a blessed coma. But they could be tricked—
if I was quick enough and careful not to let myself get side-
tracked.

"Yes," I said again, gathering my purse and getting out of
the hearse at last.

I paused inside the front door. The front door was quiet. I
held my breath and waited, trying to discern where each family member might be.

Nothing.

I moved down the hallway. Every creak and groan of the
old wood floor vibrated through my very bones, but no one
in the too-still house seemed to notice. If someone did, if they
stuck their head out or yelled at me to come and join them
in fulfilling Fawnie's death-list work, I'd beg off. A headache.
Or cramps. Or head cramps. I'd play that one as it cropped
up—and declare a nap in the sun would take care of everything.

Out the back I'd go, and amble down to the pond. And
when I knew for certain they had forgotten all about me out
there—*splash.*

Jump, Charma!

My stomach lurched, but in a good way. I could do this. I
could take control of my life and never again surrender it to
guilt or rage or the petty whims of people who—

"Whatcha doin', Charmika?" Min's voice carried loud and
clear from Bess's make-do bedroom near the back of the house.

The petty whims of people that I loved more than life itself. Who the hell *was* I kidding? Not myself. Not anymore.
If I could jump all the way into the Gulf of Mexico, I'd never
jump clear of the hold my family had on me. And maybe that
wasn't the worst thing in the world to know about myself.

"I was headed out back." And I did not plan to let anyone deter me. Then I peered through the half-open door of the room now divested of years worth of collected cotton sheets, tablecloths and kitchen towels. "What are you two doing?"

"*I'm* hiding from Mommy and Aunt Fawnie." Minnie plunked down cross-legged on the floor beside the rollaway bed we'd pushed up against the shuttered window. She held up a huge plastic tumbler filled with amber iced tea. "Bess is supposed to be resting—Fawnie's orders."

I moved into the doorway but not into the room. I was not staying, after all. "Okay, it was hard enough to believe you'd started obeying God's edicts, Bess, but Fawnie's?"

Afternoon sunlight slid through the cracks in the window shutters and shot slivers of light on the wall and bedpost and over the hills and valleys of the quilt bunched around Bess's wan body. She herself remained in shadow. "If I said I didn't have the strength to fight her, would you leave it alone?" she murmured.

I didn't want to, but as Bess had pointed out earlier, dying comes with its own set of unique privileges. "Where are the old gals, anyway?"

"Primping," Min said.

"Primping for what?" Warning bells went off inside my brain.

"For each other, mostly." The ice in Min's tumbler popped and cracked. "You know how they always have to outdo one another."

Warning: Don't ask. The answer will only detain you. Warning: If the two Mrs. Georges have something up their proverbial sleeves, you'd be wise to know about it.

I strained to integrate the two ideas and for a second

thought I might just have accomplished a head cramp for real. It's the only explanation for my blurting out, "But why the outdoing today in particular?"

"Because they're Fawnette and Shugi *George*. It's what they do. It's all they know. Slop sugar. Swallow your pride. Spill blood if you have to, but grab the spotlight for yourself and don't let go, because she who dies with the most attention wins!" Bess laughed. "That's why they dressed you up like a hillbilly-ho to go see Guy, you know."

I would have protested her description, but when I raised my hand to hush her, the ruffles on my sundress flipped up and tossed a pink crystal necklace down into my exposed cleavage.

"They think we're like them." Bess laughed, or did she cough? Maybe a little of both. "They think as long as we draw breath, we'll compete over Guy. As if everyone hasn't always known which one of us he loved, which one he would always love."

Who? I didn't ask it because I didn't really want to hear the answer. Either way.

"I guess they'll go to their graves as rivals," I said.

Like us, I left unsaid.

"And the best of friends," Bess whispered.

Also like us. I hope. Again unsaid, but just as clear between us.

I could not meet Bess's gaze, though. If I did, I might not keep moving, and if I didn't keep moving, I'd never get anywhere at all.

I turned to Minnie and asked, "So what's the rivalry about today?"

"Their boyfriend is on his way over." She batted her eyes and fussed with her snaggled topknot as if it was a bouffant complete with a red velvet bow.

"Boyfriend?" I asked ever so nonchalantly, when I really wanted to clench my teeth and screech, *Please, Merciful God in Heaven, tell me they have not invited Guy out here again!*

"Sterling." Min wicked the condensation off her glass with one hand, flinging the droplets every which way.

Some hit me on the calf, and I flinched. "Hey!"

"What? You made of sugar all of a sudden? You're not going to melt." She took a sip, then smacked her lips. "Though I don't know, in this heat I sometimes think *I* might."

Hmm. A perfect opening to suggest we all go out by the pond to cool off. Perfect, if we weren't about to be invaded by the enemy. "Sterling's coming, huh? His idea or theirs?"

Min made a nondescript sound. *Uh* or maybe *Phuf.*

Guess it didn't matter how Sterling came to come calling today. It only mattered that starting my new life would have to wait until he'd gone.

Min stretched her arms and arched her back, then rolled her sweating tea tumbler along the side of her neck. "Going to loiter there in the doorway like a spook, or come in and sit down like a member of the human race?"

I considered for only a moment before crossing into the bedroom-turned-linen-closet-turned-deathbed-to-be. What the hell, if I couldn't go and drown myself, I might as well go for a baptism by fire. "Human, I guess."

"Good." Bess pulled her legs up tight against her chest. She looped her arms over her knees. "This house doesn't need any more spooks haunting the hallways."

Min wriggled around to look at her. The scatter rug scooted beneath her bottom and her ice clinked. "You think the Aunt Farm is haunted, Bess?"

"Haunted by memories." Her spindly wrists stuck out from

a sweatshirt that ballooned around her. She grasped her hands together. "Yes, I do."

"That why you want it for yourself?" Min did not shy away when she asked it. In fact, she propped her elbow on the side of the bed like a child readying herself for her favorite story and asked, "Do you want to own those memories?"

Baptism by fire, indeed. Only I wasn't the one fanning the flames. And that didn't sit well with me.

"Sit here, Charma." Bess kicked Min's arm away. "You won't disturb me."

But I wanted to disturb her. I wanted to shake her. I wanted to bring her to her senses and scare her half-silly. I wanted to startle her into feeling...something. Anything. I wanted to be the one to make Bess realize that her lifetime of scheming had cut us all to the bone but had not bled us dry. We were a family of substance, of hope, of strong-willed, right-minded women—and like it or not, she was one of us.

But nothing seemed to have that power.

Like the lost cause of my jumping into the pond, I resigned myself to not reaching Bess. At least not today.

I sank onto the end of the bed and tucked one foot up under my cushy behind.

Everything went quiet. So quiet I could hear my cousins breathing. Minnie, slow and regular. Bess, like she couldn't quite fill her lungs before she had to sigh, lost momentum and had to try again.

I took the long, deep breath that Bess could not take and held it. The room smelled of old wood and wallpaper, with just the hint of linen fresh from the clothesline on a breezy summer day. "I love the way this room smells. You know, sometimes after I'd moved away, I'd still stop in just to take a whiff."

"You know, if I had a habit of sniffing around old people's houses, Charma—" Bess stifled a yawn "—I don't believe I'd have told anyone."

"Do you have to take everything to do with this place and give it your own vicious little twist?"

"For the last time—fiction! My book was fiction."

"It didn't read like fiction. It read like a bunch of lies strung together with just enough family folklore for everyone around here to think it just might be all true."

"Like the story about the time Aunt Dinah turned a shotgun on Guy."

"Yeah, only in Bess's story she had Guy coming round *after* the two of them had run off instead of before."

"That's how it happened." Bess shifted. The bedsprings protested. "He came out here the day we got back from..."

"My honeymoon." I kindly filled in the blank for her. "That's not the way I remember it. And since Mama isn't around to set the story straight, pardon the hell out of me if I take my own version over yours."

"Little helpful edit—your *age-addled* version. And pardon the hell out of me if I suggest we could always ask Guy."

"Over my dead body."

"Charma!" Min set down her glass with a thunk.

"Better you than me."

"Bess!" Up the tea glass came and down again like a judge's gavel.

We both turned on our goody-two-shoes go-between. "Minnie!"

She glared at us. "I was going to tell you two to act your

ages, but given that you've forgotten the details of something so momentous as Aunt Dinah climbing out onto the balcony and firing a shotgun over the head of your beloved, the man who changed both your lives forever, maybe you *are* acting your ages."

I blinked. "Did you just call us old?"

Min sipped her tea.

"You are only six months younger than me, you know."

"Not in girl math, she's not." There was a smile in Bess's tone. "In girl math, Min is about..."

"Twelve?" I stuck my tongue out at her.

"Twelve." Min beamed. "Good age. No hot flashes and a perfect excuse for the petty, immature way I've dealt with Abby of late."

"You have hot flashes?" Bess snuggled farther into the thin quilt, totally missing the nagging detail that could not be ignored.

"For your information, Min, when Mama shot at Guy, he was hardly my beloved. That doesn't even make any sense. She shot at him because he'd just gotten back from..." Uh-oh. "And he had the balls to show up after..."

"Uh-huh." Min nodded.

"Oh, shit." I slumped back against the window shutters, setting them rattling.

"Remember it now?" Bess poked at my behind with her pointy toes. "That happened just like I said. He came here after we got back from running off together."

"In glorious full-screen Technicolor with surround sound and Smell-O-Vision." I rubbed my forehead.

"I'll accept your apology whenever you're ready." Another toe poke.

"I'm sorry, hon." I patted her leg, or the lump under the covers that was probably her leg, then let my hand rest on the soft cotton fabric nubbed with hand stitching and French knots. "I can't believe I had that out of order all these years."

"I can," Bess scoffed.

"It's so like you, Charma." Min translated in a way that only left me more confused.

"How so?"

"Because you sequence your life in accomplishments. Nurse, mother, getting rid of that rat-bastard Boyd, and every tiny triumph in between. You lump all those together and hope that's enough to make everybody love you. And you know what?"

"What?"

"Everybody does love you," Bess said, so soft, it felt more like air over my skin than actual words. "But it's never enough. Not for you. It's the people and situations you couldn't change—you lump all those together and let them weigh on you. How can you ever hope to put them into perspective, timewise or otherwise, when you carry them around with you always? Someday you have to get out past that, Charma."

Go to hell, I wanted to say. And then quickly rush to add, *And don't you dare let yourself become one of the people I fail to save. Don't you do that to me, Bess. It will I never, ever, get past that. Ever.*

Instead, I glanced around us, sat up straight on the bed and said, "So, this is what you distilled your life down to? Your laptop. Your favorite music." My eyes moved from the portable CD player to a slender wooden figure, and I smiled. "Your soul."

"My what?"

I nodded to the elegant Kokeshi doll sitting on the nightstand.

"Oh, *that*." She picked it up and curled it close to her chest. "It's just a cheap souvenir, you know."

"Shut up." Minnie set her tea aside. "You love that little doll and all it represents and we all know it, you big softie."

"Don't make me throw this thing at you again. Over the years, my aim has only improved."

"Look how scared I am." Min rubbed the scar by her eye with her middle finger.

For once *I* stepped in to play peacemaker. "So, Bess, you still—"

"*Have* a soul?" She chuckled.

"Are writing?" I finished what I had meant to ask.

"Of course. I still have my soul. If I had sold it to the devil, I'd have more to show for my efforts."

"You have plenty to show for your efforts."

"Right." She shifted on the bed, lying back on the plump pillows until shadow hid her entire face. "That from someone who just pointed out all I've distilled my life down to—my favorite music, my words and my soul. What more could a girl need?"

"Your family," Minnie said.

"You're here," she answered in the Bess equivalent of a verbal shrug.

"We're hardly your whole family." I crossed my ankles, trying my best to appear laid-back and self-assured when, in fact, I wondered how far Bess would let us push this before throwing more than a wooden doll at our heads.

"I'd tell you to go jump in a lake but—"

"She knows there's not a chance in hell of that." Min bounded in with her opinion.

"Show's how much you know," Bess muttered.

"Charma? Jump in the pond? Are you nuts? Never."

"That's why you went out there that night I found you on the dock, isn't it?"

I might have answered her if my heart hadn't risen up into my throat and all the oxygen drained from my—how did Bess describe it? *age-addled?*—brain.

"No. That's crazy talk, Bess." Min swatted at the bed, her knuckles making a quiet *whomp.* "She's paralyzed with fear of that place. Why would she ever want to go there, at night, much less jump in?"

"Because she's paralyzed with fear of it." Bess pulled herself up again, this time swinging her legs off the bed and scooting over until her lean thigh pressed against my plump one. "Isn't that right, Charma?"

What are you waiting for—God Almighty to kick you in the butt?

It would take God Almighty to get me to break down here and now and blubber about my fears and failures. No, thank you. I did not need another round of psychoanalysis from a genuine psycho. "It was just a whim. Nothing, really."

"You mean she's right? You went out there the other night to jump into the pond?"

"I wouldn't call it nothing." Bess looped her arm around Min's shoulders and leaned in close and turned her head to confront me. "To face your greatest fear? That's something. Trust me on this one, that's something *very* big."

I tipped my head. "You speaking as someone who's done it?"

Bess did not look away. A sure sign she had no intention of telling the truth.

"Have you faced your greatest fear, Bess?" I pressed.

"If I hadn't, do you think I could have refused chemo?"

"Not an answer."

"How about you, Charma—you ready to face your fear? You ready to go jump in that pond finally, after all these years?"

I could not take my eyes from hers. I don't know what I thought I might find as I searched them. Remorse? Compassion? Even an inkling that she had played some role setting into motion the events that cost my daddy his life the day she had pushed me in and given birth to my phobia?

Nothing.

Suddenly, and I have no idea why, Min leapt up. "Well, if Charma's going, I'm going."

"I never said—" And I never got the chance. Min had me jerked to my feet and stumbling toward the door before I could finish.

"Bess, you in?" she called over her shoulder.

"Into the pond? Wouldn't Charma love that?" Bess laughed and threw the quilt aside. Again before I could get a word out of my mouth, she shoved up the sleeves of her sweatshirt and stuffed her feet into the flip-flops by her bed, men's tube socks and all. "Solve all your problems, and in such a fitting way, wouldn't it?"

"Don't be an ass, Bess," I muttered, ever the queen of the witty comeback.

"You inviting me to come along then?"

Come? I didn't even plan on going myself. Except I had to, didn't I? I'd been headed toward that damn pond since the first night I arrived in my aunts' home. If I refused to go now, how would I ever get past this horrible mired-down place I'd gotten myself into? "Yeah. You can come, Bess." I held my hand out to her. "Just don't stand behind me."

18

"I don't think I can do this." I stood stock-still on the dock.

"If *I* can do it, you can." Bess held on to Minnie's arm beside me.

"Can you do this?" Min asked her.

Bess stared at the lightless water and shook her head. "No."

"Let's go back to the house." Min shifted her feet. The slight motion sent the boards pitching.

"No. Not yet." Bess had braided her hair—well, in retrospect, she'd probably allowed Shug to do it after hours of fussing and pouting—and she suddenly tucked that braid inside the back of her baggy sweatshirt. It practically screamed that she was going in. "If I played any role in Charma chickening out of this, I couldn't live with myself."

"Pardon me if I don't make a tacky joke about that right now." My bare toes pressed hard against the rough wood to hold my ground. I bent my knees and held my arms out from my sides for balance. I even spread my fingers, as if that would somehow give me an edge and make the rocking and the creaking cease. "Does that mean you're jumping?"

The toads croaked.

The grass along the banks rustled.

"It means I'm staying. Jumping? Hmm." Bess leaned out and over to peer down into the clear spot just past the edge of the dock. "You?"

"I'm *thinking* about it," I hedged. "As good as I can think in this awful heat."

Lord, it was hot. And muggy, too. The air lay lethargic right on top of a film of sweat, so that the wind, when it did roll through, drew goose bumps for a second but did nothing to really cool you off.

The sun stung my bare arms and made my eyes water. That didn't keep me from seeing everything, though. How small the pond had grown. How weathered the dock. How stagnant the water.

It broke my heart.

It mocked my memories.

It diminished my resolve.

Moonlight. That was the only real venue for a mission like this. The magnanimous moon would have set the mood perfect—veiled the whole scene in awe and mystery. And kept me from seeing that all these years I'd built up a whole mythology around something so damn unremarkable.

"It doesn't smell as bad as I remember," Min said.

"You have to admit Shug and Fawnie have really let it go, though." Bess shaded her eyes and looked toward the opposite side of the fair-size pond. "Aunt Dinah would never have stood for it getting so overgrown and nasty."

"I suppose that job should naturally have come to me. I

have the name of their pond man," I said softly, thinking of Mama's once chic leather address book crammed full of labels torn from envelopes, business cards and even napkins with names and numbers sketched out in unreadable blurs. Where had I last seen it among the piles and packing boxes crammed into my apartment? I sighed. "Someplace."

Min inched toward the edge of the dock. "Surely, it's clean enough that we could dangle our feet in it."

"My apartment?" I blinked.

"Focus, Charma." Bess snapped her fingers. "The whole reason we are standing here this very minute is so you can..." She pantomimed diving.

"I know. I know. Don't push me." Water sloshed against the dock. "And I mean that literally."

I stepped beyond Bess's reach.

"Nobody answered my question. Do we dangle or not?"

Bess frowned and openly eyed Min's chest, then mine. "Well, neither of you is as perky as you used to be."

"You're just jealous because you never grew boobs yourself." Min threw her chest out proudly.

"*Dated* a few boobs," I added, ever watchful for a chance to be helpful. Then I, too, pulled my shoulders back. "But never had any of your own."

"Remember how she used to sit out here on this very dock and do those bust exercises?" Min pressed the heels of her palms together, grunted, then threw back her elbows and screwed up her face à la Bess at thirteen. "Is it working, y'all? Can you see any difference?"

"Ooh, remember this classic? Flopping down on her belly, popping open her bikini top and saying, 'I don't care if your mothers think it's common, when I grow up, I won't have a single tan line on my entire body.'"

Bess held out the collar of her sweatshirt and, looking down inside, said, "Hey, I finally got my wish."

"What? You growing some boobies, hon?" I tipped my head up and peered down my nose as if I thought I might steal a peek.

"No, but I don't have any tan lines."

"I know." All kidding fell away just like that. "I was trying to spare you from the inevitable comments that Min or I would feel compelled to make about all that time you spent in the sun in pursuit of the perfect tan and how maybe that started everything downhill."

My gaze went to the scar on her neck, the site of her first cancer.

"Yeah." She let go of her sweatshirt, then looked away off into the distance. "But I wouldn't change it. The history, not the cancer. I wouldn't have done anything different."

"Worn sunscreen," Min whispered.

"Since it wasn't even invented yet and I wouldn't have used it if it was, why agonize over that?"

"Like you ever agonized over anything," I teased, realizing too late it might come off more like an accusation.

Bess glared at me, her head high. I could imagine the grand speech forming in her brain. One about how I had never really known her, how deeply she felt things. About how she had come to terms with her mistakes, and at this stage of things no longer had any use for regrets. About how I should respect her life and honor her feelings for this little time we had left.

"Bitch," was all she said.

I laughed. "Never use ten words when one or two will do."

"I thought she'd throw that silly old vow in your face." Min rolled her eyes. "You know—about living, about laughing about living and loving without limits, and making sure no one gets buried like Nana Abbra did."

"Live without limits. Love without question. Laugh without apologies." Bess's jaw hardly moved as she repeated it word for word, hard and clear.

"And *then* that part about not getting buried like Nana," I added quickly, usurping Min's usual role as referee.

"I can't believe you don't remember that, Min." Bess took a ragged breath. "I put it in the dedication of my book."

She had, and just under the vow she had added, "For C.D. and M.A.—my cousins, my best friends, the bane of my existence and the very people who keep me sane."

"I remember it because after the book came out, so many people around Orla accused me of falling down on the job," I said.

Bess cocked her head in question.

"Keeping you sane," I explained.

She laughed, just a little bit, then wrestled in another breath and reached for my hand and then Min's. "Sane or not, I want you two to understand that I wouldn't trade a day of the summers I spent here, even knowing now what price it cost me."

I couldn't meet her eyes.

I think I heard Min sniffle.

"It did cost me, but it also made me. How could anyone want to change the thing that made her who she is?"

For once Bess did not need Min to translate for her. She was saying she'd made peace with her situation.

"That is, if you *like* who you are." Bess gave my fingers a squeeze.

And again I heard her loud and clear.

Jump, Charma! If you ever hope to be the woman you so desperately want to become, you have to. *Jump!*

"I can't," I whispered, looking out at the pond.

"Let's put our feet in, then." Min let go of our hands and slid off her plastic sandals. "Give Charma the chance to acclimate herself to the water. It's a start, anyway, right?"

I nodded.

Bess looked down.

"You need help getting your socks off, Bess?" Min asked.

"I think I can manage that." She eased herself down to sit on the dock. The splintered wood rasped at the jersey fabric of her pants when she worked herself around to look back up at me. "Charma?"

Jump, Charma!

I raised my head and drew in the moist, hot air. All I had to do was peel away this ruffled sundress, step to the edge and let go at last.

"Let's sit," I said. When you think the only thing that can bring you back from the brink is to fling yourself into the abyss, as it were, dangling your feet in skanky water is a damn poor substitution. I knew that. Somewhere deep in my being I knew it. But maybe this small compromise...

A sound from the drive drew my attention—Sterling roaring up to the house in the compensation-mobile. It should have spurred me on, but it knocked the wind right out of my sails. How was my jumping in this water any different than him driving that repulsively expensive car? All show, no substance.

"You okay, Charma?" Min held out her hand to me. "Because if you're afraid..."

"I'm not afraid." I lowered myself to the dock, and with no further thought or enthusiasm, stuck both feet in the cool, dark water. "It's not..."

Not *enough,* my mind screamed.

"...bad," I concluded.

"I thought you could handle it." Min settled down beside me. "All the hours we spent out here as kids. You weren't afraid of the pond then, were you?"

"The hell I wasn't." I wriggled my toes, wondering when the panic would begin. It didn't, so I went on. "Don't you recall what it took to get me down here the first few times every summer?"

Bess joined us. Her pants rolled up to her calves, she kicked at the water's surface instead of sinking her feet in. "We had to promise not to throw you in under threat of giving you our firstborn girl child."

"Funny how that doesn't feel like much of a threat these days." Min swished her feet around and braced both arms behind her. "If you still want my girl child, Charma, I think we can strike a deal."

I opened my mouth to say something, but Bess beat me to it.

"Okay, Charma has stuck her toe in the water, now it's your turn, Minnie."

"My turn?" She jiggled her legs. The water swished. "I'm in up to my big fat anklebones."

"It's a metaphor, Min." Bess slipped her braid out of her shirt and let it fall over her angular shoulder. "Charma came a little ways toward dealing with whatever the hell has crawled up her butt and stolen away all her old heathen ways. More than once now you've made reference to hard feelings between you and Abby. Spill it, girl. What's up?"

Min's shoulders lifted, then lowered slowly. She did not make eye contact as she said, "I have issues with Abby's...life choices."

"Life choices?" I raised an eyebrow. A shallow response, I'll grant you. But in this day and age one can't throw out a term like "life choices" without piquing a little curiosity.

"Romantic entanglements," Min said like that explained anything.

"Romantic entanglements?" Both my eyebrows raised now, and if I'd been a dog, my ears would have pricked up and my nose lifted in the air, trying to sniff out the quarry.

Bess played it all real cool, of course, laying her hand on Min's and saying, all serene and supportive, "Like what?"

"Stupid, stupid stuff. Prejudices that go back to and beyond my mom, I suppose." She shook her head, swirled her foot in the water, then looked back toward the house. "But it speaks to the core of who I am, y'all. Who my mother is, too. And who Abby will be."

"Who Abby *is,* you mean." Bess reached up and plucked out a silver strand in Min's coarse hair.

"No." She winced and pulled her head away. "I mean who Abby will be. She doesn't see it this way, but she's still unformed. Not finished." Min faced me, her eyes searching. "A work in progress, you know?"

"Better than anyone." Only I didn't feel that way about my children. I felt that way about myself.

"A couple years away at college and she thinks she knows everything."

"She'll learn better." Bess patted Min's back, as if that ended it all.

I ached to rush in and articulate just the right solid, comforting words, but two things held me back. One was the over-riding, hard-won belief that parents cannot and should not try to live their children's lives. The other was that I had no idea what Minnie was talking about.

So I just gave her the best advice I could, the advice I desperately wanted to be true. "Sometimes, Min, you just have to let go and believe everything will be all right."

"That might have more credibility if you were saying it sopping wet," Bess muttered.

I'd have argued, but she was right. I hate it when Bess is right.

So I stood up.

Min's eyes got huge. "You going to do it, Charma?"

I bit my lip. I glanced back at the gleaming convertible parked in front of my family home. Then I stared at the glom of weeds and water stretched out beyond my bare feet. "Maybe."

The dock dipped, sending ripples to the shore. They sifted through the tall plants that bent and bowed in the sun-warmed breeze. Not the *whoosh-whoosh* of my dream but soft, like a snake slithering through the grass.

I took a deep breath and...

"Stay right there, ladies. I have something for you." Sterling strode down the path right toward us, waving a paper.

I should have jumped then.

To hell with him and whatever nonsense he had come to spout at us. But my legs would not move. And in my mind I knew that to jump to spite a man and not for *myself* wouldn't accomplish a damn thing, life-renewal-wise.

As the only one already standing, I folded my arms, took a defensive posture and spoke for us all. "I know it's a scum-filled pond, and as a lawyer you seek your own kind, but this is a private moment, Sterling. You're not welcome here."

He stopped short of the dock, his feet firm on the broken slab of concrete. He held his precious piece of paper up the way a rookie cop brandishes a badge. "No, Charma Deane, I regret to inform you that you are the ones who are not welcome. I have a restraining order. You and Miss Halloway are out. Mrs. Raynes can stay."

Bess sighed and started to push herself up.

Min rose to help her.

"You're not going to leave, are you?" I asked Bess.

"She doesn't have a choice, Charma. Neither do you."

"Come on, Charma." Bess gathered her socks and shoes. "This isn't the time or place to make our stand."

"Maybe not the time, but I can't think of a better place."

The dock rocked.

Bess grabbed my arm to steady herself. "Okay, not the right time, then."

Min walked her to the end of the wooden boards.

Bess stopped only long enough to smile at Sterling and murmur, "I'm impressed."

I wasn't impressed. I was pissed. I didn't budge an inch. "You bastard. How could you do this?"

"How could I protect your aunts from a person set on taking away their home and security? Easy, I just imagined how I might feel if someone threatened the people I loved."

You're threatening someone I love, I wanted to yell at him. Of course if I did that, I ran the risk of Bess contradicting me or making a smart remark to undercut my outrage. So I huffed out a beleaguered sigh and inched toward the shore. "Okay, we'll be out as soon as we pack."

"I don't think you understand the nature of a restraining order, Charma. You can't go back inside. You can't even go as far as the front porch."

Five months ago I'd have shouted "Halleluiah!" at that news. But now...I looked at the Aunt Farm through a sudden wash of tears.

"It's not fair," I whispered.

"Life's not fair." Sterling took my arm, helped me off the wobbling dock, then stood there, his expression staunch and sorrowful all at the same time. "Your aunts have gotten some things together. You should leave now before I'm forced to call the police to have you removed."

19

"Welcome to my home." I practically strangled on the last word.

If Bess noticed, it didn't show. But then nothing showed on Bess but the years. The years she had lived. The years the cancer had cut out from under her.

What the hell had I done? Pried her out of her safe cocoon at the Wycliff only to haul her home so Sterling could toss her out on her brittle-boned ass.

And now to bring her here.

"It's only temporary." I set our suitcases down just inside the door.

"So you say. From the looks of things, you've stretched temporary into a long-term living arrangement."

I tossed my keys into one of the few things I had unpacked, Mama's crystal fruit bowl. I had perched the thing on top of a stack of cardboard boxes by the front window to try to give the outward appearance of someone actually living in the place. "I meant temporary for you."

"Charma, honey, at this stage, everything is temporary for me."

"Because you plan to get back into the Aunt Farm?"

"Yeah." She brushed my hand with hers. "If that's what you need to pretend I mean, we'll go with that."

I squeezed my eyes shut and rubbed my forehead. "I'll make this work somehow, Bess. You'll see."

"Uh-huh." Bess edged her way between the rescued-it-from-the-rec-room, let-my-sons-furnish-their-apartments-with-the-good-stuff sleeper sofa dominating the one-room apartment, and the towers of still-sealed cardboard moving boxes lining the walls. "So this is what you distilled *your* life down to?"

"Distilled? Hardly." I worked to fit my bag into the few square inches between the microwave and the telephone on what the landlord called a spacious kitchen counter. "Bottled, maybe, but without the boiling down and refinement process."

"I can see that." She shoved the pile of winter clothes draped over my vacuum cleaner to one side and made her way to the empty office chair crammed against the boys' old air hockey table, which served as my computer desk/dinner table.

I lunged for a plate and glass. "Sorry. Guess these didn't quite find their way to the sink."

"Aww, and you left a trail of bread crumbs for them and everything."

I glanced down at my grubby floor and crinkled my nose. "I got called out unexpectedly to observe a home birth and just left things as they were."

"Judging from the state of your house, that baby must have started kindergarten by now."

"Actually, I went from there straight out to the farm because I got this panicked phone call from Aunt Fawnie. Something about her beloved niece serving her with an eviction notice."

"Excuses, excuses."

"A million times better than spilling the truth," I muttered.

"Why? What difference would spilling a few more things around this place make? A little truth scattered here and there might do a world of good."

"Which should I scatter? The grubby little details of why I really ran out on the home birth? Or the great grimy under-the-surface truth of how I came to let my home and my life fall apart around me?" I folded my arms and studied her as she tried to find a place to sit. "You figure centrally either way."

She gave a dismissive grunt, heaved a pile of unread self-help books off the end of the sofa and settled in. "I suppose I should feel flattered that you would think I hold that kind of power over you."

"Don't play coy with me, Bess." I should have been kinder. But the whole situation had me frazzled down to my last nerve, and the fact that Bess refused to get worked up over it got to me. "You not only know that you hold that kind of power over our family, you relish it. You seek it out and cultivate it."

She laid her head back and closed her eyes. "How?"

"Hello? Evicting our elderly aunts from the place so synonymous with them that everyone in the county calls it the Aunt Farm? If that move doesn't have a big old Power Play stamped across it, I don't know what does. And then there's always the issue of your book."

"Water under the bridge." She yawned, covered her mouth,

but went right on speaking. "I've totally distanced myself from that book since then, by the way. No one ever seems to mention that part."

"Because that's the part that pisses everyone off the most." Set our whole family up as a laughingstock, cash in on it; then, when the publicity dies down, blithely go around to writers' conferences and the odd cable TV show saying none of it had a shred of meaning? How could that not hurt? "Sometimes I think you don't know anything about us at all."

"Us? You mean *'the family.'*" Without moving her head or opening her eyes, she raised her fingers in the air and made invisible quotation marks every time she mentioned the term. "You all are 'the family' and I am...I'm just me. An outsider. You say I never knew 'the family'—maybe I feel like y'all never knew me."

"Not because we didn't try."

"Yeah, by blaming me for everything from your problems with home births to your lousy housekeeping."

"Damn it, Bess, if you'd just once—"

"You're making too big a deal out of this, Charma Deane."

"Well...yeah. Making too big a deal out of stuff is what our family does best—yourself included."

She chuckled, sat up and looked around. "What the hell have you done with your life lately, girl?"

"Oh, you know, grieve, pout, eat junk food, watch crappy TV shows, feel sorry for myself. The usual." I kicked some shoes and things out of my path, came around to sit on the sofa's arm and gazed down at her.

She looked tired, but our time in the sun had put a little color in her cheeks. It gave me the sense that maybe she felt better. Maybe my prayers had been heard. Maybe that miracle wasn't so far out of reach.

"Bess, we never talked about your treatment."

"I've had treatment, Charma, and I'm done with it. Talking won't change that." She put her hand on my knee. "I was hoping that, as a nurse, you'd be there through the whole thing, but if you can't do it, we can call in Hospice."

"Hospice." I couldn't seem to force the word out completely. It stayed in my mouth, in my mind long after the sound of it had faded.

"I have the number of the county headquarters stored on my laptop." She wet her lips, paused, then inhaled hard, forced a smile, turned around and said, "Undo this braid for me, will you? It's giving me a headache."

"Shug's doing?" I asked, working the rubber band loose with my fingers.

"The hair or the headache?"

The band snapped and popped my knuckle. "Damn! I've told her a thousand times not to use these rotten old rubber bands."

"You can't change people, you know. No matter how hard you try or how much you love them."

Just watch me. I shook the sting from my hand and went back to Bess's hair. "Maybe not, but at least once in a while I can keep them from doing something totally self-destructive. So I have to try, don't I?"

"Charma saves the world."

But she cannot save herself.

It was the loudest thing I'd ever heard not said.

I combed my fingers through her hair, scrubbing at her scalp to try to ease some of the tension there. "Given my superhuman world-saving duties, I guess I better check my phone messages pretty soon and see if anyone needs me."

"Oh, speaking of the phone." She tilted her head forward so I could better work my fingertips over every bump and nerve. "You said you had the number of the pond man? Let's give him a call. Oh, and, uh, maybe a housekeeping service."

"There, all done." I gave her head a little push. "And for your information, I can clean up around here myself."

"I kind of get the feeling you can't, Charma." She folded her legs up on the sofa and gathered her wavy black hair in one hand alongside her slender neck. "Not really. You've created your own stagnant swamp here."

"I need to check those messages." I turned my back.

"And you're getting pulled under, deeper and deeper every day," she added.

"Cut me some slack, will you? You don't know what I went through when I found out Mama had died and you—" I froze.

"I only did what Aunt Dinah asked of me. I guess I was the only person on earth she could trust to do it, me being so close to having to make my own similar choices."

"She knew about you?"

"Yeah. I'd gone to her for advice about how to handle it. She told me what she wanted and I guess that sort of sealed both our fates."

"Didn't it surprise you? Her suddenly making plans for the end of her existence? I mean, we're not talking Fawnie here."

"Surprise me? Why?"

Why? I blinked. "Because I didn't even know Mama was sick."

"Honey, she smoked since before Lucky Strike went to war."

I managed a smile at the reference. Mama and Fawnie tended to measure time in their own particular way. Things in their lives happened "after smoking became criminal" or "back when a doctor's office had ashtrays." Talk of some far-flung future event might be prefaced with, "long after I've gone to the smokers' section in the sky."

"But Mama saw a doctor regularly. She said she'd cut way back. Said the doctor told her a few puffs a day wouldn't do her any harm."

"Well, either he was lying to your mama or your mama was lying to you. Which do you suppose?"

I didn't have to suppose, of course.

"Damn it, Dinah." I borrowed Fawnie's favored phrase. A doctor telling a patient with chronic pulmonary disease that smoking wouldn't hurt. Ludicrous.

Of course Mama had lied to me.

For my part, I had made it easy. I wanted so badly to believe her. After all, she said it so frequently and with such firm conviction that I didn't dare doubt. And Mama's word was sacrosanct, wasn't it?

I put my hand up. The wall remained intact, even beyond death. Me and my hurt on one side, Mama and her lies and choices on the other.

I swallowed hard and curled my fingers into a ball. "I won't ever get over my mother's death, Bess."

She nodded. "And what about me?"

"I'll get over your role in the way she died." I dropped my hand to my side and glanced her way, grinning just enough to dilute the venom when I added, "Just like I've gotten over every other time you knifed me in the back."

"Yeah, right. You've been a real marvel getting over those."

She wriggled lower on the sofa, strained, then reached beneath the cushion to pull out the proverbial pea that had kept the princess from getting comfy. An empty plastic soda bottle. She threw it at me.

I ducked, and it bounced off the wall and fell into a pet dish for a cat I hadn't owned in six years. Why I had unpacked that and not my own dishes, I couldn't say.

"That's not what I was asking, doofus."

I looked up from the bottle in the bowl to find her sitting on the edge of the skewed cushion, gripping it like it was the last life raft on the *Titanic*.

"What I wanted to know was…Charma, will you get over *my* death?"

"Don't go there." My mind reeled. I wanted to run from her or poke my fingers in my ears and sing to blot out her words. Or maybe sink to my knees and start pouring my heart out in prayer. Anything to get her to stop. "Not now, Bess."

"I guess I just can't help but wonder." She dropped her gaze. If she had looked at me, I could have endured it, because I'd have known it for a manipulation. But when her eyelids fluttered and she bowed her head, I knew she was the one issuing the heartfelt plea to God. *Don't let my life be for nothing.*

And to me.

"After I'm gone, will you miss me, Charma?"

"Oh…God, Bess." I choked on my own sudden, overpowering tears. Mama's wall had stayed intact but Bess's had just come tumbling down. "Yes. I will. I will."

I went to her, arms open, and folded her in close to me.

A deep breath—I don't know from which one of us.

And I drew her closer still.

"Yes," I whispered again. "You don't know how much."

"That's..." She swallowed so hard it racked her entire cancer-ravaged body, and for the first time it all became real to me.

Not *true;* I had known from the beginning it was true. But *real.* Feeling her body shudder with the most simple of functions, the movement of her bones beneath her skin. This was going to happen, and nothing I said or did would stop it.

"Oh, God," I sobbed.

"Charma, please don't—"

"I'm not talking to you, Bess. I'm talking to *God.*" I laid my head on her shoulder and buried my nose in her brittle hair.

My heart ached. *Ached.* All my life I'd used that term, and now I knew I'd used it wrong. Nothing I had ever known had hurt this deep. Nothing had ever felt so beyond my ability to bear it alone.

"Dear God... God, we're such unholy messes." I rocked her body slightly, as if she were my child, not my elder cousin. "We're so flawed. We're so pretentious and flawed and, oh, stubborn and foolish. We've hurt people who never deserved it. We ignored people who needed us and ridiculed people who loved us. We have been selfish and prideful and eaten alive with anger and fear. But, God..."

I raised my hand to Bess's cheek and used my thumb to wipe a tear away.

Forehead to forehead, I closed my eyes. "But God, we have loved. *Loved.* Not just played at affection. We have stretched our souls to encompass others, knowing we would lose a little of ourselves in the bargain. We have lived and loved and laughed just as we vowed. Surely, God, if you are merciful, that will all count for something."

Bess nodded and sniffled, quietly adding, "Yes."

"Hold your daughter Bess in your hands, Lord. For what she has to go through, give her strength."

"And serenity," Bess murmured.

"And a sense of humor," I added.

"Oh, hell, yes," she countered.

I pinched her.

She laughed.

My heart lifted, just a little, as I pulled away to meet her dark eyes, even as I spoke to the only one left for us to turn to. "Because this is Bess, God. And she has loved. She *is* loved. Amen."

20

"Hey, girl! Hang on a sec." I could hear Inez taking off her earring, then her voice came back as strong and nasal as ever. "Your cell phone's not working. Turn it on or charge it up or whatever, okay?"

I'd grabbed the phone on the first ring in hopes of not waking Bess. I checked the clock on the microwave. "Inez, what are you doing calling me at nearly midnight?"

"Were you asleep?"

"Hardly." I may have told Bess I could sleep anywhere, but an inflatable pool raft on the kitchen floor just wasn't cutting it. "But you didn't know that."

"Sure I did. How many times have you told me that you can't sleep nights? Sheesh, you fall asleep in the middle of the day all the time, girl."

I'd have argued, but since she'd actually caught me doing just that, I merely got cross with her. Quiet, but cross. "Look, Bess is staying here with me tonight and she needs her rest, so I can't stay on the line yakking."

"Yeah, I heard about loverboy tossing you out."

"You heard about that? Where?"

"At the police station. Word there is they called the sheriff and hauled you off in an ambulance."

"There was no sheriff. And I drove off under my own power in the hearse."

"The hearse? Trust me, girlfriend, you should go with the ambulance story. It was getting you lots of sympathy down at the station."

"The...what were you doing at the police station, Inez?"

"Oh, that's what I called you about. I need a favor."

I held the phone close to my mouth. "Bail?"

"No! Nothing like that." She laughed, then muttered something in Spanish. "Jeez, it's not like I'm related to *you* or something."

"Sorry."

"No, it's RoryAnne."

"RoryAnne?" It felt as if someone had just dragged an icicle down my spine. "Is she okay?"

"Yeah."

I relaxed, but not entirely. "The baby?"

"Fine."

"Okay." I exhaled, sat up properly, then scooched over to put my back against the stove so I could see if I disturbed Bess. "What's the problem then?"

"That jerk of a husband of hers turned up in town."

"But she and the baby are okay?"

"Yeah. He hasn't done nothing—yet. But it's only a matter of time until he either talks her into leaving with him or, if she keeps turning him down, gets really crazy."

"Has he made any threats?"

"No. Best behavior. You know the drill. Those guys can be real charmers when they want something bad enough."

"Preaching to the choir here, Inez. I grew up in a house where women came to hide out from men like that. I saw plenty of them walk right back out the door on the arms of those men before their busted lips and broken bones had even healed."

"I went to the police, but they say if he hasn't done nothing, *they* can't do nothing. I thought maybe if you called up the station and threw your weight around?"

"I thought you said they were all gossiping about me down there. Maybe I don't have the kind of influence you think I do."

"Are you kidding? They was all on your side, Charma."

"Really?"

"If I was Sterling, I'd watch my back—and my driving— for the next few days."

I had to smile at the image of Sterling sitting in his Jag pouting while an officer who thought I'd gotten a raw deal wrote him a ticket for going thirty-six in a thirty-five-mile-an-hour zone.

"Please, Charma." When Inez spoke again, her voice had gone hushed and serious. "I'm scared for RoryAnne. Scared for the kind of life her and her baby will have if she goes with that man. Scareder still for what he might do if she *doesn't* go."

I wrapped my arms around my chest and fought off a shudder. "Okay. I'll call first thing in the morning."

"Tonight."

"But it's late."

"So what? They got someone to answer the phone down there."

"Who values her job too much to bother the chief at this hour. I'll get further if I wait."

"If you call tonight, they can send a cruiser around by the house off and on. What else have they got to do, anyway? You'd be doing them a favor, giving them something to do."

"Okay. I'll call tonight."

"And tomorrow."

"And tomorrow."

Suddenly a thin white figure loomed over me. "Call who?"

"Oh, shit, Bess!" I almost dropped the phone. "I didn't see you there."

"Call who?" she said again, rubbing her lower back in a way that made her cotton nightgown bunch up and show her pale, bruised shins.

Poor thing. The smallest bump or bumble left its mark, and I had brought her to a place where a cat couldn't walk without banging into a box or piece of furniture. There had to be a better solution.

I started to hang up the phone, remembered what little I had left of my manners and bent down to say, just before the receiver hit the cradle, "Good night, Inez."

"Call!" If she shouted anything else after that, I didn't hear.

"Call who?"

"The police."

"Why? Something wrong?" Bess yawned.

"It has to do with the girl with the home birth and the abusive husband she'd run away from."

"That's the most dangerous time."

"You don't have to tell me." I picked up the phone and started punching in the familiar number. "I swear, if this town ever gets itself modernized and changes phone numbers, my head will explode."

"You're calling them now?"

"And again tomorrow. Wife beaters don't keep regular hours, you know." The dispatcher answered, and I made my case quickly. And after only a modicum of swearing and mere trace amounts of implied threat, she saw things my way and agreed to send the patrol car through the specified neighborhood.

I hung up to find Bess with a glass of water in one hand, a slice of buttered bread in the other, and a shit-eating grin on her face.

"What?"

"Look at you." She shook her head. "Carrying on the family tradition."

"I do what I can to help those who aren't in a position to help themselves." I pushed myself up off the floor with all the grace and some of the sounds of a set of inflating bagpipes. "For instance, I am now going to help you help yourself to some sugar for that bread. You could use the calories."

"Buttered white bread with sugar on top. I'd forgotten y'all considered that a delicacy around here."

I ignored the snide remark, dug out some of the paper packets I'd swiped from dives and diners all over the county, and started tearing them open.

"Aunt Dinah would be proud of you, you know."

"Yeah, yeah. It's an old family recipe. Get off of it, okay?" I handed her back her bread sprinkled with the fine, sweet crystals.

"I meant about you making that phone call. Getting involved. It's a hell of a lot more than I'd do—more than most people would do—at this hour of the night." She took a bite, swiped a dab of butter from the corner of her mouth and licked it off her thumb. Head nodding and still chewing, she said, "It just seems like the kind of thing Aunt Dinah would have wanted you to do."

"That's not why I did it."

"I know."

I grabbed the butter from the fridge and started slathering my own piece of bread. "You really think she'd be proud of me?"

"I know she would be."

I pinched a sugar packet and began to shake it. "Why?"

"Because...you're *you*."

"Okay, aside from that not being a real answer, what I want to know is, do you know something I don't?"

"Like?"

"Did Mama talk about me at the end?"

"She didn't talk about anything in particular, Charma, except retelling for the millionth time those old stories about Uncle Jolly. Did you know your daddy once told Nana Abbra he was going out to wash her car, drove it to see Aunt Dinah at college, and when he got back four days later, he told Nana he'd had taken the car to Hot Springs for the superior water?"

"Everybody knows that, Bess." I rolled my eyes and bit into my bread. Sugar and butter melted on my tongue, and I shut my eyes to savor the old childhood treat.

"*I* didn't know it," Bess grumbled.

"You know what I didn't know?" I set my snack on the counter and brushed the sugar from my hands. "I didn't know about—and I'm hoping you can shed some light on this for me—did Mama happen to mention making a choice about Daddy the day he died?"

"Choice? No. Why?"

I studied her face, unsure I'd even know if she lied to me anymore. Finally, I swallowed the last of the sweet flavor and shook my head. "Something Fawnie said."

"Oh, there's a credible source."

"Maybe." I leaned my hip against the cabinet and folded my arms.

"Look, Charma, I wish I could give you what you want, but all Aunt Dinah said about you was that you'd had a wonderful visit at Christmastime."

"Did we?" I tried to conjure up the image of a Norman Rockwell Christmas with me and Mama at the center, but all I could recall was Shug folding every kind of origami shape out of wrapping paper and Fawnie making some vile mix with a carton of eggnog and her precious sloe gin.

"For the life of me, Bess, all I remember is her sitting there in her favorite sweater—the champagne-colored cashmere with the seed pearls?" I brushed my hand over my thin cotton T-shirt and would have sworn I could feel soft knit and intricate beading under my fingertips. "Just sitting in her usual chair, her feet in her Christmas slippers propped up on the hassock, holding court over every little thing."

Dinah McCoy George. The queen bee in her natural element. I couldn't help but smile.

"See?" Bess nodded. "I think she wanted you to remember her just that way. She told me that you two didn't have any great unresolved issues, and to bring you back from seeing your sons just to watch her die wouldn't accomplish a damn thing."

"*A damn thing.* That's just how she'd have said it, too." I pressed two fingers to my temple and didn't look at my cousin, but I had to ask, "But how could she have known she'd die then, while I was away, unless..."

"She was under a doctor's care for a long while, Charma. Maybe she sensed the end. Maybe she held on long enough to get through the holiday, then just let go. It happens."

"Did she suffer? At the end?"

"Don't, Charma. Please don't ask me for those kinds of details. That's exactly what Aunt Dinah wanted to spare you, what she went to great lengths to keep from you."

"Gone nearly six months now and still the queen bee."

"Yeah, well, it's not such a bad trait, after all, is it?"

"Bzz."

"I'm glad that's out of the way, though." Bess set her glass in the sink. The other dishes there clattered. She braced her arms against the counter and stared down into the clutter of unwashed cups and cutlery. "I've been expecting you to ask, and dreading it. Other shoe dropping and all."

I picked up my sugared bread and picked a corner of it off to eat. "I'm surprised you didn't realize that I didn't ask because I didn't want to know."

"Really?"

"Sure." Another piece, another nibble. "If I didn't know Mama's part in it, I could keep blaming you. I like finding new stuff to blame on you. Keeps my reflexes sharp."

She threw a quick boxer's one-two jab at me, missing my nose by a mile, then winced and pressed her hand to the small of her back.

"What? Is it the cancer?"

"The cancer? In my butt?" She rubbed her hand lower. "It's the bed, Charma. Here I thought you were being generous taking the floor, and then come to find out you had the more restful of the two arrangements."

My eyes went to her legs again, and I sighed. "We have got to do something about this. At our age, sofa beds and swim floats are not going to cut it for long."

"Actually—" she jerked her hand up to cover an enormous yawn "—I have an idea. I was going to tell you about it in the morning. You too tired to hear me out now?"

Another yawn.

"No." I surrendered and did the same. "What are we going to do?"

She crooked her finger for me to follow, and headed for the sofa. "We are going to do what any proud George woman would do in a time of chaos and calamity."

"Get our hair done?"

She threw back the covers and climbed onto the foldout bed. "No, play to our strengths."

"Ahh, shopping." I threw the blankets back over her and sank down on top of them at her side.

"Very funny." She propped her head on her hand and tugged the sheet up to her chin. "No. Think, Charma. What have women of our family done for decades when confronted by seemingly insurmountable obstacles?"

"Mount something?"

She smiled at last. "Now you're talking."

Except I wasn't. Talking, that is. What the heck could I say in the face of a statement like that, anyway?

"I'm going to start with that golden boy the old gals conned into working for them."

"Golden boy? Sterling?" I sat cross-legged, my back rigid. "Tell me you have not just hatched a plan involving mounting something or *someone*...namely the man I've shared a quasi-romantic relationship with this last year."

"Quasi-romantic?" She scratched her nose. "You dress up as hunchbacks when you have sex?"

I looked heavenward—well, ceiling-tile-ward. "We don't *have sex.*"

"All right then, make love."

How long has that water stain been there? I tried to think back to the last rain and if it had been there before that even as I answered absently, "We don't do that, either."

"Oh? Good." She rolled onto her back as if she suddenly wanted to know what I found so all-powerful fascinating overhead. "All the better for my purposes."

"Purposes?" *Water stain be damned.* "You have *purposes* that involve poor Sterling? Hasn't the man suffered enough at the hands of my relatives?"

"I promise not to hurt the boy."

"To heck with him, what about me?"

"I plan to help *you,* cousin. But I can't promise it won't come at a cost."

"Your help always comes at a cost, Bess."

"Everything worthwhile does, Charma."

"What do you want me to do?"

"It's not so much what *I* want. It's what you *have* to do. Where you have to go. Who you have to deal with in order to move forward with your life."

"But I'm not worried about my life right now, I'm worried about yours."

"Or what's left of it." She said it like a joke.

I didn't laugh. "Whatever is left, you can't spend it in this place. We have to get you home, Bess."

"The farm?"

"Yes, the farm. That's where you belong right now, not in some storage unit masquerading as an apartment."

"If you really mean that, then let me deal with this Sterling fellow and you go do what you have to do."

"Narrow it down for me, will you?" The sheer magnitude of options overwhelmed me. "What do I have to do?"

"I don't know. But when you figure it out? The past won't have any more hold over you. You might even be able to finally go out to that pond and jump."

21

"Tell me the truth." Bess glanced over her shoulder.

"We've survived two weeks now in the same house without bodily harm. Let's not risk our record by telling the truth now." I held up my hand.

"About this outfit." She grabbed the hem of her dress and fluffed it.

As the crinkled fabric went floating down to her calves again, I lay back on her neatly made bed in the linen room. "Lord, that's even scarier territory than truth-telling about our lives."

She spun around and put her backside to me. "Shut up and tell me if my butt looks big in this."

I sat up, looked and spread my hands wider than an old man telling a fish story. "Enormous."

"Bless you, dear." She did a half twirl in front of the mirror, then moved to the dresser and began foraging through the odd lot of jewelry we had all gathered to loan her.

"So, how many dates is this now with Sterling?" Min asked

me, because Bess still pretended the outings with my former would-be lover were business-related.

"Let's see. She wormed our way back into the house two weeks ago. She's had dinner with him almost every night. Then there are the lunches and the long drives in the country."

"Don't forget the breakfasts." Min, standing next to Bess at the dresser, didn't even look up from the tangle of necklaces she'd started to unravel. "Provided he does feed her breakfast."

"I don't know. Bess, when you stay over at Sterling's for one of your extended business meetings, does he serve you breakfast in the morning or just kick you out the door on your enormous ass without so much as a bowl of cold cereal or a piece of burned toast?"

"He serves me a big, steaming platter of mind-your-own-business-O's. You should try some." She held a pair of golden hoops with pearl studs up to her earlobes. "I think I'll wear these tonight. What do you think?"

"Can't talk now." I pointed to my mouth and pantomimed chewing. "Gagging down a big wad of mind-your-own-business-O's. Yu-u-um."

She glared at me.

"They're gorgeous and so are you." Min smoothed the underside of Bess's plastered-in-place chignon.

As it had gotten harder and harder to do anything becoming with her once-lustrous hair, and as Bess did not want to cut it, Min and I had taken to devising more and more elaborate hairstyles for her.

"You will totally wow the man. Not like you haven't already, of course." Was that a hint of jealousy creeping into my tone? Hell, yes. Sterling had been *my* toy, and once again Bess shows up and... "What'd it take you, a whole hour, to get him to re-scind the restraining order?"

"What can I say? I dazzled him with my brilliant legal logic."

"Bullshit," Min muttered.

I blinked in surprise.

Bess did, too.

"Oh, come on, it's *us* here, Bess. We know you played on his sympathies big-time."

"Okay, okay. I admit it." Bess put on the earrings. "I may have mentioned that I had health issues and felt I would re-cuperate much faster in familiar surroundings. But I also agreed to sign a document recognizing that my presence in the house prior to the date of my legal possession did not con-stitute a claim of—"

"Oh, blah, blah, blah." Min handed Bess a necklace, then moved behind her to fasten the clasp. "Why don't you throw in some Latin and a party of the first part while you're at it? He let you back in because he felt sorry for you...and he felt attracted to you. Then he felt—"

"You." I chimed in with a wicked smile. "Guess he's not a breast man."

She grinned at me over her shoulder. "Why do you think I asked if my butt looked good in this?"

"You asked if it looked big, not good. It ain't necessarily the same thing, you know. Just like 'health issues' are not exactly the same as stage-four cancer." Yeah, I said it. Sterling deserved to know what he had signed on for, and in order for that to happen, someone had to be able to say the words.

Bess raised her chin and met my gaze, all petulance and puppy eyes—always a clue she was about to lie like a dog. "I don't know what you're talking about."

"I'm talking about that coming to the farm to recuperate nonsense." *My* toy. The games I had played with him had hurt no one. But Bess, when she toyed with someone—well, I certainly knew how devastating the results could be. I would do anything to spare Sterling that kind of pain. Except—maybe—ratting out my dying cousin. "You have to tell him, Bess. It has to come from you. Now. A good man's heart is at stake."

She opened her mouth, still making eye contact, but before she could spin out her latest nasty little untruth the doorbell rang. She smiled, tossed her head as if she'd just been exonerated of all charges, and said, "That's him!"

"Mommy'll get it." Min finished brushing down the back of Bess's dress. "This is so fun."

"Oh, yeah, this is a regular laugh riot," I muttered, knowing that Sterling's arrival and Min pushing mediator mode into high gear had ended my hopes of persuading Bess to do the right thing.

"I mean, we haven't all been together doing the getting-ready-for-a-date thing since that summer after Charma and I graduated high school." She directed Bess to do another turn for one last going-over. "Bess, you had that job writing travel pieces for the state tourism bureau, and you convinced them you had to do an in-depth piece on Orla, remember?"

"I remember," she said softly, centering her necklace and letting her fingers linger a little too long on her old skin cancer scar. "Do you remember that, Charma?"

"Yeah, I remember." How could I not? It was, in essence, my last innocent summer. If you count losing your virginity in the bed of a pickup while your mother thought you'd gone to a college orientation meeting as innocent. "It was the summer Guy and I got 'engaged to be engaged.' A ring at Christ-mastime, a wedding under the trees at the Aunt Farm the fol-lowing spring."

"Things don't always work out the way we plan." Bess only glanced my way before snatching up the vintage purse she'd glommed from some long-forgotten closet in the house, and threw the strap over her shoulder.

"Tell Sterling, Bess. Don't blow off his potential feelings by telling yourself that people shouldn't count on things work-ing out as they planned."

She moved to the doorway, then turned and looked in my general direction. "Why don't you fix yourself another serv-ing of those mind-your-own-business-O's, Charma?"

I opened my mouth with what I can promise you was a brilliant and scathing retort, but the ringing of the phone shut me up.

Hey, we're over forty, we're not dead. The phone rings in *this* house, we all stop and listen to see if it's for us.

"Charma Deane? Lamb? Honey, it's for you! It's that dar-ling Inez."

"Oh, shit." I leaped up off the bed as fast as my tingling little pudgy feet and popping knees would allow. "If she's call-ing me to observe another water birth—"

"She says she's out at RoryAnne's mother's house."

Suddenly I wished it were a home birth call and not this. I'd done what I could to get the police to patrol, but twice now they'd stopped her abuser in the vicinity only to have Rory-Anne swear she'd invited him. I couldn't seem to make Inez understand that in the face of that, even I couldn't convince them to keep up *the protection*.

Of course, that wouldn't stop me from trying. I pushed past

Bess in the doorway—okay, squeezed past. "Excuse me, but I have a *family tradition* to uphold."

Just then Fawnie hollered out the rest of the message. "Says to tell you they need you there to throw your weight around."

"Well," Bess called as I hurried down the hall away from her, "at least they picked the right member of the family to do it!"

I don't know if that was a compliment or a comment on my weight.

Either way, did it matter?

Whether dealing with Bess or a battered woman, I could only do so much.

And that really pissed me off.

22

"Guess we'll all sleep better from now on. The bastard's dead," was how Inez, her arms folded over a yellow tank top, had greeted me.

I'd barely climbed out of the hearse in front of the home where weeks ago we'd come to witness the beginning of a new life when she shouted it.

A second patrol car had just come screeching to a halt cattywampus across the drive, narrowly missing the rust-speckled hatchback and a commanding black Crown Victoria already parked there.

Heart pounding, I picked my way through the dark yard toward my friend's side, calling out, "If I step on a severed body part, Inez, I swear you are buying me a new pair of shoes."

"Aww, you're all right. He's all in one piece over there in the bushes." She pointed to where the two officers stood shoulder to shoulder at the side of the house.

Light from the window glinted off their badges, buttons

and the slick leather of their gun holsters. The taller of the two, the one who had been on the scene first, pointed down at something in the scruffy snarl of evergreens and boxwoods.

Neither RoryAnne nor her mother were anywhere in sight.

"Okay, out with it." I reached Inez just as the tall officer's gestures grew more animated. "Did you kill RoryAnne's husband?"

"No, Charma, honey." She looped her arm around my shoulders. "*You* did."

Though it was too dark to see the body, the neighbors had begun to cluster around trying to get a look—or at least hear something interesting.

"Would you watch your mouth?" I grabbed Inez by the arm and yanked her over to one side, whispering, "What do you mean, *I* killed him?"

"Simple. By keeping on to the police."

The taller figure raised his hand with something in it.

His companion nodded.

"They told me they hadn't planned to swing through the neighborhood again tonight, but you called the chief and asked for the patrols to continue."

The beam of a flashlight probed the bushes. The tall man prodded something with his boot.

A limp arm flopped out into the moonlight, and where the first officer shone his light, blood drenched the sleeve and pooled in the palm.

The newly arrived officer jumped back, put his hand to his mouth, then turned away.

An unmistakable sound filled the still night.

Inez elbowed me in the side. "I think he got some on his shoes."

"Blood or puke?" I went on tiptoe to see what she saw, and couldn't make out anything but a silhouette.

"Go check it out." She jabbed me again.

Though I was jaded by my profession, made cynical by my life experiences and encouraged to hone the convoluted sense of humor of a borderline sociopath by my family, there were still some things that even I wouldn't do. "I refuse to go up there and snoop."

"No, I don't want you to snoop. I want an excuse to tag along and see for myself."

"That's why you called me out here, isn't it? You're under the mistaken impression that I can somehow get you on the inside of this investigation."

"Investigation? Who said anything about an investigation?"

"Whenever there's a crime—"

"That's the beauty of it all, Charma. It was an *accident*."

"An accident? Are you sure? Can that be proved?"

"Does having a cop as an eyewitness count as proof?"

I glanced back in time to find the first officer whacking the second one on the back, saying, "Never give me shit again about making you direct bingo traffic while I go on patrol. Lucky you weren't here when it happened. You'd have crapped your pants, too, the way it all went down, slow and gorylike."

"Yeah." Inez nodded. "I had come by to bring the baby some things and hadn't been in the house ten minutes when we heard the car drive up."

"The husband's car?" I racked my brain to remember his name, but couldn't. "How'd you know it was him?"

"Did you see it? It don't exactly purr when it runs. Anyway, RoryAnne says he's just coming to talk and to see the baby, and she can't deny him that. You know, don't he have a right to see his own baby?"

"Yeah, yeah. How does all that result in the man lying dead in the bushes?"

"I'm getting to that. It was one of them moments, you know?"

"Moments?"

"Pee or get off the pot."

"So you wet your pants?"

"I had the cops on speed dial, so I whipped out my phone and made the call like that." Her long fake nails muffled the effect of the finger snap, but the sound still sent a tiny chill through me.

There had been no time to contemplate. No standing on the dock agonizing over anything. The moment called for decisive action, and Inez had risen to it.

"What if you had been wrong?"

"RoryAnne would have stood up for him. They'd have been mad at me. You'd have had to make another call to the chief, and maybe next time the police wouldn't have come." Inez waved her hand. "But this time, they did come. Because of you, the cops were already in the vicinity, and they came by just in time to see this guy standing on a folding lawn chair, trying to pry the screen off the bedroom window with a nine-inch screwdriver."

"Could you hear him inside?"

"Not the screen stuff, but we did hear this cussing and then a loud sound like metal twisting, and a crash."

"Metal?"

"Yeah. It was weird. So, we're inside wondering what's going on. Why hadn't he come to the door? Did the cops get here and talk to him? RoryAnne is all, 'If they harass him, he'll take it out on me,' and 'He didn't do nothing.' And her mama and I are all, 'He's no good for you,' and 'You should let the cops handle it,' you know?"

"Uh-huh." I made the universal let's-hurry-this-story-along gesture. "And?"

"And long story short, I go out into the driveway to see what's up, go over to his car and hear this cop getting out of his cruiser saying, 'Don't move.'"

"That's when you wet your pants." I sure as hell would have.

"That's when I ask him, 'What's up?' and he says he thinks someone's been hurt, and I can see by the look on his face while the car door is open, it's bad."

"Yeah?" Again with the hurry-this-up gesture.

"Okay, turns out the amazing jerk-husband was holding on to the downspout for support while he's working the screen loose. When the cop car came down the street real slow and shines the light on him, hubby panics and makes a dive into the bushes. Only his watch is caught on the downspout." She tugs at an imaginary watchband around her own wrist. "And so he gives it a yank to get free, and it tears down the whole gutter, which throws him off balance, collapses the lawn chair, and he does a header directly into the bushes."

"Which kills him, how?"

"He lands—" she smacked her hands together in one sharp clap "—right on the screwdriver. Straight through the heart."

I gasped. "What an awful way to die!"

"I know." She bowed her head, made the sign of the cross, then raised her face, her eyes glinting. "Ain't your aunts going to love that story?"

"Inez, the man is dead." A minute ago he'd been alive, a man. Now he was a body, a thing to be poked at by the toe of a boot, to be carted away and buried. "He might have been a creep but—"

"Might have been? Oh, wait till you hear the rest of the story."

I lifted my hand.

"I know, I know." She supplied the gesture for me. "Quick and to the point. The chief comes—he's in there with Rory-Anne and her mama now—and the cop makes me stay out here. You know, to make sure our stories match up and all. And anyway, he and I are standing in the drive, and I happen to look into hubby's car finally, and you know what I saw?"

I gazed toward the star-scattered sky. "Oh, God, I hope it was the end of your story."

"End of my story. End of RoryAnne's story, her mother's, her baby's. Anyone's who was in that house tonight."

"Why? What did you see?"

"Only some rope, some of that, uh, you know that tape stuff." She made a motion across her mouth. "A semiautomatic, lots of ammunition and a shovel."

"Wow." My stomach dropped. After weeks of adjusting to the idea of losing Bess in increments, to consider losing Inez and the others in a single night, and so horribly, made my knees weak. "You saved some lives tonight, Inez."

"I just made the call. You made sure they'd take it seriously."

"They would have taken it seriously, Inez, if you had told them."

"Told them what? And in this accent?" she scoffed.

I opened my mouth to tell her that it wouldn't have mattered, but before I could, she took my hand.

"No, you made this possible. The chief himself said so. That they would have stopped coming by after the first time Rory-Anne backtracked on her story. But you dogged him. That's what he said, you dogged him."

I didn't actually say, "Ah shucks, t'weren't nothing," but I suspect my body language did.

Her face softened and she patted my cheek. "He also said you asked him to do it for your mama."

"I asked him to do it for *his* mama." I patted her cheek right back, only just once and with just a little oomph.

She cocked her head, her earrings swinging. "His mama?"

"She'd been out to the Aunt Farm a few times, and so..." I lifted one shoulder.

Inez shook her head. "You know, Miz Fawnie told me she thinks you guys need a big funeral to remind people about your family, but what you really gotta do is have a rebirth."

"I don't want to hear it, Inez." I started to walk away. To where, I had no idea.

"Well, you're going to hear it." Inez stepped in front of me, arms folded, and would not budge. "You guys need a rebirth, and as someone who has rebirthed herself all over the place, I know what I'm talking about. You gotta use that house and that name of yours the way it ought to be used. The way it has been used. The way you're doing with bringing Bess home and taking up for a brown-skinned Yankee buttinsky trying to protect a beat-up-on girl no one in town knows."

A car drove up and Waymon Foley, the one and only reporter for the *Orla News Press* clambered out, his camera flashing.

One of the officers cut him off before he actually reached the death scene.

Waymon kept snapping pictures as if he was in an old black-and-white movie, all the time barking out questions. "Coroner pronounced yet? Why's the chief here? What's with the screwy hearse? Didn't you call Chapman's?"

I wanted out of there. I should never have come, after all. And now Waymon would probably see me and want an interview. Worst of all, he'd dredge up the George family past, the speculations about the house, maybe even Bess's book. Wouldn't that all make a mundane if grisly story of an accidental death all the more newsworthy?

I closed my eyes—like maybe that would make it so Waymon wouldn't see me?—and turned toward the my '72 Cotner-Bevington golden chariot. "I can't do this now, Inez. I can't."

"It's already done, girl. You *did* it." She pulled me to her side for a hug. "And because you did, three women and a helpless child are safe. You tell that Aunt Fawnie of yours that your family don't need no fancy-ass funeral to restore honor to your name—they have you."

"Golly gosh, Inez, that's so sweet I don't know whether to cry or join that nice officer over there barfing on his shoes."

"I'd give you such a pinch if I didn't know you meant that as a good thing."

The headlights of two more vehicles cut across us in quick succession.

"Thanks, Inez. It really does mean a lot to me. A lot of BS."

"Ha! I'm getting to you, girl. Gradually wearing you down. Before you know it, you'll be believing in yourself again."

"Yeah? And then what?"

She did this wringing her hands thing like an evil villain, which totally didn't work with her jewelry clacking and her standing there in sequined flip-flops. "And then the Aunt Farm will be mine."

"How many times do I have to tell you? You cannot get to that house through me. I have no claim on it. In fact, day after tomorrow Fawnie and Shug might not have any claim to it, either."

"Why tomorrow?"

"Day after tomorrow. There's a hearing. Being basically alienated from both sides on this issue, I don't know any details except that if it goes in Bess's favor, my aunts will have seventy-two hours to relinquish the property."

Inez muttered something in Spanish, crossed herself again, then shook her head. "I'll remember your aunts in my prayers tomorrow."

"Not tomorrow, day after tomorrow."

"What? I can't pray for them a day early? You don't think God can sort it all out?"

"Inez, honey, considering the awful mess everything in my life has become, I'm counting on God to do just that. I sure can't do it for myself."

"You hear that, Father? Charma is finally asking for help."

"Don't you go and get God involved in this."

"Are you kidding?"

"I just mean, I happen to be a very strong believer in the adage 'Be careful what you pray for because you just might get it.'"

"What's the matter, Charma? You afraid the Lord might have something different in mind for you than you have for yourself?"

"Since I am drawing a total blank on what to do, and who to be for myself, it is at the very crux of my fragile faith, Inez, that God has a better plan for me."

*What are you waiting for, Charma Deane? For God Almighty
to kick you in the butt?*

"It's also my biggest fear," I confessed, my jaw tight, "that
he will do something about it."

"Young lady? Hearse driver?" A stooped-shouldered man
wearing a golf shirt tucked into plaid Bermuda shorts strode
up to me. Beyond his clothes, the only way I could describe
Dr. Mark Macintyre was in dairy terms. Milky-blue eyes. Hair
the color of butter. And legs—now that I saw them out in the
open this sultry summer evening—the finely veined whiteness
of blue cheese. And a disposition as pleasant as curdled cream.

"Dr. Mac. It's me, Charma Deane Parker? We ran the sco-
liosis clinics together for years when you worked for the health
department."

"Did we?"

"Yes, I used to be the school nurse, remember?"

"Hmm. So you've got a new job, too?" He eyed me up and
down, though I cannot say he actually saw much.

Dr. Mac has been a fixture on the Orla medical scene since
I was a grade-schooler getting checked for curvature of the
spine myself. When he'd grown too old to continue running
the county health department, some brilliant politician suggested he'd be a good coroner. You've heard of the blind leading the blind? Having Dr. Mac in charge of sealing the affairs,
then sending off Orla's most recently departed felt a little like
the dead loading the dead.

"No, Dr. Mac. I don't have a new job. I—"

"Oh, that's right. You married a Chapman, right? That's
right. Well, you know then. Case like this, we got to have a
Chapman transport the body. County has a contract. C'mon
then, let's get this over with. My supper's getting cold."

Inez looked at me. "Married a Chapman?"

"Don't laugh. And don't you even dare suggest this is somehow the answer to that prayer of yours." I raised my hand to the retreating man. "Dr. Mac? There's been a mistake. I did drive a hearse here, but that's for personal use only. I am not now, nor have I ever been, a Chapman."

"Put your arm down, Charma. It's not a senate hearing." A large hand grasped my shoulder lightly, and instantly the tension of the moment seeped out of my body.

"Hi, Guy." I looked back at him. He wore a gray suit, a dark tie and a kind smile despite the tinge of weariness around his eyes.

"I didn't expect to see you here," he said. Then he touched my hair and shook his head. "Though I should have guessed. Because when someone needs help in Orla, they call a George."

"And what are you doing here?"

"When someone's past all help in Orla, they call a Chapman."

"You mean they call Chapman and Sons Funeral Home." It was a small but significant distinction.

"Do I?" He rubbed his neck.

I wanted to step back, to distance myself, to get a better perspective on the man and the situation. But as Minnie had pointed out not so long ago, nothing would give me perspective until I stopped keeping my fears and failures at the forefront of my emotions. In other words, until I let bygones be bygones. That's the rub, though, isn't it? I didn't want Guy to be a bygone in my life.

I wanted to trust him. I almost felt that I could. He'd *said* I could. Why was it so hard to push aside the old hurts and believe?

He shook his head. "Didn't you hear the doctor, Charma? Got to have a *Chapman* transport the body. County has a contract, and the people in town have an expectation."

"But I didn't think you did this kind of thing."

"I don't." He brushed his knuckle down my cheek.

Dathan and another young man I didn't recognize rolled a gurney past us toward the bushes where the officers and the chief of police stood in a semicircle holding flashlights up for Dr. Mac.

"I do *this* kind of thing." He dropped his hand, gave Inez a wink and a nod, then plastered the biggest, phoniest smile on his face I'd ever seen. "Waylon! You sure got there fast, man."

A flash. Another, this one aimed at Dr. Mac's activities. Then Waylon pivoted and shook Guy's hand as if they were old war comrades.

"No." I put my hand over my heart. Heat began to rise from there up my neck and cheeks. I clenched my jaw and cursed.

"What is it?" One of Inez's bracelets bounced against my arm as she gave me a shake.

"Got to be a Chapman," I muttered, even as I looked at Dathan doing his work without once meeting the eyes of the men of Orla authority. "Guy's nothing but a front man, Inez."

"What are you talking about?"

"I'm talking about almost believing someone whose whole existence in Orla is about hiding behind a wall of lies." My stomach turned. "That's why Guy doesn't have to be there for meetings, and why Dathan is always afraid someone will find out and everything they've worked for will sink like a stone."

"Charma?"

Guy patted Waylon on the back, his face solemn.

Waylon jotted something down on his pad.

"That bastard."

"Who? Charma, what are you talking about?"

"Guy." My eyes did not tear up. A person can only be kicked so many times before everything goes blissfully numb, I guess. I stared at the man I knew I would always love as Fawnie loved Kel, and who I would always trust about as much as I could Bess, and snarled, "He promised me he'd never lie to me again, and all the while he was living the biggest lie of his life."

23

"What did you expect me to do? Go over and confront him while he glad-handed a reporter, and see it all played out on the front page?" I peered through the doorway at the clock on Min's nightstand. Half past nine. I'd been home from RoryAnne's mother's house long enough to clean up and realize I couldn't wriggle my way out of spending the remainder of the evening with the family. "Or wait until he was pretending to oversee the removal of a dead body, then march up, slap him in the face like some overwrought soap opera vixen and scream, 'Impostor!'?"

Actually, I wish I had thought of that second one.

"No, Min. Not the right time or place." I sighed and stared at the staircase spilling downward from where we stood.

Right time. Right place. Was there ever such a thing for Guy and me? "Besides, Dr. Mac thought Guy and I were married, and I didn't want that particular demon rising up there in front of everyone."

Min, who was taking her time changing back from her

nightgown into something that would not throw Fawnie into a flaming hissy fit if Min wore it to the formal dinner table, called out, "Not to mention that man with the screwdriver protruding from his chest."

"No, we didn't want him rising up, either."

"I meant, a man had died, Charma. Right there. Blood oozing, his body growing cold when just minutes earlier he had been—"

"Attempting to break into the house and do who knows what vile thing?"

"Still..."

"Yeah, I know." I glanced down the stairs. I did not want to do this. I wanted to crawl into bed and pout about the lousy hand I'd just been dealt. I wanted to feel miserable about Guy and angry about Bess and the eviction. I wanted to wallow in self-pity that, for all my best efforts, I hadn't been able to change either one of them. I did not want to go downstairs and act civil as a favor to women who hadn't done a damn thing to help me deal with Bess or Guy or Mama or myself. "If he had just stayed away."

"Seems like that type never does, though."

"Maybe that's the definitive way to tell the good men from the louses. If you tell them to go away and they do, you should have hung on to them." I chuckled, wondering what ailment I could come up with to beg off going down those stairs.

"Guy keeps coming back. What does that make him?" Min asked.

"A fool?"

No answer. I thought about saying it louder, but figured it might bring Fawnie or Shug running to see what the shouting was about.

"What?" Min appeared at the door barefoot, with her shoes in her hands.

"Guy doesn't keep coming back. He sure as hell didn't the first time, and lately we've been more thrown together by fate and our own choices than by him coming back. And, of course, there is that more than twenty year gap in between."

"The first time? When?"

"The night before our wedding." Min had known about that. She'd helped me sneak out to do it. "You know, when I went to call it off and—"

"Wait a minute, all these years you told me you went there that night just to ease your anxieties about getting married so young."

"Yeah. And being young, I did that by telling him I wanted to call off the wedding." Duh. Why I went was not the point. Didn't she get that? "I never thought he'd actually tell me we'd do whatever I thought was best. Jeez, I was a kid *and* a George. I went expecting angst, drama, make-up sex."

She slid one shoe on. "And you've blamed Bess, let *all* of us blame Bess, for that fiasco ever since?"

"He said he'd be waiting for me when I came back, Min. I came back the next morning, and he was gone. With Bess. Let's not forget who the bad guy is here." *Bad girl? Bad person?*

"Still, Charma, that's a pretty important piece of the puzzle you've been holding back all these years. To have never taken any responsibility for Guy's choice that day? I'm surprised at you."

To take responsibility, to direct my own soul. It was and always had been my charge in life. Could that have been at the root of my anger at Bess and Guy for what happened?

That I had made a poor choice, and they had not loved me enough to see it? To help me make a better one? The thought was staggering.

And awful.

Two people I loved had left me to flounder. I *wanted* to stay mad at them.

"So maybe I'm not who you think I am," I snapped at Min, again misplacing my resentment. "Maybe Guy isn't who people around town think he is. Maybe none of us is who we think we are or, uh, who anyone thinks we should be. Or maybe some of us aren't who we wish we were but don't want anyone to know." I shut my eyes. "I don't know."

"It's okay." She laid her hand on my back. "It kind of made sense to me."

"It did?"

"Yeah, but I'm not myself these days."

"Oh, Min." I hugged her close and laughed.

"Girls?" Fawnie's voice drifted up, sweet and delicate, from the hallway below. "Have you forgotten our special—"

"Dinner!" Shug screamed, so loud it brought on visions of her tonsils shaking and her hair standing on end.

"Shitfire, Shug!" Fawnie thumped her cane so hard a picture fell off the wall. Or maybe she took a swing at her counterpart and knocked the picture off. "Where are your manners?"

"This is not time for manners, old woman. This is time for *dinner*. Girls, get down here!"

"Oh, they give me such a headache." I had barely brushed my warm forehead with my cool palm when Min yanked my hand away.

"Oh, no you don't. We promised them we'd be here for this

special dinner of theirs. I've been here all night listening to them alternate between bitching about you and Bess going AWOL, and berating me for not having anything better to do tonight than sit with a couple of old women. The least *you* can do is sit and make nice through a couple courses of crab wiggle and salmon croquettes."

She glared at me, waiting for an answer.

What could I say? "I thought a wiggle was made with shrimp?"

She stuck her other shoe on and directed me to the stairs.

"Where's your darling friend?" Fawnie grasped the finial, waiting. "I thought you invited her to join us for our special dinner."

"I did, but she thought that after everything that happened tonight..." I sighed and started down.

Min followed. "I guess, unlike certain people we could point fingers at, death must put a damper on her appetite."

"I like that Inez. She got class." Shug circled her thumb and fingers and put them up to her ears like a pair of the giant earrings Inez preferred.

"Class." Fawnie overaccentuated the *l.*

"That's what I say." She jiggled her finger-earrings as if that proved her point.

Fawnie rolled her eyes. Actually, she rolled her whole danged head—that's how disgusted she was and how much she wanted us to know it.

"I like her." Shug took Min's arm and patted it. "I like that she isn't just sitting around waiting for her kids to call. You know, she's learning new stuff, midwife stuff. It's very good."

"I'm thinking of going back to college," Min blurted out.

"You are?" I asked.

"Yes." Everything from the tightness of her lips to the flames shooting from her eyes said "Shut up and play along."

"That's news." Shug stepped back as if she needed the distance to put Minnie in focus. "You gonna go to the same school as Abby?"

"Oh, yeah. What was I thinking?" Had I totally forgotten that the not-being-able-to-stand-someone-else-getting-the-admiration-and-attention-I-so-desperately-crave trait was genetic? It might not often raise its head in Min, but when it came to winning Shug's approval... "She talks about it all the time."

"What are you going to study?" Fawnie asked, even as she turned and started toward the dinning room.

"I, uh..." Min looked to me for help.

"She going to study taxi-a-dermy. Then we have someone who know what to do with you when you finally kick the bucket, old woman." Shug laughed and winked to let Min know she was off the hook, then motioned for us to follow, and hurried after her friend.

Light from every chandelier and sconce in the downstairs poured into the foyer. The hallway practically glowed a rich honey gold.

Because it was a special occasion, Fawnie had put on little jewel-toned beaded flats and had dug out an antique mahogany walking stick with a carved ivory handle. The shoes and unfamiliar cane had slowed her progress over the polished hardwood floor. Hair coiffed, decked in her finest and without a cigarette in hand, she had the appearance of some kind of grande dame of Southern society moving gently through her elegant old home.

"Don't be such a horse's patoot, Shug." Fawnie paused outside the French doors that opened onto the formal dining room. "I hope to high heavens you wouldn't act like that if sweet little Inez did show up."

"Inez happens to like me, patoot or not."

"Of course Inez likes you. She likes herself and a person does that, well, what do they give a damn if they don't have a lick of good taste in who else they like?" She stopped to fuss over Shug's collar, getting it smoothed down just right. "That Inez, now there's a gal who has truly embraced her sacred self."

"Her what?" I asked, even as a voice inside me warned I had probably just postponed dinner by twenty minutes.

"Go into the dining room and sit." Fawnie prodded the fleshy part of my shoulder.

I led the way, everyone else on my heels.

"Oh, wow. Y'all have outdone yourselves." Min spoke first.

Fawnie swept her arm out to offer us the full view of the table, set with the family's finest right down to finger bowls and flowers in crystal vases illuminated by two dozen candles in silver candelabra. The warmth from the flames had forced the buds to open, making the room smell like a rose garden.

"Well, hell." Fawnie clunked her cane against the cherry-wood buffet and eased herself down in the chair at the head of the table. "We thought *company* was coming."

"Should have known you wouldn't do anything this nice for just us." I snuck a quick hug from Shug, then kissed Fawnie on top of her hair—I don't think even modern technology could penetrate the layers of AquaNet and bouffant—and moved around to take my own seat. "I haven't seen the place looking like this since, I don't know, my divorce party?"

"We should have had a real party tonight, Shug." Wistful didn't begin to describe the depth of the longing in Fawn-ette's tone.

The legs of my chair snagged on the carpet. "You talk like you think you won't have a chance do to that after tonight."

"After tomorrow night," Fawnie corrected, referring to the meeting Sterling had with a judge roughly thirty-six hours from now regarding Bess's eviction plans.

My stomach knotted. I wrestled my chair out and sat, whispering, "After tomorrow night."

We had spent the better part of the last couple weeks painstakingly going through years of accumulation. Well, Min, Shug and Fawnie had. Being the only one endowed with the power to drive the hearse, I drew hauling duty. Loading up and making a run to the dump, another to the donation center, one to my apartment for storage—what would another box or two matter there, anyway? So I couldn't say they hadn't planned for the worst. But hearing Fawnie say it out loud like that…

"I guess y'all saved packing up the good dishes and silver for the last."

"And the linens."

Both Fawnie and Shug rubbed their palms over the surface of the supple damask tablecloth.

I found myself doing the same, and when I glanced up, caught Minnie at it, too.

"One of your rescues?" she asked.

"Wedding gift," Fawnie said. "Your grandmother gave it to me when I married Kel."

"I got one just like it still in the box she give it to me in." Shug leaned over and put her hand on her daughter's. "You want it? I give it to you."

Min blinked. "Nana Abbra gave you both the exact same wedding gift?"

"Yeah. Said since we marry the same man, she don't want to play favorite." Shug slid the silver ring from the napkin on her plate.

"We found out later they were left over from when your grandfather had a restaurant. She had cases of them."

"Damned old biddy." Shug frowned.

"Maybe she was just embracing her sacred self," I teased.

"Nana's sacred self was a damned old biddy?" Fawnie edged her chair in. "Makes sense to me."

"Not to me." I glanced over the table, looking unsuccessfully for a platter of meat, a soup tureen, an appetizer tray. "I have no idea what you are talking about with this sacred self gobbledygook."

"It's not gobbittyguck!" Shug protested.

"Gob-ul-dy." Fawnie sounded each syllable out. "Not gobbitty."

Shug snapped her napkin, placed it in her lap and let out a few choice words in Japanese. Then she turned to Min and me and jerked her thumb toward the first Mrs. Kelvin George. "That's her sacred self—be a great big pain in the ass."

"Really? And what's yours, Mommy?" Min grinned and threw a knowing glance my way. "To torment Aunt Fawnie? To learn and remember the death story of everyone in the county? To—"

"To be an American," she said softly.

The flickering candle flames reflected in Shug's dark eyes. Not a laugh line or wrinkle marred her smooth, sun-darkened skin. Shoulders back, white hair bright in the dimming light, she commanded everyone to listen with a mere raise of her hand. "I get on a plane and fly halfway around the world with a man I know only a few months, understanding maybe I could go to jail if they say our marriage not legal."

She glanced at Fawnie.

"You gave Kel the one thing I never could—a baby." Fawnie smiled at Minnie all maternal-like. Then she cleared her throat, reached for a smoke, found nothing beside her place setting and so folded her hands in her lap. "It had to be legal. If not court legal, then God legal."

"Yeah, but I didn't know if that would matter to anyone. It wouldn't have matter to that damn Nana Abbra, if she'd had anything to say about it."

"Don't kid yourself, Shug, the fact that your presence galled that mean biddy went a long way toward soothing my hurt." She exhaled as if she'd just finished a particularly satisfying drag on an unseen cigarette.

Shug accepted Fawnie's words with a gracious nod.

For the first time in my life I saw something that had been under the quibbling and quarreling all these years—mutual respect. Who knew?

"I barely spoke English. I didn't speak Southern at all." Shug laughed. "I come to a place called Arkansas to live with people who were nothing like my family. Just to have my baby and hope to live in the place of my dreams, America."

"Just like that?" Min whispered.

"That's who I am, Minami." Shug patted her hand high on her chest. "That's how I want everyone to know me. As an American."

"But you're more than that, Mommy."

"Sure. Everybody is a whole lot of things, but only one thing is sacred. One part, they draw a line and say this is where

I stand. This part, I risk everything for." Shug held her head high. "I risked everything to come to America. I would have died for that chance."

"Wow, I never heard you talk about this, Aunt Shug." I mean, yeah, we knew Shug was crazy for America, but I always thought of it more in terms of the things she adored about her adopted country—*Cinderella*, baseball and *The Price is Right*. I didn't ever consider it was who she was. I turned in my seat to my other aunt. "I suppose you have one of those sacred selves, Aunt Fawnie?"

"We all do, lamb. Shug and I were just lucky to find ours early in life."

"Kel, I don't know if he ever knew himself good enough to say that." Shug rested her chin in her hand. "Men, if they think about that stuff long enough to figure it out, most of them don't say. Sometimes you know, because they do something, show you. Like Jolly did."

"God rest his soul," Fawnie murmured.

"Daddy? Figured out his sacred self? How could you possibly know that?"

"Because you're here, lamb. Jolly George's sacred self, the thing he would risk everything for, was to be your daddy."

I tried to gulp in some air, but the heat from the candles had grown suffocating. I reached for a drink of water, but there was none in the delicate stemware by my plate. I blinked, and to my surprise my eyes were as dry as my water glass. All my life I'd known the truth in what Fawnie was telling me. But there was one thing I didn't know.

"You said the other day that Mama made a choice the day Daddy dove in after me, Aunt Fawnie. You said it changed her?"

Fawnie looked at Shug.

Shug nodded.

"I always thought that Dinah told you. Then, how I got that notion, I can't say. That woman never told anybody anything that might make her appear weak, or somehow less than the almighty queen of everything."

I braced myself.

"When they got your daddy up to the house and the doctor came out—doctors still came out to houses like ours back then, you know."

"I know." I inched to the edge of my chair. "Go on, Aunt Fawnie."

"The doctor said Jolly had..." She motioned, moving her hand over her head in the place where Daddy's had been gashed open. "And it was all another one of them Kel-and-Jolly-produced disasters, you know."

"What?" I asked

"Fawnie, Daddy had been dead two years by the time Uncle Jolly..." Min's voice trailed off.

"Yeah, but if he and Kel hadn't been doing their mother's bidding five years earlier and screwing around as usual..." Fawnie pursed her lips and shook her head at Shug, who mimicked the gesture. "Your grandmother had wanted them to put in a permanent dock, instead of the floating kind we've always had. Jolly and Kel, God knows what got into them that day."

"Probably the same as every other day that they had to come out here and try to please their wives and mother," I muttered.

"Hmm. Bourbon," Min said.

"Don't matter. Point is they never did get that dock built, and in the end it was the remnants of that—that old jaggedy piece of concrete by the pond's edge—that done your daddy in."

"That's what he hit his head on?" It made sense. "I thought maybe he'd drowned, but that didn't make sense. If he'd drowned how could he have gotten me to the surface?"

"That's the thing, Charma, hon. That's how we know your daddy knew his sacred self. He shouldn't have gotten you to the surface. You know that expression, dead in the water?"

"Dead in the water," Shug echoed.

"That's exactly what the doctor said. Jolly couldn't have gotten you out of the water with that kind of blow to the head, but he did. For you. Your daddy chose to stay alive somehow, to save you."

My lips contorted in the effort not to gasp or sob or whatever ugly sound comes out when someone tells you that somebody did the impossible because they loved you. Tears stung my eyes. I covered my mouth.

Fawnie reached out, maybe for me, maybe hoping to find a pack of cigarettes. Either way, her hand faltered. She bowed her head.

"He saved you, but nothing could save him." Shug reached out and laid her hand on Fawnie's. "They probably got a political correct name for it now, but what they called it back then, he'd be a vegetable."

"I understand," I murmured, hoping she knew I understood more than just the physical details.

"Well, your mama saw for herself two clear choices, lamb." Fawnie pulled herself up in her seat, looking regal and removed from it all again. "Either she let the ambulance take your father to the hospital, knowing Nana Abbra would exert her supreme power over the situation, spend every last dime of the family fortune to sustain her son against all hope, and Dinah would live her life not quite married, not quite free."

"Or?"

"Or she could do what she did best—take control."

"What are you saying, Aunt Fawnie?" Min asked the question I didn't have the guts to ask. "That Aunt Dinah...?"

"We don't know." Shug folded her hands on top of her empty plate. "She went in to sit with him while we called the ambulance, and by the time they got here, Jolly had stopped breathing."

"If she did anything, lamb, you have to know Shug and I both think it was the right thing," Fawnie rushed to assure me. "You don't remember how he looked that day. You don't know what kind of place they'd have taken him to. Even with the best of money, it wasn't good."

"The name, the money, the house, the stories. She chose what she needed." It should have crushed me, I suppose, but it all made a sort of lovely logic. Mama had a made a choice. She had taken responsibility for her own soul, and in some ways, for Daddy's as well. "And then she shut herself off from everyone. Why? To keep her secret? To protect y'all from possible repercussions? To shelter me from the ugly truth?"

"Well, we never gonna know that, Charmika." Shug's round shoulders sagged.

"Damn it, Dinah," Fawnie muttered.

I couldn't have agreed more.

The doorbell rang.

"Maybe Inez changed her mind." Min threw her napkin onto the table and pushed back her chair. "Want me to get it?"

"I go with you." Shug shot up. "It could be the pizza."

"Pizza?" Min stepped aside so her mother could shuffle by.

"Yeah, we order it while you up changing. What? You think me and Fawnie gonna *cook?*"

"You all right, lamb?"

"I, uh..." I blinked. "I have no idea what I feel right now."

"Don't be too hard on your mother, okay? You young people, you've had it easy." Glancing to make sure Shug couldn't see her, Fawnie reached inside her neckline and withdrew a lone cigarette. "No trial by fire. Not the way we had it. Makes it harder to discover who you really are at the core, because who you are never gets tested."

Know my sacred self? Lord, I didn't even remember the password on my computer.

From the hallway, the aroma of pizza drifted in.

I could hear Shug flirting with the delivery boy.

Min tried to pull her in line.

Fawnie lit her cigarette on a candle in one of Nana Abbra's antique candleholders.

As if nothing had happened. As if the whole world hadn't up and reordered itself in the span of a few sentences. My mother had kept an unthinkable secret. My father had known his sacred self.

Shug walked in bearing the pizza box like a lady-in-waiting might carry a crown.

Guy was a fraud. My aunt was an American. And I was...

I was the one who was totally screwed up.

24

Sacred self? How the heck was I supposed to find my sacred self? I needed Bess to find my mother's address book so I could call the pond man!

The pond.

Bess.

Mama.

Suddenly I longed for the days when those were my three leading sources of emotional upheaval.

Ugh. *Upheaval.* The perfect word. For the last few days I'd felt like I could up and heave at any minute.

I picked up my Kokeshi doll and ran my finger along the smooth painted wood.

To own yourself.

To be yourself.

To have faith in something beyond yourself.

I wondered how a person did that, without, as Aunt Fawnie described it, trial by fire. I wondered if these kinds of thoughts kept Minnie awake.

Mostly, I wondered if there was any pizza left.

Yes, finally what drove me from my room in the wee small hours of this steamy summer morning was not the drive to birth my sacred self, but the eternal quest for comfort food.

Pulling an old worn pair of scrub pants on under my sleep T-shirt, I headed downstairs. Yes, straight downstairs. No stopping by Min's door to see if she was awake and wanted to help me raid the kitchen. First off, at 2:00 a.m., I thought she'd be asleep. Second, if she wasn't asleep and tagged along, and there was only enough pizza left over for one, Min could probably whup my ass.

The kitchen floor chilled my bare feet. A blast of air from the fridge cooled my sweat-dampened body. The sight from the kitchen window warmed my heart.

Seconds later, holding the pizza box—contents: six slices, assorted toppings—aloft, I marched up to the old claw-footed bathtub in the backyard. "If you came out here to get away from everyone, you're S.O.L., Min."

"Hey, Charma." She drew her legs up and pulled her baby-doll nightie over her raised knees. "Hop in."

"What in heaven's name are you doing?"

"Ain't it obvious? I'm moonbathing."

"Are you loony?" I set the box on her knees and climbed in. "That's only a three-quarter moon. Everyone knows that to moonbathe properly there has to be a full moon—*and* you have to be naked."

She pinched the strap of her nightie. "I'm three-quarters naked. It all works out."

"Do you hear that, Lord?" I raised my hands to the star-scattered sky. "It all works out. My only question is...when?"

"Now who's loony?"

"I'm not loony, I'm...okay, maybe a little loony. But what do you expect? I just found out my mother may or may not have killed my father."

"I don't believe it."

"I don't know what to believe, which pretty much leaves me where I've always been with my parents."

"You okay with that?"

"I guess I have to be."

"I think you need to confront somebody."

"From the mouth of the woman hiding from Travis and Abby for almost three weeks now?"

She put her hand to her ear. "Who?"

"Your husband and daughter."

"No, that's your line. You're supposed to ask *who* you should be confronting."

"How about I ask what's up with you and Abby instead?"

"If I tell you, do you promise not to laugh at me?"

"No."

"I didn't think so." She slid a piece of pizza from the box, bit down on the tip and talked as she chewed. "Okay, here's the deal. Abby is dating two guys."

"Guys." I took a slice for myself and set the box on the rusty lawn chair just behind the tub. "That's good."

"*Two.* That's not."

"She's young, Minnie."

"Exactly. Too young for as serious as things are getting. There has been talk of marriage."

I caught a mushroom as it fell toward my chin. "All three of them?"

"No. Just one. The wrong one."

"The one you disapprove of?"

"I don't disapprove of either of them, but whichever one she picks, it will be the wrong one."

"Because she's too young?"

"She doesn't know who she is yet."

"Oh, don't start with the knowing who you are business again. It makes my head hurt. Sacred self? Who knew Fawnie and your mom had that in them?"

"I did."

"You did?"

"Yeah. That's what makes the whole situation with Abby so hard. Charma, one of the guys Abby is involved with is Japanese."

"So?"

"Real Japanese. As in going back to Japan to live after he graduates next year."

"And you don't want Abby to live so far away?"

"I don't want Abby to negate what my mother risked everything to realize. She wanted to be an American with American children and grandchildren and—"

"Tell me about the other guy."

"Her high school sweetheart. Great kid. All-state basketball. Going for a law degree so he can join his daddy's firm."

"And?"

"And if she marries him, she'll end up living less than five miles away from the house she grew up in. Not that that's a bad thing—eventually."

"Got it. If Abby goes with one guy, she betrays your mama's dreams. If she goes with the other, she betrays *her* mama's dreams."

"Betray? Awfully strong word."

"Awfully strong reaction."

"I just don't want to say the wrong thing, Charma. Don't you see? I don't want for Abby years from now to agonize over choices based on the expectations I've placed on her."

"What expectations did Aunt Shug put on you?"

"That I be an American. That I marry an American." She held her fingers up as she counted them off. "That I pretend that I was nothing less than one-hundred-percent American made. That it all worked the same way for me as it did for her and for you and for everyone else in this family. That I embrace the whole fairy tale she saw as life in America, like some flag-waving Cinderella."

"You don't like being an American?"

"Why am I even talking to you?"

"Because we're in the same boat, uh, bathtub. Eating the same pizza. Because we grew up together in the same house."

"In the same house but different worlds, Charma."

"What?"

"I grew up in the same world where Guy has to front for Dathan and where Inez has to call you to get the police to do their job. And where you don't even see what's going on and why."

"Was it so bad, Min?"

She inhaled, looked toward the house, then exhaled long and slow. "The point is, Abby is about to make a choice that I spent my whole life doing everything to avoid, and it scares the hell out of me. Maybe that's my sacred self—coward."

"I don't believe that for one minute, Min." I gave her hand a squeeze. In another time, on another day, I might have rushed in with some kind of lifeline, the need to save my sweet cousin all this pain. I had nothing now but a question. "What you going to do about Abby?"

"You think staying here and hoping she gives up both guys is a realistic option?"

"She's twenty. Falling out of love is not the worst way to bet." I smiled. "But doing it while your mom is providing you with the high drama of not speaking to you? Huh-uh."

"Oh my gosh, Charmika. You're right. She's a kid."

"And a George woman," I hastened to add. "And you know how us George women love our angst and drama and—" I stopped abruptly at the sound of a ruckus in the back porch.

"Don't you dare follow me into this house, Sterling May-house, or I swear I'll get my aunt Dinah's shotgun and blow you clean to kingdom come."

"I wonder where Abby gets it?" Min drawled.

I cocked my head. "What do you suppose that was about?"

Doors slammed.

"You going to eat the last piece?" I asked, reaching for the box.

"You're going to just let all that go?" Min's eyes were big with astonishment.

"What can I do?"

"Sterling is out on the back porch. You can go and talk to him."

Rescue him. She didn't put it that way, but clearly that was the expectation here.

"Me? The person who doesn't see what's going on and why?"

She gave me a look.

"Okay, but I'm not sharing my pizza with him."

"I'll go see if I can get anything out of Bess."

"Talk about someone who doesn't know what's going on," I muttered as I made my way to the porch.

"Shouldn't you be getting some rest?" I said more loudly as the screen door creaked open, then slapped shut behind me.

Sterling stood by Mama's rocker looking out toward the pond.

I hesitated a moment, unsure if I wanted to wade in. "Big day tomorrow. Got that hearing in the morning. My aunts are counting on you to—"

"There is no hearing tomorrow."

"Why?" I took a step toward him. "What's wrong?"

"Nothing is wrong. From our vantage point. Can't say the same for Bess and her eviction plans."

"You stopped it." It came out sounding odd—a mixture of awe, disbelief, triumph and, yeah, regret. "How?"

"Technicality." He put his hand on the back of Mama's chair and set it rocking gently. "Bess's name wasn't on the legal deed. She had some paperwork, but when it got right down to it, she didn't have the right to throw your aunts out. She has to correct that and start the process all over again."

I took another step toward him, my bare feet silent on the cold, cold cement floor. "And you waited until the eleventh hour to tell her that to give my aunts the most time possible."

He didn't look at me.

"No wonder Bess is pissed. That little maneuver cost her time. And time's one thing she doesn't...like...to, uh, waste."

"I know, Charma."

I shut my eyes. "She told you?"

"No. What Bess told me was to go to hell."

"Seems to be a recurring theme with her tonight. She told me basically the same thing."

He nodded, his face still turned downward.

"I decided to leave her alone until morning," I said, not because I cared that he knew what I'd done, but because I wanted to ask him. "You?"

"I decided to leave her alone indefinitely."

We stood there in silence.

Maybe some frogs or crickets chirped, and the wind rustled in the trees. I heard the distant lap of pond water, but nothing more from him.

One of us had to say something. And as my manifest destiny was my role as rescuer, it fell to me. I wet my lips and somehow managed to whisper, "Bess doesn't have indefinitely, Sterling."

"Forever then." His shoulders rose and fell again. He moved around and sank into the rocker, a defeated figure.

The sight of him, of anyone sitting there, made me recoil.

"Bess made it perfectly clear she doesn't want to see me again."

And the pain in this good man's voice drew me in again. "She doesn't mean that, Sterling."

"I don't know. I'm not much use to her now. Not that I proved much use at all if she thought she could influence what I did for my clients."

More quiet. More sounds rising from the vicinity of the pond.

"This is where you jump to the defense of your cousin," he said, his gaze on his hands, which rested between his knees. "'Oh, no, Sterling,' you're supposed to say, 'Bess would never try to use you to improve her case.'"

Jump, Charma. The man was sitting in the very chair where my mother had died, and he was dying inside. I knew it. I couldn't stand back and watch that without trying to help.

I went to him. "I hate for you to think that, Sterling."

"Do *you* think it?"

"No." I knelt so I could meet his gaze. "I don't want to think it."

"But you do."

"I can't tell you it's not possible, but I don't believe it. No, Sterling, I don't believe it at all. You should hear Bess when she talks about you."

"Yeah?" He raised his head at last.

"Yeah," I said softly, meaning it. "You have to know this about Bess, she's...pushy."

"There's a news flash."

"No, I mean she pushes people. Now, it seems like she's pushing them away, but I think, maybe..." I couldn't believe what was coming out of my mouth. Moreover, I couldn't believe that I believed it. But I did. Even as the words formed, I knew I believed it with all my heart. "I think maybe she's pushing them toward something better. Toward becoming something better."

"How do I know if that's what she's doing with me?"

"You come around here tomorrow. You look her in the eye and tell her how you feel. If she's pushing you toward that, you'll know."

"And if she's not pushing me toward something better?"

"Then be prepared to run like hell. And for my part, I'll hide Mama's shotgun."

25

"What are you doing up so early?" I found Min where I did most mornings, sitting at the table disassembling the tiny Orla newspaper.

"It's not so early." She pointed to the clock over the door. "Sterling already called to say he'd be out in half an hour."

"Yeah, the phone woke me." I staggered in, yawning, and wondered which stung more, the glare of the morning sun bounding off the chrome edge of the table or the smell of the rich black coffee warming on the counter. "Bess up yet?"

"I knocked on her door and told her Sterling was on his way. I figure she's spending the time before he gets here making herself look devastatingly gorgeous."

"Or pitifully pathetic. Whichever one will win more points in round two of the argument." I went to the cupboard to find a coffee mug. "Get any sleep at all last night?"

"Not really. I kept thinking about Mommy. And Abby. And Abby's boyfriends. About Japanese-American relationships in the postwar era. And, of course, about Cinderella."

"Of course. So, you going to call?"

"Naw. Ever since she married that prince, Cinderella's been too stuck-up to answer the phone."

"Abby." I glanced over at Min, then back to the shelves of mugs and glasses. On a whim, I pulled out two juice glasses, then shut the door. "When are you going to call Abby?"

"When I'm sure I won't say the wrong thing."

"Then you will never speak to your daughter again, Min."

She laughed and rattled the paper.

I plunked the glasses down on the table.

"What's this for?"

"Celebrating. The house is safe, at least for now. Sterling is on his way over to appease Bess. The resolution of the Rory-Anne situation has freed up considerable phone time for me. Which means it will be free for you when you call your daughter. God is in heaven and all is right with the world."

She eyed me over the Ag and Sports section.

"Okay, all is tolerable with the world, sort of. Seems like grounds enough for breaking out Fawnie's special morning brew." I flung open the fridge and held the glass pitcher aloft. "You in?"

"Tomato juice and sloe gin? I don't think so."

"It doesn't have sloe gin in it." I lifted the lid and sniffed. "I think."

"Hello?" Thanks to Fawnie's death list duties, the front door no longer squeaked when someone walked in, but Sterling made his presence known with a shout. "Everyone decent?"

"If you wanted decent, you've come to the wrong house." I poured the red liquid into one glass and then the other.

"Bess is still in her room, Sterling," Min called out. "But she knows you were on your way over to see her. Go on back."

I lifted my glass. "Let's drink to finally having one normal day."

"Bess!" Sterling's pounding on the bedroom echoed down the hallway. "Bess, don't be this way. Let me in so we can talk."

Min picked up her glass by the rim. "Define normal."

"Okay. How about one death-list-free day?"

"Hmm." She swirled the thick juice around slowly. "How about we drink to this as the day you finally face your issues and make a trip to Chapman's?"

"Go jump in a lake, Min."

"You first, but not until after you—"

"I am not going to Chapman's. Nothing to be resolved there, not since I now know for a fact that Guy Chapman is a big fat liar."

"Guy is a decent man doing what he has to do to keep his family business thriving—not to mention meeting the payroll for his whole staff and providing an indispensable service to the community."

"I'd hardly call what he does indispensable to the community. In fact, the very nature of what he does is to dispense with the community." I laughed, but not because I found myself particularly clever.

"Okay, I've had enough, Bess." Judging from the sharpness of his tone, Sterling didn't seem to find his situation all too amusing, either. "I'm coming in."

"Anyway, I wasn't talking about you chasing after Guy Chapman, I had more in mind that it's about time you—"

Jump, Charma, my mind supplied. I shut my eyes as if that could stop her from saying it, but it was Sterling's voice, not Min's, I heard.

"Charma! Minnie! Come quick. I can't rouse Bess."

* * *

For all its age and cumbersome build, the old hearse kept right behind Sterling's Jag the whole way to Orla's tiny hospital.

"I should never have tried to make a toast to having one normal day. It was a jinx." Or a portent. My throat tightened. I leaned back in the hard plastic seat and shut my eyes. "Please, don't let this be the last normal day. Don't let this be the start of—"

"We should have had them take her to a real hospital." Min dropped into the seat beside me, the sundress she'd thrown on in a hurry billowing out and over the only thing I'd had that was clean and that I could get into in less than thirty seconds—a pair of scrubs.

"This is a real hospital, Minnie." I opened one eye to sneak a peek at the portrait that took up almost one entire wall in the waiting area. The hospital's first benefactors loomed above us, dour-faced and disapproving—our grandparents. "A real small one, but it will do the job."

The job. Bess had come to me first to be the one who would stand up for her wishes. We'd made a vow, after all. She trusted me.

Besides, Sterling was with her, and he had insisted we honor whatever arrangements Bess had already made. Damn it.

"Bess has a living will, Min." I touched her hand. "We could take her to the best hospital in the country, and it wouldn't let them do any more for her than they can right here in Orla."

"But this isn't it. This isn't the time," she murmured, her head bowed.

"You don't know that."

"I *do* know. This...this is a fever. A virus she was too weak to fight off. This is treatable. It's too soon, Charma."

"You *don't* know that, Min, and neither do I."

She'd just been rattling off the things I had suggested might be wrong, on the drive into town. Funny, I had said them then as a comfort, but hearing them parroted back, I found them anything but comforting.

"Maybe we should call Mommy and Fawnie."

"And tell them what? Inez should be there by now—let's trust her to take care of things on that end and concentrate our thoughts on Bess."

"If you mean we should pray, that's all I've been doing ever since I walked into her room and saw her on the bed like that. For a second I thought..."

I clenched my fists as if to strangle my own gut reaction. "I know."

"And when you got a pulse and we started scrambling, even then, Charma, I couldn't shake it from the back of my head. One day, we'll walk in and—"

I nodded. "No pulse."

"No *Bess*."

Our grandparents looked on, sour-faced and forbidding.

"But that wasn't today, Min, and there's nothing in Bess's will that says we can't pray for her to recover today."

"Or recover for always—you know, to get healed."

"Well, yeah." It shamed me that I'd given up on that awhile back.

"Have you talked to her any about, you know, soul stuff?"

The sweet, simple face of my Kokeshi and the responsibility it represented to me came to mind. No one had to tell Bess that she must direct her own soul. No one *could* tell her. "She got carted off to church with us every Sunday morning and Wednesday night when she stayed with us summers. She's heard the message. What she does with it..."

"Yeah. I've been too chicken to say anything, either."

I started to argue, then laid my head back against the wall. I could have banged it a few times to illustrate my point. "And there's always that annoying sense that whatever you say to Bess, she'll take up the opposite side just to...to..."

"You. Whatever *you* say to her. Me? She'd smack a big kiss on my forehead and tell me how cute I am."

"Her rules."

"What?"

"You can't do anything with Bess unless you play by her rules." I glanced up at Nana Abbra in the portrait, standing over my seated grandfather, her hand on his shoulder, and noted dryly, "Wonder where she gets that?"

"Charma?" Guy pushed through the swinging doors that led from the parking lot reserved for hospital personal. "How's Bess?"

"Overbearing," I retorted before I could stop myself, or realize that no one had tried to stop Guy or to tell him to move his car.

They would, of course, if he hadn't come in his company car, in his official capacity.

I stood up even though my knees did not feel as if they could support me. The room around me shrank down to just the three of us, maybe just the two of us, when I asked, "Why are you here, Guy?"

"I called him." Sterling stood in the hallway, his hair and clothes rumpled and his expression weary.

Min stood, her fingers wound around my arm. "Is Bess...?"

Sterling held his hand up. "Resting."

"In peace?" I asked, determined to get a direct answer.

"What?"

"Holy crap, Sterling." I made the kind of gesture the moment called for—a big one, flailing both arms out, breaking contact with Min and whapping Guy in the back all at once. I wish I could have reached Sterling and given him a shake on top of it all. "You called the family mortician."

Sterling moved in, totally unimpressed with my antics, and said softly, "I called a family friend, Charma."

"Friend?" I gave Guy the once-over. It had been a long time since anyone had referred to this man that way, especially around me. "I guess I can see that, you know, because of his history with Bess."

"Because of his history with *you.*" Sterling slipped his arm around me, presumably to render comfort and aid. But I suspected he might also have hoped to preempt my overreacting to what he said next.

"I have to hold everything together for Bess now, Charma. And you have to hold everything together for me."

"And me," Min said softly. "And Mommy and Fawnie and Aunt Ruth and Uncle Chuck and the boys."

"The boys are forty-year-old men, Min." I inhaled the scent of Bess's lavender body lotion on Sterling's clothes where he'd picked her up like a child and carried her to the car.

"Not in a situation like this they're not, Charmika."

"See, you have to hold the whole world as we know it together." Sterling turned me toward him. For the first time I noticed the circles under his red-rimmed eyes. "And in order for you to do that, somebody has got to have a hold on you."

And that somebody was Guy.

Had to be.

No one else could do the job, not with Bess incapacitated and Mama gone.

Sterling had known it. Almost as an instinct.

I placed my hand along his smooth cheek. "When did you get so damn wise and mature?"

"About twenty minutes ago, when I realized I was probably going to lose the only woman I have ever really loved."

I pulled away, blinking. "You...you *love* Bess?"

"Yeah, I do. And I need to get back in there with her. I just came out to say they are admitting her." He turned to walk away. "I suppose there are some people you need to call?"

I caught his sleeve and tugged. "Did she say anything to you about contacting her parents? Her brothers?"

"No. She hasn't said a thing."

My pulse flared up. Sterling didn't know about Bess's request not to contact her family. Her rules for the tidy little death she'd ordered up. I glanced at Min.

She stood there with Nana and Grandpa looking over her, and chewed her lower lip.

Min didn't know, either. Bess had purposely left her out of that bit so she couldn't mediate it.

Only I knew.

And Guy.

I met his gaze.

"Your call," was all he said.

Jump, Charma.

What are you waiting for?

What was I risking here? That Bess would not forgive me if I called? That I could not forgive myself if I didn't? Maybe that didn't qualify as trial by fire, but it was a test of who I was at the core of myself. A person who keeps a promise at all costs, or a person who keeps true to herself, to what she knows to be right?

"Let's find a phone." I grabbed Guy by the lapel and headed for the lobby. "I need to call Aunt Ruth."

26

"**Y**ou know, when Bess gets here and realizes you're the one who convened practically the entire family?" Guy set a vase filled with deep red roses on the bedside table in the vacant hospital room. "She is going to kill you."

"Don't care. This was my defining moment. The time when I called upon my sacred self to choose."

"What?" He winced. "Oh, hell, Charma, don't tell me I have to learn about some other George family invention like girl math."

"No. But thanks for mentioning girl math. From this moment on, I am hereby giving myself two years off my age as a reward for putting up with all this crap." Which only felt fair. Everything I'd gone through just since Bess went into the hospital had probably *put* two years' worth of worry on to my face. Two years in two days.

Two nights, three days, in actuality.

Just long enough for Aunt Ruth and Uncle Chuck to fly in. Long enough for Bess's fever to break and for her to come around. For her parents to learn Bess would recover from the virus but not from the cancer. Long enough for them to move from disbelief to denial and on into anger, and for them to direct that anger not at God but at me and my aunts.

Mostly my aunts.

The bickering with Fawnie and Shug for not letting them know how sick Bess was started a few hours ago, after it was decided to move Bess into a regular room and then home if she stayed stable for twenty-four hours.

"You did just fine, Charma."

I kicked at the brass doorstop on the dense gray carpet. "I broke my promise."

"You did the right thing."

"Did I?" I asked, my question overlapping his reassurance. "One person's right thing is another person's betrayal. Of course, that doesn't make it any less right."

He folded his arms, his pale-blue shirt bunching over his flat stomach, and set his scuff-free tennis shoes wide apart, like a man anchoring himself against the breaking surf. "I don't know what you mean."

Lord, he looked adorable in his immaculate jeans, sport coat and pressed dress shirt. An adorable liar. Just the kind I can't seem to resist. Or tolerate. "I think you know exactly what I mean, Guy. Having to choose between a wrong and a right, that's not so hard. But give a person two rights, or in my case, two wrongs—to keep a world-shattering secret, to tell a world-shattering secret…it's a defining moment."

Maybe not in the same way or to the same extreme as Mama had faced, but significant just the same. Yet for the life of me, I couldn't say what it had defined about me. Standing here waiting for them to bring Bess into this stark, cold environment, with her mother and father in tow, trying to be brave about it all, I felt anything but definite about what I had done.

"I don't envy you having made it, Charma, but you did and it's done. Now you have to gather your strength and go from where we are now."

"We?"

He made a circular gesture with one finger. "All of us who love Bess."

"Of course." I nodded.

He shifted his weight and ducked his head a moment. Then his smile broke out, slow and unsure, but cocky all the same. "What? You thought I meant..." he pointed to me, then to himself "...*we?*"

"There is no..." I repeated the pointing gesture.

"Don't kid yourself, Charma. There will always be this." Again he pointed to me, then to his own chest. "Just like despite everything that has gone on or will go on, there will always be a..." He made the circle again, the "we" who are linked by our love of Bess, by our history.

"Hard choices notwithstanding."

He lowered his head, his eyes filled with a kind light. His mouth lifted on one side and he held his hands open, palms up. "You got it."

"Yeah, I got it. I've got you, too. Got your number, so don't give me that bullshit about not understanding what it means to make a life-defining decision."

"You know I do, Charma."

"And do you think it defined you?"

"I think it came to define me, at least in the eyes of... It defined me to a lot of people." He pushed his fingers through his hair. As it fell back into place, the silver took on more prominence. "Listen to me, talking all around it."

"That's okay. I don't want to stand here and rehash our past anyway, Guy."

A nurse walked a patient attached to a rolling IV pole down the hallway. I acted as if I found them fascinating, but I just didn't want to look at the damn adorable liar when I whispered, "What good would it do?"

"Maybe you'd come to better understand Bess."

I watched the nurse guide the patient around the corner. "I understand Bess plenty."

"Okay. Then maybe you'd find room in your heart to finally forgive me."

Forgive him.

The words should have cut me. Should have burned or stung or...mattered. I took a breath. The air smelled sick and sterile all at once. I blinked, thinking I might conjure up a tear. Nothing.

Forgive Guy Chapman?

"I don't know if I can, Guy." I swallowed and leaned back on my hands, which still held the door handle. "Not unless I know for sure that you can forgive me, too."

"Forgive you? Charma, for what?"

"For playing games all those years ago and thinking I could make you play by my rules. I'm not like that. I'm not Bess. And I should have owned up to my part in what happened a long, long time ago."

"All you had to do was—"

"Don't." I held my hand up. I could not stand those words coming from his mouth again. "I did walk in the door. And you were gone. With Bess."

"But I didn't stay with Bess. You could have come anytime this last year. Was that part of the game, Charma? Your never coming for your mother's ashes?"

"No. Not a game, Guy. A choice." My only choice, as I saw it. "Do you think a choice like that changes who you are? In that sense, defines you?"

"Maybe. Or maybe it just solidifies who you are."

"How so?"

"You know, it's that old story. You have a cup of water and someone bumps you, why does the water come out of the cup?"

I shook my head.

"Because there was water in the cup. Whatever comes out during times like these, Charma, that's what was inside. I guess it's up to you to decide what it was that came out when you decided to tell your family about Bess."

"I wanted to save her."

"Bess?"

"I guess, or Aunt Ruth, maybe. I mean, I know firsthand how it is to have something like that—no, not something *like* that, that *very thing*—kept from you until it's too late. Maybe I wanted to save her that kind of pain. She's family. I owed her, you know?"

"You're asking a man who up and got off the fast track, walked away from bonuses, travel, perks, just to come home to Orla, Arkansas, to keep a funeral parlor afloat, if he understands the meaning of being indebted to his family?"

"You didn't have to do that, Guy."

"Yes, I did." He didn't just meet my gaze, he commanded it. His eyes darkened, his cheek twitched. He rubbed his neck, and his whole body shifted, seeming ill at ease in any position. "As long as my brother was here overseeing things, I didn't have to face it, but the truth is, I was a lousy son."

"No."

"I was a lousy everything, Charma. A lousy son, a lousy sibling, and I would have made a damn lousy husband."

I clenched my jaw to keep from blurting out a denial that I didn't really mean. If a man like Guy stands before you, humbled, and tells you he would have made a bad husband, you know he means it. You could hope it would have been otherwise, but you can't refute it. So I swiped away the fleeting dampness along my eyelashes and nodded.

"My dad was a good man, Charma. He did the kind of work he did because he believed in it. The way I wish I could. The way Dathan does."

"I can tell that about Dathan. He's a special man."

"He is." Guy looked down at his hand. "So, I chose not to let everything my father worked so hard to build cave in on itself over my brother's rash impulse. I came back to act like I'd taken the reins. Dathan runs the whole thing, Charma. I greet and glad-hand. That's all."

I watched the top of his head and waited.

He looked up. "You're not shocked?"

"No, you big, adorable...doofus." I finally smiled. "I had it figured out awhile ago. But I am glad you told me outright like that. That's a pretty character-defining quality in itself."

"Thanks." His posture visibly relaxed. He even chuckled a little. "I'd feel pretty shitty about the whole thing if it wasn't for knowing that without me, Dathan would still be night manager of a pizza place."

Okay, that was news. I cocked my head. "You mean he's not licensed or whatever you have to be to do that?"

"Licensed, degreed, second generation in the business. His wife, Rebecca, too. You know they can make folks integrate the schools and the work force. But in those most private places, where you have to lay your hands on someone..." He opened his own large hands, his fingers spread. "Where souls are tended and people are the most vulnerable..."

I knew *exactly* what he meant. "Churches, mortuaries and beauty shops."

He smiled, nodded and dropped his hands to his sides. "In those places, color still matters. That's a human thing, and the law can't change it."

"So you and Dathan play by your own rules."

"The African-American mortuaries didn't have enough work to hire Dathan, the white ones didn't have the balls."

"But you did."

"I did what?" He narrowed one eye at me. "Have work or balls?"

I just smiled at him and finally walked into the room. "You really think I did the right thing? Calling everyone?"

"Bess may hate you, but she'll get over it. And I'm sure, deep down, your aunts and Chuck and Ruth appreciate all you've done."

"I don't know." I shook my head. "Do you know how many times in the last forty-eight hours I've wanted to scream at them, 'Y'all are the grown-ups! Act like it!'?"

He didn't scold or try to talk reason to me, just pulled me close and placed a kiss on my forehead.

I leaned into him and shut my eyes, gripping the lapels of his sport coat and inhaling deep the smell of his skin and clothes to chase away the smells of the hospital. "But then I remember that Aunt Ruth and Uncle Chuck have just been handed the unimaginable reality of losing a child. How can anyone be expected to act rationally in the face of that?"

"You have Fawnie and Shug to help you."

I pressed my face to his shirt and laughed. "Rationality—not their forte."

"You might be surprised."

"Why?" I stepped back just enough to allow me to look up at him. "What do you know?"

"For one thing, the Death List has finally come into its own—on Bess's behalf, not your aunts'."

I shoved at his chest. "If this is your way of cheering me up—"

He didn't let me push him away. Hands on my arms, he gave me a gentle shake. "No, it's my way of letting you know your aunts have found a way to feel like they are contributing."

"I guess that's sweet."

"Of course, the things they could do themselves were already done in preparation for the possible eviction. Now they've called in the experts. Bess's lawyer, the one she used to send the eviction letter, is getting together a list of all the paperwork we'll need to have on hand. Painters rolled in this morning. And the pond guy was there yesterday."

"The pond guy? I *am* impressed. When I called him, he said he couldn't even get out to look at it until August."

"Apparently you don't share your aunts' persuasive powers."

"Oh, which powers would those be? Bribery or bourbon?"

He brushed my hair back from my temple. "You'd be proud of the old gals, Charma."

"I am, Guy." I turned my face into his open hand. "They drive me out-of-my-skull crazy, but I am proud of them. Even if I do find it terribly morbid that they'd use Fawnie's Things That Have to Get Done Before I Die list to get things ready for when Bess—"

"When Bess does what?" Bess demanded as the nurse pushed the wheelchair into the room.

"Well, lookie here." I stepped aside to make room for her, the nurse, and Sterling, who was trailing behind with a plant in one hand and a balloon bouquet in the other. "All she needs is a cane to poke us in the fanny, a cigarette to puff smoke in our faces and a hairdo that reaches halfway to heaven, and the transformation of Bess into Fawnie will be complete!"

"Shut up, Charma Deane, or I swear, you're not invited."

The nurse struggled to get Bess into the bed, not because Bess weighed anything at all but because my dear cousin kept shoving away even the smallest overture of help.

I lurched forward and caught her ankle so she didn't roll out of the bed before she could get in it.

Guy shook his head.

I gave him that "What was I supposed to do, let a helpless person fall on her ass?" look, settled Bess in and swept her hair off her forehead. "Invited where?"

"I, dear cousin, and my former insignificant other—" she sneered most pleasantly in Guy's direction "—have found my Prince Charming. A little late in coming, but I'm in love, y'all. Sterling and I are getting married."

"Married?" I looked at Guy, who repeated the word right back at me.

"Married?"

"Yep, it's true." Sterling set the plant down and began untangling himself from the curled ribbons on the balloons. "I

proposed this morning in the hospital atrium, and Bess said..."
He glanced at her, cleared his throat, then tossed me a pat-
ented Mayhouse grin. "Well, never mind what she said. Eventually, with some gentle persuasion on my part, she said yes."

I think, given the circumstances, I'd have been more in-
clined to go with Bess's first suggestion. Whatever it was, it
had to be more realistic than... "Marriage?"

Guy thrust his hand out to Sterling. "When's the wedding?"

"If they let me out of here tomorrow, then this coming Saturday." Bess tucked the covers over her thin midsection, then
twisted around to put the call button close at hand. "In fact,
if they let me out of here anytime before then, next Saturday."

"Next Saturday, no matter what." Sterling slashed his hand
through the air to end the discussion.

The nurse moved in to fluff Bess's pillows, and got swatted
away even as Bess batted her eyes at me and cooed, "Charma,
honey?"

Honey? Why did hearing Bess say that send a chill down
my spine?

I didn't have to ask myself that. I had had a defining moment, I knew something about myself that I had not known
before, and that was...that Bess didn't have to use sweet talk
to get me to do her bidding. So when she tossed it around so
lightly...

"As a reward for your faithful devotion to doing what's best
for us all—even when we don't want it done to us, I mean *for*
us—I am letting you make all the wedding arrangements."

"Oh, goodie," I said, glancing at Guy. "I can't think of anything I'd rather do."

27

Bess's wedding day.

Or rather evening. In less than half an hour she and Sterling would take their vows. The house shone. The yard sparkled, literally. The pond...well, it didn't stink anymore.

The guests were seated in beribboned folding chairs borrowed from the Baptist church. Bess's brothers and their families. Abby and Travis, saving a seat for Min. Inez and RoryAnne, baby in tow. They took up the first rows. No one had shown up from Sterling's family, so we had friends move over to flesh out the groom's side.

Aunt Ruth and Uncle Chuck waited in the hallway for my signal that Sterling and his best man, Guy, had taken their places at the altar. Then they would escort Bess out to the backyard and give her away.

I didn't know whether to laugh or cry. What made that different from *any* day revolving around my cousin, I couldn't say.

No. Wait. Yes, I could.

Today Bess had asked us all to hope with her and *for* her, for whatever time she had left. By this simple act of faith and trust in the most unlikely soul, Sterling, she had brought light into the darkness of the last of her days.

Joy in the midst of heartache.

My miracle had happened.

It wasn't the miracle I'd had in mind, but somehow I can't fault God for what he had brought us to today.

Sterling and Bess. It was crazy and impossible.

And perfect.

I couldn't have wanted anything more or better for either of them. I could only hope for something nearly as right for myself.

Guy.

Yeah, how could I go through a wedding here at my home, in the place Guy and I were supposed to be married so many years ago, and not have him on my mind the whole day?

Bess's day. I would focus on her.

And Guy, a little voice deep inside me murmured.

"Charma! Save me!"

"Oh, Lord of Mercy, Sterling!" I turned to the man standing on the back porch in front of the hall mirror, which we'd taken down without Fawnie's knowledge to lean against the wall out here. "What have you done to yourself?"

"What have *you* done to me?" He pulled his fingers from the silk bow tie that went with the white dress jacket of his vintage suit. "This getup sure wasn't my idea."

"Shut up and stand still and see if I can remember how to do this." I grabbed the ends and examined them. "I haven't had to help a man with a tie since my youngest went to the prom."

Sterling raised his chin. "I wish your sons could have come. I would have liked to meet them."

"You will." The black silk whispered through my fingers. I poked the tip of my tongue out to help me recall the way it went. Over and around and tugged into place. "You're family now."

"Family." He did not make eye contact. "But for how long?"

I knew what he was asking. How long could this last? Bess had come back strong after the virus. Too strong, some people thought. It didn't feel right. It didn't bode well. A last rally before the worst.

But this was a happy day, and I'd sworn to keep it that way. So I pretended to straighten the tie without messing it up too much, and smiled. "How long? Sterling, I hate to tell you this, but once you're in this family, it's a forever kind of deal. If you don't believe me, ask Fawnie. She got in when she was just fourteen years old, and neither death, nor divorce, nor divine intervention has put her asunder from us."

He took a deep breath and fixed his gaze in the direction of the pond.

"Hmm-mm. There." I stepped back and tried not to let my voice waver as I said, "You make a pretty damn fine-looking groom, you know that?"

"Groom." He shook his head. "In a few minutes I'll be a husband." He touched his left hand, where his wedding ring would soon belong. "And not long after that..."

"Turn around for me. I want to see the total effect."

He obliged, and the second his back was turned, I shut my eyes and willed myself not to cry.

"Charma?"

I forced my eyes wide and my expression bright. "You are too handsome."

"You don't think this is all a bit corny? The wedding? The getups?"

"They aren't getups. Look, Bess had her choice of every wedding dress we had in storage in this place. You're lucky she didn't go kimono on your ass."

He nodded sheepishly. "Fawnie may be a lot of things, but a bad dresser isn't one of them."

I chewed at my lip. Size had dominated Bess's choices more than the elegance. The white suit Fawnette Faubus had worn to wed Kelvin George in 1945, with its padded shoulders, peplum jacket and rhinestone buttons, tailored to fit Fawnie at fourteen, was the only dress that readily fit Bess at fifty. At fifty, and five months into the final stage of cancer.

"She's absolutely going to hate those, you know." He pointed to the hundreds of tiny white lights twinkling in the low branches of the trees.

"I know, but we made up for it with that." I gestured to the old claw-foot bathtub.

"Roses?" He nodded, his gaze seemingly fixed on the palest pink and deepest red roses drifting among lighted candles in the water-filled tub.

"No, what's underneath the roses."

He lifted his head to peer down through the crushed ice below the surface. "Beer?"

I smiled.

"Guess you thought of everything."

"No, if I had thought of everything, I'd have put Fawnie and Shug on a plane for parts unknown."

"They'll be fine."

"They'll pull something."

"I hope so."

I touched his cheek. I wanted to tell him how much he meant to me. How much he meant to our whole family. How when this whole maddening adventure had begun, I could never have seen in him the man standing before me today. I wanted to tell him...

"Thanks," I whispered, knowing that didn't come close to covering it all.

He nodded, his eyes misty if only for a moment. "How's Ruth holding up?"

"She's not."

"You did the right thing in calling her, Charma. Bess will never tell you, so I'm telling you. Thank you."

I nodded, too, and that seemed to say everything. And then, because I wanted to change the subject and because, being a George, for me the most natural thing to bring any subject around to was myself, I brushed a curl out of my eyes and looked up at him, all coy and guileless. "Can I ask you something?"

"Have I ever been able to stop you?"

I put on a pout, but not much of one.

He chuckled. "What do you want to know?"

"I want to know why, Sterling."

"Why Bess?"

"No. Why marriage? Why now?"

"You mean is there some kind of nefarious plot lurking under all this wherein I suddenly inherit the family home and fortune?"

"No." I hadn't thought of that. "I guess what I'm really asking is, why not me?"

"Given your staunch refusal ever to have sex with me, I would have thought that us getting married might not be all that satisfying an endeavor." He laughed. Looked away. His shoulders rose and fell. "Besides, I have this crazy notion that when two people get married, more than one of them should be in love."

I pressed my fingers to the spot between my eyes, as if his words had just given me an ice-cream headache. "You can't stand there and try to tell me that you loved me."

"I wouldn't dream of it."

"Oh." I dropped my hand and raised my chin. He could have pretended, even a little.

"Look, we had some fun. And it wasn't for nothing. I gave you—well, I'm not sure what I gave you. But you gave me a whole new sense of family."

"Family? You got my sense of family?" I asked softly. "Scary, but sweet. But scary."

"Yeah. Scary as hell. For the first time in my life, because of you, Charma, I saw a family as a safe place to screw up. As people who love you even when they want to strangle you. As people you'd sometimes do anything to get away from and always do anything within your power to help."

"I can see that."

"And Bess. You gave me Bess."

"Nobody gives Bess to anyone. That's what makes this all so remarkable. Bess is giving herself." I took both his hands in mine and looked deep into his darling blue eyes. "After all these years, after all this time, even when to any reasonable person it would appear that time had run out, Bess is giving herself to you."

"Yeah. But I'd never have had that chance if you hadn't dragged me into all this mess."

"Bambi to the Buckmasters."

He chuckled. "And I love you for that. But not in the way that could ever have made a marriage between you and me."

"But you said you had the idea more than one person should be in love...?"

"And *you* were. Only not with me."

"Hey, Bess wants to know what we're waiting for." Guy leaned in.

"What are *you* waiting for, Charma?" Sterling murmured as he leaned down and kissed my temple, then turned to Guy. "We're ready."

"We'd better get to it. Time's awasting."

Sterling moved through the door.

Guy caught me by the elbow. "What was that all about?"

"Nothing," I whispered. I started to move on by him, then pivoted, went up on tiptoe and kissed him hard on the mouth.

If he intended to kiss me back, I didn't know. I certainly didn't give him the opportunity. Pulling away, I looked down, pressed my lips together to reset my lipstick, and said, "Go take your place next to Sterling. I'll signal them to start the wedding march."

It all went by in a blur from that point on.

Bess looked beautiful.

Sterling looked...sad.

And happy.

But mostly sad.

Every time the breeze blew, the lights twinkled overhead. They reflected in the rose petal strewn water. The candles in the rented candelabra flickered.

Aunt Ruth and Uncle Chuck cried. Silently. Openly. Without any attempt to put on a brave face. I don't know if they would have cried like that if Bess had simply married Sterling because she loved him and planned to spend a long and happy life with him.

I kind of like to think they would have.

Fawnie and Shug behaved beautifully. At Bess's behest, they had donned matching gowns. To complement the ambiance, she'd told them, or some such bullshit. In fact, we figured it was the only way to keep them from trying to outdo each other in who could look the prettiest, or the pluckiest, or the most pathetic or whatever effect they would be going for under the circumstances.

And as Sterling and Bess drove off in a golden hearse covered with tissue-paper roses and shaving cream, Guy put his arms around my and Min's shoulders and said, "And they lived happily ever after."

To which I couldn't help but add, "Yeah, if you can count your ever afters in weeks."

28

Weeks turned into months.

Two.

Two months.

But the best of Bess's days were behind her almost as soon as she and Sterling returned from their honeymoon.

We moved the twin bed from the linen room into the front parlor for Sterling, and called Hospice to get a hospital bed for Bess.

Bess's brothers and their families went home after the wedding, but each of "the boys" came back to visit once more by themselves. My boys came, too.

Selfishly, anytime they weren't with Bess, I kept them to myself. I miss being a mom. Not that I won't always be their mom, but not in the way it used to be.

Sterling did get to meet them, but I stayed clear of Guy, both as a reality and as a topic of conversation. Even grown boys don't want to hear their mother speculate about the chances of her getting back together with the man she should have married instead of their father.

I did not see Guy socially. I didn't return his calls. I did not bring up his name. That's how I wanted to play it.

But not everybody played by my rules.

"Why aren't you out with Guy tonight?" Bess opened her eyes, then shut them again.

I slipped my hand under her pillow to straighten the pillowcase, then plumped a bit, smoothed the sheets. "Because I'm here with you."

She rolled her shoulders toward the wall, her version of turning away these days. "I don't need a babysitter."

"And I don't need a matchmaker."

She lay flat again and fixed her hollow-eyed gaze on me. "You ever going to go out with him?"

I poured some water from the crystal pitcher by her bed into her glass. I held it to her lips, one hand behind her head for support. "I don't know. It all seems so...pointless."

"Wow. It must be near the end, Charma." She took a sip, another, then nodded to let me know she'd had enough. "We're now living in a time when the only thing I find worth hanging on to in the world is love, and you think it's futile."

"I didn't say futile. Pointless. As in, what's the point in going out with Guy? I don't have the energy to commit myself to that kind of thing right now."

"How much energy can it take? You aren't the only person in this house who can sit and keep me company."

"If you were the only one I had counting on me, maybe."

"Don't let them drag you down, Charma."

"What?"

"If you want to do anything for me, grant a dying wish or

whatever you want to call it." She held her hand out to me. "Promise. Promise me you won't let them drag you down."

I took her hand. Her fingers were like ice. So I rubbed them as if that might make some kind of difference, restore some life, even as I asked, "Who?"

"Fawnie and Shug."

"Oh, yeah." Poor old things. They looked as lost and helpless as I felt. Wandering around this house that had suddenly become both cavernous and cramped all at once. They hardly even bickered anymore, or laughed, and if they wept, they wept in private. "Poor old things," I whispered.

"Afterward…" Bess curled her fingers around mine.

"Don't, Bess."

She gripped my hand as tightly as she could. I barely felt it. "Afterward, Min will go home. Sterling may stay on awhile, but in time he'll pick up and carry on with a new life."

"Oh, Bess."

"No, that's okay. I want him to. I couldn't stand the idea that he'd never be happy or in love again."

"Ahh." I folded my hands under my chin and batted my eyes like a cartoon animal in love. Make a joke or fall apart. I took the latter path. "I'm getting all gushy inside."

"Shut up and listen to me." She smiled-*ish*. "After everyone else has gone, you'll be the one left here in Orla. The gatekeeper at the nuthouse."

"Or just another nut."

"And they are just going to get older."

"As opposed to me, who will girl math myself into a second childhood?"

"They'll get more needy."

"That's possible?"

"You know it is. And when that time comes, you, being who you are, will step in. You'll come to the rescue full-time. You won't have a life of your own anymore. You'll just be—"

"Me, Bess. I'll just be me."

"That's what I mean. Just you, Charma. Min will have Travis. Sterling will have at least a memory of someone who loved him very much. Mom and Daddy will have each other. And you'll just have yourself. It's not fair. I want more for you."

"Haven't you heard the song? We can't always get what we want." I laughed, hummed a little, laughed some more. She wasn't buying it.

"I want more for you," she whispered. "Damn it, Charma, why do you think I did all this?"

"All what?"

"Trying to take control of the farm. I told you I came here to help you, Charma."

"By evicting two old ladies?"

"By forcing Fawnie and Shug to take responsibility for themselves, to make a plan for their old age. No one else was going to do it. I had to. Don't you see? For you. I did it for you, Charma."

I couldn't grasp it. But there it was, plain and simple. "You were trying to save me, Bess."

Her expression softened, but the old glint came into her eyes. "Just like when I pushed you in the water, remember?"

"Remember?" I edged my chair back from her just a little. "How could I ever forget that? You pushed me in the water before I was ready, and Daddy had to jump in and—"

"What the hell are you talking about?"

"That day at the pond when Daddy—"

"I pushed you in the year after Uncle Jolly died."

I tried to fit that version into the puzzle, the mix of bad dreams and convoluted memories. "The year after?"

"Because I couldn't stand the idea of you spending your whole life with that pond just a few feet away and you terrified for your life."

"Are you sure?"

"Ask Min."

I didn't have to. I didn't want to. If I did ask Min, I'd just get that lecture about lumping the bad stuff with the good stuff and never feeling as if the good stuff won out. And she'd probably also tell me to call Guy.

"Oh, Bess, I am so sorry."

"What for?"

"For always believing the worst about you. For wanting the worst to be true so I could stay removed from it. I did it with Daddy—if you pushed me, none of it could be my fault."

"It wasn't your fault, Charma. You were a kid. He told you to jump and everything would be all right."

"Everybody here loves you. We wouldn't let anything bad happen to you. You're safe and strong and free. Jump out beyond your fear." I repeated what Daddy had said, or at least the way I remembered it. "He told me to. I jumped and he..."

"He lived up to his promise. He didn't let anything bad happen to you," she murmured.

"And after that, *you* decided to start looking out for me?"

"Not always."

I stared at my hands. "I let you take the whole blame for Guy."

"And you were right to do it. Of the three of us, I had the least to lose and the most to gain. No altruism there, honey.

I ran into the man that night. He was loaded, confused and had two plane tickets out of Orla. Pretty much made him my dream date."

That was the most honest explanation anyone had ever given me about what happened. "It was a long time ago."

"Not so long it doesn't still hurt."

"A little."

"Then do something about it. Heal the hurt, girl."

She made it sound so easy. But I hadn't been able to heal anything. Life-defining moments, choices, sacred selves. It didn't mean a damn thing if you still felt lost. I couldn't begin to think that a relationship with Guy Chapman was the answer. "I'll think about it."

I nestled down in the chair again and pulled a tattered paperback from my bag. "Hey, Bess?"

"What?"

"Look what I'm reading." I held up the book she had written about our heathen ways here in Orla.

"How do you like it?"

"It's trite and trashy and full of damn lies." I cracked the spine open wide and put my feet up. "I love it."

All went quiet for a few minutes, then Bess shifted to face me. "Hey, Charma?"

"What?" I didn't look up from my reading.

"What are you going to do without me?" she asked, the way a kid asks "Why is the sky blue?"

I shut the book and sat there looking at the parlor wall. "I don't want to know."

"I know what you're going to do." She labored to sit up. "You're going to have to help yourself. You're going to have to push yourself."

"But that's the last thing I want to do." I leapt out of my seat and reached to assist her.

She slapped my hands.

I slapped her right back, softly.

"Either learn to push yourself, to do the things you have to do to jump out past your fears, or climb in here with me and die." She lifted the covers up, exposing her birdlike legs and feet in heavy socks.

I scooted up next to her and threw the blanket over us both. I rested my head on her shoulder, knowing I should be ashamed to take comfort from her instead of giving it, but I couldn't help it. I was scared, and it had always been this way. I wanted it go right on being this way.

I didn't want things to change. I didn't want to jump beyond a time when I did not have Bess to do battle with me—to do battle *for* me.

"Bess?"

"Hmm?"

"You never did tell me."

"What, Charma?" She bent her neck to look at me, her features still and her eyes somber with the willingness to impart to me the deepest of all wisdom.

"You never did tell me—does Sterling really need that Jaguar to compensate for his...shortcomings?"

"Get out of here, you damn heathen." She pushed me out of bed.

It had always been just like that between us.

Within days, she no longer had the vitality to kick the covers off. Or to go to the bathroom without assistance. Or to give me orders on how to live my life.

"It's a hell of a lot of hard work, this dying," she told Sterling one evening before she drifted off to sleep.

Min had gone home with Abby and Travis after the wedding, and came back and forth from Tennessee every other week now. Uncle Chuck only came weekends. This Tuesday with Min in Tennessee. Ruth, Sterling and I were taking turns sitting with Bess, waiting, watching and whiling away the precious little time she had left.

The house stayed dark because the light hurt her eyes. And that suited most of us.

Sometimes Shug muttered about it, but since her complaints were in Japanese, we ignored them easily.

Fawnie took to smoking only in her room or on the porches. And every morning, though Bess never once had the strength or the desire to drink it, Fawnie left a glass of her morning mix on the table by the hospital bed. Like milk left for Santa, Sterling drank it down every time and told the old woman how much Bess had enjoyed it.

Summer turned to early autumn while we moved through our days without any real marker of passing time except, *Did she eat today? Did she rest last night? Did she open her eyes this morning?*

When we weren't with Bess, we haunted the hallways, the kitchen, our own dreams.

My dream, the one about the pond and the person calling "Save me, Charma!" had become so familiar that some days when I looked out at the pond during waking hours, it surprised me that it did not look like the strange, dark place I visited each night.

The leaves began to change. Fawnie and Shug busied themselves with stuffing rags in the window cracks to keep the cool air out. But Bess was always cold.

Sterling lost weight. Lost weight and gained substance with each passing day. Fawnie and Shug mothered him, and he opened himself up to their attention like drought-parched land, drinking up every drop.

I think there would have been days upon days that he'd never have left the front parlor if those two wild and wonderful women hadn't concocted some desperate need that only he could fulfill. Today they threatened to fix the bent second-story storm windows themselves, ladder climbing and all, if he didn't help.

"He need fresh air. Young man, need to make himself work or he waste away," Shug had whispered to me as she shuffled along behind Fawnie on the way out the door.

That left Ruth and me alone with Bess.

Alone with Bess and a lot of questions.

"Aunt Ruth? What do you remember about the day Daddy died?" Death was no longer a taboo subject around this house. In fact, it had become the *only* subject.

"We were visiting. I think Chuck was serving in Spain that year, and I had come home for a few weeks with Bess and the boys." She looked up and away. "It was such a normal day, and then, you know, it was the end of the world."

"End of Daddy's world."

"And my mother's," she said softly.

Should I? I wanted to say it, to ask but... No, I had to say it. "And the end of *my* mother's world, in some ways."

"Yes."

No judgment. No sense that I had tried to trump Nana

Abbra's pain, the pain of a mother seeing her child die, with my own.

"Dinah was never the same after that. Can't blame her, really."

"Because of what she did?"

"You mean the pills? She never would have done anything like that before Jolly, but after..."

"Pills?"

"Yeah. I asked Bess a dozen times if that's how Dinah had gone, saved up all her pain meds and exercised the ultimate control over her own life."

"Oh, my goodness. I never thought of that."

"I'm so sorry, honey, I assumed that's what you meant when you talked about how Dinah had changed. Please don't fret over it. I'm probably way off base. After all, the coroner ruled her death came from natural causes."

"The coroner? Dr. Mac?" I laughed coolly. "Hardly a reliable source. Not that it matters now, I suppose."

And strangely it didn't.

"No, I wasn't asking if Mama killed herself. I was asking if she killed Daddy."

"Killed your daddy? Where do you get an idea like that?"

"Fawnie and Shug said she went into the room with him to wait for the ambulance, and by the time it got there, he had stopped breathing."

"Implying she had held a pillow over his face or some such nonsense?"

"Well?"

"No, honey. I can't accept that even Dinah in her unending thirst for control would have done that. But I'll tell you what she would do, what I think she did."

"Please." I leaned in.

"I think she let your daddy know that it was okay to let go."

"Let go?"

"He'd held on to you so tight, Charma." She held her hands up. "His fingers were white. We had to pry them off. Left marks on your skin."

I touched my neck and could almost feel Daddy's grip again.

"I think Dinah went in that room and told him that you were safe. That she loved him and always would, but it was time for him to let go."

I exhaled.

"It's not such a bad thing to do for someone you love."

I looked at Bess lying there, every breath an effort.

"I wish I could do as much for Bess. But every time she hears my voice, or Sterling's, you can just see her fighting to stay with us." She looked at me, her face the picture of exhausted sorrow.

I knew what she was asking of me.

The impossible.

She wanted the one person who had started out on all of this with the single-minded mission of saving Bess to...to do what Bess would have done for me. To give her a push.

Ruth stood and went to Bess. She swept a strand of hair back, whispered something, then bent and kissed her child on the cheek like she was simply tucking her in for the night.

Aunt Ruth gave my hand a squeeze, then moved into a darkened corner of the room, leaving me with Bess to occupy a small circle of light.

"Bess?" I leaned over her. "Bess, it's me, Charma."

Her eyelids moved, maybe. Nothing more.

I drew a deep breath and slipped my hand in hers and said the words my daddy had said to me an entire lifetime ago. "Everybody here loves you, Bess. Not a one of us would ever let anything bad happen to you. You're safe. You're strong. You're free."

Her body shuddered. She went still.

I stiffened.

Suddenly she drew a deep, pained breath.

"Jump, Bess. What are you waiting for—God Almighty to kick you in the butt?" I smiled. Yeah, I know she couldn't see it, but I thought she knew. "Jump, honey. Jump way out. Jump out beyond your fears and be free."

She took a breath.

Another.

And then she didn't.

I put my fingers on her wrist to find a pulse.

Nothing.

I motioned to Ruth that it was done.

I reached over and stopped the small travel alarm clock by the bed: 3:24 p.m.

Then I went to get Sterling and call Guy.

29

"You really did her makeup?" Abby turned around to talk to me from the front pew in the empty chapel.

"Yes, ma'am, I most surely did. With Rebecca's help." I rolled my head to try to work out the knots in the back of my neck.

Min, sitting next to me, reached over and kneaded her fingers into the tight muscles.

I'd hardly slept at all last night, couldn't rest and couldn't risk another dream. Min and Abby had rolled in around midnight, I think, and it took some time to catch them up and settle them in. This morning we had come to Chapman's early to fulfill the promise I had made so many years ago. "We used her wedding photo to go by for her hair and all. She looks..."

Dead.

Get real. All that "She looks so peaceful," "She looks so realistic," "She looks like she's just sleeping" was a bunch of bullshit. The thing that had made Bess, well, Bess, had left the shell of her cancer-ravaged body, and it showed.

We sat for a moment, just the three of us in the chapel where they would hold the visitation tomorrow and the funeral the next day. A small gallery set off to one side to grant the family privacy in their grief.

Privacy.

As if you could lose someone like Bess so young and keep your pain private.

Bess would have hated that.

So I hadn't quite decided what to do about it. We didn't have to have the funeral at Chapman's. We had a church. Or perhaps we'd just do a memorial at the cemetery. It was left for me to decide.

Aunt Ruth and Uncle Chuck had said their goodbyes and felt the rest was just a formality.

Sterling was too damn young to be planning his wife's funeral. It almost took more than he could give to pick out the clothes that she'd be buried in.

"I can't believe Fawnie agreed to let them bury Bess in her wedding dress," Abby stated.

"Oh, you are so young." Min laughed and swept her hand down her daughter's long black hair. "Fawnie will be milking that for the rest of her own life."

"Really?" Abby cocked her head.

Min raised her fingers to her lips. Holding an invisible cigarette, she wheezed in, set her face to sour and gave a gravel-throated imitation. "Buried that child in *my* wedding dress, you know. Don't anyone tell *me* I'm not a real member of this damn family."

Abby laughed. "I can't believe you two aren't even more screwed up than you are, growing up with all that."

Min drew herself up, all defensive. "Growing up like what?"

"Heathen," I said softly.

We all went quiet for a time.

I checked my wristwatch, only to find that I hadn't started it up since we'd stopped the clocks yesterday. I brushed my fingers over the crystal.

"So, what next?" Min asked.

"I wish I knew," I whispered.

We all wish that, don't we? Death and then what?

But that's not what Min meant. I squared my shoulders and rattled off the official agenda as I knew it. "We check to make sure Bess is ready. Uncle Chuck and the boys and their families arrive this morning. Sterling's parents will get here—"

Min put her hand on my arm to stop me. "His parents are coming?"

I nodded and said nothing more. Whatever had gone on between them and their son, you couldn't fault a parent who would put everything aside to come when they knew their child was in pain.

"So, where are they going to bury her? Sterling is from Atlanta. Uncle Chuck and Aunt Ruth live in Dallas now. The boys, I don't even know where they live." Abby, the girl caught between two men, two countries and countless loyalties, would think of that.

"Orla," Min said without hesitation, then blinked and looked at me. "That is right, isn't it?"

I nodded again. "Mama's plot."

"You okay with that?" Min scooted to the edge of the pew, her knees touching mine.

"Sure. Why not?"

"But...if you bury Bess in..." Abby's fine eyebrows crimped together over her brown eyes. "Where's Aunt Dinah?"

"Here." Min spoke to her daughter, but her eyes never left my face.

I rubbed my temple. "Yeah. I never picked up her ashes after—"

"No. Not here at Chapman's. Here." She pointed at me. "She's under your skin, Charma. She's in your being. She's in your way. And she's going to stay there until you find out how to let her go."

I opened my mouth to launch into my old reliable "Bess took that chance away from me" speech but stopped, thought and finally said aloud, "It wasn't Bess, was it?"

"What, honey?" Min placed her hand on my back.

"It wasn't Bess who took my chance to deal with Mama's death away. Or Guy. It was me."

"You?" Abby asked, so softly I scarcely heard it.

"Me." I looked at Min, and tears filled my eyes. "That's it, isn't it, Min? My sacred self. I didn't know it, I didn't *claim* it. But Mama knew. I thought of her as having this wall around her to protect her, but in the end, it also protected me."

She slipped her arm around my shoulders and laid her head against mine.

"Mama had her trial by fire. She understood. She knew who I was more than I knew myself. I could never, *never* have done for her what Bess did. I could never have let her die. I would have had to—" a tear slid down my cheek "—save her."

Min grasped my hand.

Abby reached over and put her hand on top of ours.

"I still want to. I still want to save Mama. So much so that I have risked everything. My whole life these last months." I swallowed. Blinked. More tears fell. "And it was never enough. It would never be enough. If I had been there when Mama was dying, I'd have added losing her to my failures and lived with it like it had just happened for the rest of my life."

Min sniffled.

Abby, too.

"But I did good with Bess, Min."

"I know."

"I did enough. I saved her by loving her enough to let her go. I know that."

"Yes." She did not meet my gaze when she asked, her voice hoarse, "Now can you do the same for your mother?"

I held my breath. When I was young, Min's mother had given us all Kokeshi dolls to remind us that we directed the journey of our souls. I had forgotten that a long time ago.

I was responsible for my sacred self. Only I could reclaim it. And only I knew how.

30

"**H**e's a lily of the valley—"

"Lily, damn it!" Fawnie cast me the evil eye and waggled her cane as she hurried past me out onto the front porch. "You picked that song on purpose, missy, don't deny it."

I laughed.

"Lily of the valley!" Fawnie barked, even as Shug continued to sing the foot-stomping gospel hymn we'd all sung ten days ago as part of Bess's funeral service.

Her big-ass bountiful, biracial, Bible-thumpin' service.

It seemed only right. To take the occasion not just to celebrate the life of one of the world's greatest heathen girls, but also to embrace everyone in Orla who'd ever had to pretend to be something they weren't. Who had to hide their true selves, put up walls or endure ignorance and prejudice just to get what every one of us wanted—home, family, work, and yeah, a damn good party now and then.

Hey, it met Aunt Fawnie's wish to restore the George family name to prominence. Okay, maybe less prominence and more infamy.

I could live with that.

"Thanks for offering to take those two out to dinner before you head back to Tennessee," I said to Min as she dragged her suitcase into the foyer. "When are you taking off?"

"Now," was all Travis said as he plucked the case from her hand and headed out the door.

"Nice talking to you, Travis," I called out after him, then turned to Min. "So, you're really going to go to Japan on Abby's spring break?"

"Can't believe it either, can you?"

"Well, at least Abby agreed to hold off any wedding talk until all the families meet."

"Yeah. East meets South. Sort of looking forward to it." She crinkled up her nose. "And not."

I laughed and pulled her into a hug, then stepped back and glanced down at the small travel case by her feet. "You sure you got everything?"

"Actually, I was going through Bess's room a minute ago and thought I might take her Kokeshi with me, but I couldn't find it. Do you know where it is?"

"I do." I smiled and looked away.

"You buried it with her, didn't you?"

I gave a half shrug. "Hell, why not? I thought she might want it as a souvenir."

"Good move." She kissed my cheek. "When's Sterling coming back from Atlanta?"

"A few weeks. Says he doesn't want to get into winter before opening up his law practice here. Until then, guess it will just be me and Fawnie and Shug out here."

"Yeah. Until Inez figures out how to get you to turn it into a neonatal home-birthing house and domestic-abuse shelter."

I pushed my fingers through my hair. "She may just wear us down yet."

"Where's Daddy?" Abby came down the stairs with a backpack slung over one shoulder.

"In the car with Mommy and Aunt Fawnie." Min motioned toward the open front door.

"Oh, Mom, you didn't!" Abby rushed toward the porch.

"Yeah, you big meanie." I poked Min in the arm. "He's probably talked their ears off by now."

Abby started out. "I'm off to the rescue."

I caught her arm. "Just don't make that your life's work, okay?"

"I won't." She gave me a quick hug and hurried away.

Min moved to the doorway behind her child, then turned to me. "You going to be okay here alone for a few hours?"

"I think I can manage. Thank Travis again for helping move my stuff out here from the apartment."

"I'm sure he was glad to do it."

"And if he wasn't, it's not like he's going to say anything." I laughed.

She rolled her eyes. "I can stay if you want me to, have Travis pick me up when he drops off Mommy and Fawnie."

"No!" I gave her a push. "Go! Don't worry about me. Actually, I'm looking forward to having the place to myself."

"You've got something up your sleeve, don't you, girl?"

"Push comes to shove." I gave her a knowing wink and sent her out the door. "Maybe I do."

"Hello?" Guy answered the phone while I could still hear Min and Travis's car tires grinding down the driveway.

"Hi."

"Charma? Is something wrong?"

My heart sped up. I opened my mouth, unsure I'd have the breath or the nerve to say a word. But I did. "Yeah, something's been wrong a long, long time. Guy?"

"Yeah," he murmured.

"If you ever decided to walk through my door—I'd be waiting."

"You would?"

"And for the next couple hours I'll be waiting all alone out here."

"I'm on my way."

I exhaled, started to hang up, then rushed to add, "Oh, and Guy?"

"Hmm?"

"When you come out, bring your toothbrush."

"Charma?"

"Yeah?"

"I love you."

"Guy?"

"What?"

"Get your ass out here."

I hung up the phone and headed out the back, peeling off my clothes as I went to baptize myself at last into the self I had worked so hard and waited so long to become.